PUFFIN CLASSICS

ANNE'S HOUSE OF DREAMS

LUCY MAUDE MONTGOMERY (1874–1942) was born on Prince Edward Island, off the east coast of Canada. She lived there throughout her childhood with her grandparents (following her mother's death in 1876). Readers of the *Anne of Green Gables* series of books will find plenty of scenes drawn from the author's happy memories of the island and the farmhouse where she was brought up.

Like many a future writer, Lucy Maude Montgomery was not only an avid reader as a child, but also composed numerous short stories and poems. Her first published piece was a poem that appeared in the local paper when she was fifteen years old. Later, after she had finished school and university, she turned her love of books to good effect by becoming a teacher.

She continued to write, and was once asked to contribute a short story to a magazine. She dusted off an idea for a plot she had jotted down when she was much younger – and turned it into one of the most popular books ever written for children. *Anne of Green Gables* was first published in 1908.

Lucy herself said about *Anne of Green Gables*: 'I thought girls in their teens might like it. But grandparents, school and college boys, old pioneers in the Australian bush, girls in India, missionaries in China, monks in remote monasteries, premiers of Great Britain, and red-headed people all over the world have written to me, telling me how they loved Anne and her successors.'

The 'successors' are nine further *Anne* books, all of which are now published in Puffin Classics. Lucy Maude Montgomery continued to write under her maiden name after marrying a Presbyterian minister, Ewan MacDonald, in 1911. And, despite moving with him to Toronto, she continued to set her stories on 'the only island there is', and where her heart always remained.

Some other Puffin Classics to enjoy

EIGHT COUSINS
GOOD WIVES
JACK AND JILL
JO'S BOYS
LITTLE MEN
LITTLE WOMEN
ROSE IN BLOOM
Louisa M Alcott

WHAT KATY DID
WHAT KATY DID AT SCHOOL
WHAT KATY DID NEXT
Susan Coolidge

POLLYANNA
POLLYANNA GROWS UP
Eleanor H Porter

FIVE LITTLE PEPPERS AND HOW THEY GREW
Margaret Sidney

HEIDI   Johanna Spyri

DADDY LONG LEGS   Jean Webster

REBECCA OF SUNNYBROOK FARM
Kate Douglas Wiggins

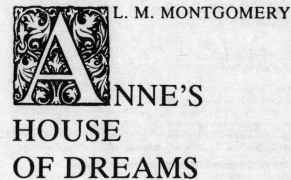

L. M. MONTGOMERY

ANNE'S
HOUSE
OF DREAMS

> *Our kin*
> *Have built them temples, and therein*
> *Pray to the gods we know; and dwell*
> *In little houses lovable.*
>
> RUPERT BROOKE

PUFFIN BOOKS

PUFFIN BOOKS

Published by the Penguin Group
Penguin Books Ltd, 27 Wrights Lane, London W8 5TZ, England
Penguin Books USA Inc., 375 Hudson Street, New York, New York 10014, USA
Penguin Books Australia Ltd, Ringwood, Victoria, Australia
Penguin Books Canada Ltd, 10 Alcorn Avenue, Toronto, Ontario, Canada M4V 3B2
Penguin Books (NZ) Ltd, 182–190 Wairau Road, Auckland 10, New Zealand

Penguin Books Ltd, Registered Offices: Harmondsworth, Middlesex, England

First published in Great Britain by George C. Harrap & Co.Ltd 1926
Published in Puffin Books 1981
20 19 18 17 16 15

Printed in England by Clays Ltd, St Ives plc
Set in Sabon

To Laura
in memory of the olden time

Contents

CHAPTER 1

In the Garret of Green Gables

'THANKS BE, I'm done with geometry, learning or teaching it,' said Anne Shirley, a trifle vindictively, as she thumped a somewhat battered volume of Euclid into a big chest of books, banged the lid in triumph, and sat down upon it, looking at Diana Wright across the Green Gables garret, with grey eyes that were like a morning sky.

The garret was a shadowy, suggestive, delightful place, as all garrets should be. Through the open window, by which Anne sat, blew the sweet, scented, sun-warm air of the August afternoon; outside, poplar boughs rustled and tossed in the wind; beyond them were the woods, where Lovers' Lane wound its enchanted path, and the old apple orchard which still bore its rosy harvests munificently. And, over all, was a great mountain range of snowy clouds in the blue southern sky. Through the other window was glimpsed a distant, white-capped, blue sea—the beautiful St Lawrence Gulf, on which floats, like a jewel, Abegweit, whose softer, sweeter Indian name has long been forsaken for the more prosaic one of Prince Edward Island.

Diana Wright, three years older than when we last saw her, had grown somewhat matronly in the intervening time. But her eyes were as black and brilliant, her cheeks as rosy, and her dimples as enchanting, as in the long-ago days when she and Anne Shirley had vowed eternal friendship in the garden at Orchard Slope. In her arms she held a small, sleeping, black-curled creature, who for two happy years had been known to the world of Avonlea as 'Small Anne Cordelia'. Avonlea folks knew why Diana had called her Anne, of course, but Avonlea folks were puzzled by the Cordelia. There had never been a Cordelia in the Wright or Barry connections. Mrs Harmon Andrews said she supposed Diana had found the name in some trashy novel, and wondered that Fred hadn't more sense than to allow it. But Diana and Anne smiled at each other. They knew how Small Anne Cordelia had come by her name.

'You always hated geometry,' said Diana with a retrospective smile. 'I should think you'd be real glad to be through with teaching, anyhow.'

'Oh, I've always liked teaching, apart from geometry. These past three years in Summerside have been very pleasant ones. Mrs Harmon Andrews told me when I came home that I wouldn't likely find married life as much better than teaching as I expected. Evidently Mrs Harmon is of Hamlet's opinion that it may be better to bear the ills that we have than fly to others that we know not of.'

Anne's laugh, as blithe and irresistible as of yore, with an added note of sweetness and maturity, rang through the garret. Marilla in the kitchen below, compounding blue-plum preserve, heard it and smiled; then sighed to think how seldom that dear laugh would echo through Green Gables in the years to come. Nothing in her life had ever given Marilla so much happiness as the knowledge that Anne was going to marry Gilbert Blythe; but every joy must bring with it its little shadow of sorrow. During the three Summerside years Anne had been home often for vacations and week-ends; but after this a bi-annual visit would be as much as could be hoped for.

'You needn't let what Mrs Harmon says worry you,' said Diana, with the calm assurance of the four-years matron. 'Married life has its ups and downs, of course. You mustn't expect that everything will always go smoothly. But I can assure you, Anne, that it's a happy life, when you're married to the right man.'

Anne smothered a smile. Diana's airs of vast experience always amused her a little.

'I dare say I'll be putting them on too, when I've been married four years,' she thought. 'Surely my sense of humour will preserve me from it, though.'

'Is it settled yet where you are going to live?' asked Diana, cuddling Small Anne Cordelia with the inimitable gesture of motherhood which always sent through Anne's heart, filled with sweet, unuttered dreams and hopes, a thrill that was half pure pleasure and half a strange, ethereal pain.

'Yes. That was what I wanted to tell you when I phoned to you to come down today. By the way, I can't realize that we really have telephones in Avonlea now. It sounds so preposterously up-to-date and modernish for this darling, leisurely old place.'

'We can thank the A.V.I.S. for them,' said Diana. 'We should never have got the line if they hadn't taken the matter up and carried it through. There was enough cold water thrown to discourage any society. But they stuck to it, nevertheless. You did a splendid thing for Avonlea when you founded that society, Anne. What fun we did have at *our* meetings! Will you ever forget the blue hall and Judson

Parker's scheme for painting medicine advertisements on his fence?'

'I don't know that I'm wholly grateful to the A.V.I.S. in the matter of the telephone,' said Anne. 'Oh, I know it's most convenient – even more so than our old device of signalling to each other by flashes of candlelight! And, as Mrs Rachel says, "Avonlea must keep up with the procession, that's what." But somehow I feel as if I don't want Avonlea spoiled by what Mr Harrison, when he wants to be witty, calls "modern inconveniences". I should like to have it kept always just as it was in the dear old years. That's foolish – and sentimental – and impossible. So I shall immediately become wise and practical and possible. The telephone, as Mr Harrison concedes, is "a buster of a good thing" – even if you do know that probably half a dozen interested people are listening along the line.'

'That's the worst of it,' sighed Diana. 'It's so annoying to hear the receivers going down whenever you ring anyone up. They say Mrs Harmon Andrews insisted that their phone should be put in their kitchen just so that she could listen whenever it rang and keep an eye on the dinner at the same time. Today, when you called me, I distinctly heard that queer clock of the Pyes' striking. So no doubt Josie or Gertie was listening.'

'Oh, so that is why you said, "You've got a new clock at Green Gables, haven't you?" I couldn't imagine what you meant. I heard a vicious click as soon as you had spoken. I suppose it was the Pye receiver being hung up with profane energy. Well, never mind the Pyes. As Mrs Rachel says, "Pyes they always were and Pyes they always will be, world without end, amen." I want to talk of pleasanter things. It's all settled as to where my new home shall be.'

'Oh, Anne, where? I do hope it's near here.'

'No-o-o, that's the drawback. Gilbert is going to settle at Four Winds Harbour – sixty miles from here.'

'Sixty! It might as well be six hundred,' sighed Diana. 'I never can get farther from home now than Charlottetown.'

'You'll have to come to Four Winds. It's the most beautiful harbour on the Island. There's a little village called Glen St Mary at its head, and Dr David Blythe has been practising there for fifty years. He is Gilbert's great-uncle, you know. He is going to retire, and Gilbert is to take over his practice. Dr Blythe is going to keep his house, though, so we shall have to find a habitation for ourselves. I don't know yet what it is, or where it will be in reality, but I have a little house o' dreams all furnished in my imagination – a tiny, delightful castle in Spain.'

'Where are you going for your wedding tour?' asked Diana.

'Nowhere. Don't look horrified, Diana dearest. You suggest Mrs Harmon Andrews. She, no doubt, will remark condescendingly that people who can't afford wedding "towers" are real sensible not to take them; and then she'll remind me that Jane went to Europe for hers. I want to spend *my* honeymoon at Four Winds in my own dear house of dreams.'

'And you've decided not to have any bridesmaid?'

'There isn't anyone to have. You and Phil and Priscilla and Jane all stole a march on me in the matter of marriage; and Stella is teaching in Vancouver. I have no other "kindred soul" and I won't have a bridesmaid who isn't.'

'But you are going to wear a veil, aren't you?' asked Diana, anxiously.

'Yes, indeed. I shouldn't feel like a bride without one. I remember telling Matthew, that evening when he brought me to Green Gables, that I never expected to be a bride because I was so homely no one would ever want to marry me – unless some foreign missionary did. I had an idea then that foreign missionaries couldn't afford to be finicky in the matter of looks if they wanted a girl to risk her life among cannibals. You should have seen the foreign missionary Priscilla married. He was as handsome and inscrutable as those day-dreams we once planned to marry ourselves, Diana; he was the best-dressed man I ever met, and he raved over Priscilla's "ethereal, golden beauty". But of course there are no cannibals in Japan.'

'Your wedding dress is a dream, anyhow,' sighed Diana rapturously. 'You'll look like a perfect queen in it – you're so tall and slender. How *do* you keep so slim, Anne? I'm fatter than ever – I'll soon have no waist at all.'

'Stoutness and slimness seem to be matters of predestination,' said Anne. 'At all events, Mrs Harmon Andrews can't say to you what she said to me when I came home from Summerside, "Well, Anne, you're just about as skinny as ever." It sounds quite romantic to be "slender", but "skinny" has a very different tang.'

'Mrs Harmon has been talking about your trousseau. She admits it's as nice as Jane's, although she says Jane married a millionaire and you are only marrying a "poor young doctor without a cent to his name".'

Anne laughed.

'My dresses *are* nice. I love pretty things. I remember the first party dress I ever had – the brown gloria Matthew gave me for our school concert. Before that everything I had was so ugly. It seemed to me that I stepped into a new world that night.'

'That was the night Gilbert recited "Bingen on the Rhine", and looked at you when he said, "There's another, *not* a sister." And you were so furious because he put your pink tissue rose in his breast pocket! You didn't much imagine then that you would ever marry him.'

'Oh, well, that's another instance of predestination,' laughed Anne, as they went down the garret stairs.

CHAPTER 2

The House of Dreams

THERE WAS more excitement in the air of Green Gables than there had ever been before in all its history. Even Marilla was so excited that she couldn't help showing it – which was little short of being phenomenal.

'There's never been a wedding in this house,' she said, half apologetically, to Mrs Rachel Lynde. 'When I was a child I heard an old minister say that a house was not a real home until it had been consecrated by a birth, a wedding, and a death. We've had deaths here – my father and mother died here as well as Matthew; and we've even had a birth here. Long ago, just after we moved into this house, we had a married hired man for a little while, and his wife had a baby here. But there's never been a wedding before. It does seem so strange to think of Anne being married. In a way she just seems to me the little girl Matthew brought home here fourteen years ago. I can't realize that she's grown up. I shall never forget what I felt when I saw Matthew bringing in a *girl*. I wonder what became of the boy we would have got if there hadn't been a mistake. I wonder what *his* fate was.'

'Well, it was a fortunate mistake,' said Mrs Rachel Lynde, 'though, mind you, there was a time I didn't think so – that evening I came up to see Anne and she treated us to such a scene. Many things have changed since then, that's what.'

Mrs Rachel sighed, and then brisked up again. When weddings were in order Mrs Rachel was ready to let the dead past bury its dead.

'I'm going to give Anne two of my cotton warp spreads,' she resumed. 'A tobacco-stripe one and an apple-leaf one. She tells me they're getting to be real fashionable again. Well, fashion or no fashion, I don't believe there's anything prettier for a spare-room bed than a nice apple-leaf spread, that's what. I must see about getting them bleached. I've had them sewed up in cotton bags ever since Thomas died, and no doubt they're an awful colour. But there's a month yet, and dew-bleaching will work wonders.'

Only a month! Marilla sighed and then said proudly:

'I'm giving Anne that half-dozen braided rugs I have in the garret. I never supposed she'd want them — they're so old-fashioned, and nobody seems to want anything but hooked mats now. But she asked me for them — said she'd rather have them than anything else for her floors. They *are* pretty. I made them of the nicest rags, and braided them in stripes. It was such company these last few winters. And I'll make her enough blue-plum preserve to stock her jam closet for a year. It seems real strange. Those blue-plum trees hadn't even a blossom for three years, and I thought they might as well be cut down. And this last spring they were white, and such a crop of plums I never remember at Green Gables.'

'Well, thank goodness that Anne and Gilbert really are going to be married after all. It's what I've always prayed for,' said Mrs Rachel, in the tone of one who is comfortably sure that her prayers have availed much. 'It was a great relief to find out that she really didn't mean to take the Kingsport

17

man. He was rich, to be sure, and Gilbert is poor – at least, to begin with; but then he's an Island boy.'

'He's Gilbert Blythe,' said Marilla contentedly. Marilla would have died the death before she would have put into words the thought that was always in the background of her mind whenever she had looked at Gilbert from his child-hood up – the thought that, had it not been for her own wilful pride long, long ago, he might have been *her* son. Marilla felt that, in some strange way, his marriage with Anne would put right that old mistake. Good had come out of the evil of the ancient bitterness.

As for Anne herself, she was so happy that she almost felt frightened. The gods, so says the old superstition, do not like to behold too happy mortals. It is certain, at least, that some human beings do not. Two of that ilk descended upon Anne one violet dusk and proceeded to do what in them lay to prick the rainbow bubble of her satisfaction. If she thought she was getting any particular prize in young Dr Blythe, or if she imagined that he was still as infatuated with her as he might have been in his salad days, it was surely their duty to put the matter before her in another light. Yet these two worthy ladies were not enemies of Anne; on the contrary they were really quite fond of her, and would have defended her as their own young had anyone else attacked her. Human nature is not obliged to be consistent.

Mrs Inglis – *née* Jane Andrews, to quote from the *Daily Enterprise* – came with her mother and Mrs Jasper Bell. But in Jane the milk of human kindness had not been curdled by years of matrimonial bickerings. Her lines had fallen in pleasant places. In spite of the fact – as Mrs Rachel Lynde would say – that she had married a millionaire, her marriage

18

had been happy. Wealth had not spoiled her. She was still the placid, amiable, pink-cheeked Jane of the old quartette, sympathizing with her old chum's happiness and as keenly interested in all the dainty details of Anne's trousseau as if it could rival her own silken and bejewelled splendours. Jane was not brilliant, and had probably never made a remark worth listening to in her life; but she never said anything that would hurt anyone's feelings – which may be a negative talent but is likewise a rare and enviable one.

'So Gilbert didn't go back on you after all,' said Mrs Harmon Andrews, contriving to convey an expression of surprise in her tone. 'Well, the Blythes generally keep their word when they've once passed it, no matter what happens. Let me see – you're twenty-five, aren't you, Anne? When I was a girl twenty-five was the first corner. But you look quite young. Red-headed people always do.'

'Red hair is very fashionable now,' said Anne, trying to smile, but speaking rather coldly. Life had developed in her a sense of humour which helped her over many difficulties; but as yet nothing had availed to steel her against a reference to her hair.

'So it is – so it is,' conceded Mrs Harmon. 'There's no telling what queer freaks fashion will take. Well, Anne, your things are very pretty, and very suitable to your position in life, aren't they, Jane? I hope you'll be very happy. You have my best wishes, I'm sure. A long engagement doesn't often turn out well. But, of course, in your case it couldn't be helped.'

'Gilbert looks very young for a doctor. I'm afraid people won't have much confidence in him,' said Mrs Jasper Bell gloomily. Then she shut her mouth tightly, as if she had said what she considered it her duty to say and held her conscience clear. She belonged to the type which always has a stringy black feather in its hat and straggling locks of hair on its neck.

Anne's surface pleasure in her pretty bridal things was temporarily shadowed; but the deeps of happiness below could not thus be disturbed; and the little stings of Mesdames Bell and Andrews were forgotten when Gilbert came later, and they wandered down to the birches of the brook, which had been saplings when Anne had come to Green Gables, but were now tall, ivory columns in a fairy palace of twilight and stars. In their shadows Anne and Gilbert talked in lover-fashion of their new home and their new life together.

'I've found a nest for us, Anne.'

'Oh, where? Not right in the village, I hope. I wouldn't like that altogether.'

'No. There was no house to be had in the village. This is a little white house on the harbour shore, half-way between Glen St Mary and Four Winds Point. It's a little out of the way, but when we get a phone in that won't matter so much. The situation is beautiful. It looks to the sunset and has the great blue harbour before it. The sand-dunes aren't very far away – the sea-winds blow over them and the sea-spray drenches them.'

'But the house itself, Gilbert – *our* first home? What is it like?'

'Not very large, but large enough for us. There's a splendid living-room with a fireplace in it downstairs, and a dining-room that looks out on the harbour, and a little room that will do for my office. It is about sixty years old – the oldest house in Four Winds. But it has been kept in pretty good repair, and was all done over about fifteen years ago – shingled, plastered, and re-floored. It was well built to begin with. I understand that there was some romantic story connected with its building, but the man I rented it from didn't know it. He said Captain Jim was the only one who could spin that old yarn now.'

'Who is Captain Jim?'

'The keeper of the lighthouse on Four Winds Point. You'll love that Four Winds light, Anne. It's a revolving one, and it flashes like a magnificent star through the twilights. We can see it from our living-room windows and our front door.'

'Who owns the house?'

'Well, it's the property of the Glen St Mary Presbyterian Church now, and I rented it from the trustees. But it belonged until lately to a very old lady, Miss Elizabeth Russell. She died last spring, and as she had no near relatives she left her property to the Glen St Mary Church. Her furniture is still in the house, and I bought most of it – for a mere song, you might say, because it was all so old-fashioned that the trustees despaired of selling it. Glen St Mary folks prefer plush brocade and sideboards with mirrors and ornamentations, I fancy. But Miss Russell's furniture is very good and I feel sure you'll like it, Anne.'

'So far, good,' said Anne, nodding cautious approval. 'But, Gilbert, people cannot live by furniture alone. You haven't yet mentioned one very important thing. Are there *trees* about this house?'

'Heaps of them, O dryad! There is a big grove of fir-trees behind it, two rows of Lombardy poplars down the lane, and a ring of white birches around a very delightful garden.

Our front door opens right into the garden, but there is another entrance – a little gate hung between two firs. The hinges are on one trunk and the catch on the other. Their boughs form an arch overhead.'

'Oh, I'm so glad! I couldn't live where there were no trees – something vital in me would starve. Well, after that, there's no use asking you if there's a brook anywhere near. *That* would be expecting too much.'

'But there *is* a brook – and it actually cuts across one corner of the garden.'

'Then,' said Anne, with a long sigh of supreme satisfaction, 'this house you have found *is* my house of dreams and none other.'

CHAPTER 3

The Land of Dreams Among

'HAVE YOU made up your mind who you're going to have to the wedding, Anne?' asked Mrs Rachel Lynde, as she hemstitched table napkins industriously. 'It's time your invitations were sent, even if they are to be only informal ones.'

'I don't mean to have very many,' said Anne. 'We just want those we love best to see us married. Gilbert's people, and Mr and Mrs Allan, and Mr and Mrs Harrison.'

'There was a time when you'd hardly have numbered Mr Harrison among your dearest friends,' said Marilla drily.

'Well, I wasn't *very* strongly attracted to him at our first meeting,' acknowledged Anne, with a laugh over the recollection. 'But Mr Harrison has improved on acquaintance, and Mrs Harrison is really a dear. Then, of course, there are Miss Lavendar and Paul.'

'Have they decided to come to the Island this summer? I thought they were going to Europe.'

'They changed their minds when I wrote them I was going to be married. I had a letter from Paul today. He says he *must* come to my wedding, no matter what happens to Europe.'

'That child always idolized you,' remarked Mrs Rachel.

'That "child" is a young man of nineteen now, Mrs Lynde.'

'How time does fly!' was Mrs Lynde's brilliant and original response.

'Charlotta the Fourth may come with them. She sent word by Paul that she would come if her husband would let her. I wonder if she still wears those enormous blue bows, and whether her husband calls her Charlotta or Leonora. I should love to have Charlotta at my wedding. Charlotta and I were at a wedding long syne. They expect to be at Echo Lodge next week. Then there are Phil and the Reverend Jo –'

'It sounds awful to hear you speaking of a minister like that, Anne,' said Mrs Rachel severely.

'His wife calls him that.'

'She should have more respect for his holy office, then,' retorted Mrs Rachel.

'I've heard you criticize ministers pretty sharply yourself,' teased Anne.

'Yes, but I do it reverently,' protested Mrs Lynde. 'You never heard me *nickname* a minister.'

Anne smothered a smile.

'Well, there are Diana and Fred and little Fred and Small Anne Cordelia – and Jane Andrews. I wish I could have Miss Stacey and Aunt Jamesina and Priscilla and Stella. But Stella is in Vancouver, and Pris is in Japan, and Miss Stacey is married in California, and Aunt Jamesina has gone to India to explore her daughter's mission field, in spite of her horror of snakes. It's really dreadful – the way people get scattered over the globe.'

'The Lord never intended it, that's what,' said Mrs Rachel authoritatively. 'In my young days people grew up and married and settled down where they were born, or pretty near it. Thank goodness you've stuck to the Island, Anne. I was afraid Gilbert would insist on rushing off to the ends of the earth when he got through college, and dragging you with him.'

'If everybody stayed where he was born places would soon be filled up, Mrs Lynde.'

'Oh, I'm not going to argue with you, Anne. *I* am not a B.A. What time of the day is the ceremony to be?'

'We have decided on noon – high noon, as the society reporters say. That will give us time to catch the evening train to Glen St Mary.'

'And you'll be married in the parlour?'

'No – not unless it rains. We mean to be married in the orchard – with the blue sky over us and the sunshine around us. Do you know when and where I'd like to be married, if I could? It would be at dawn – a June dawn, with a glorious sunrise, and roses blooming in the gardens; and I would slip down and meet Gilbert and we would go together to the heart of the beech-woods – and there, under the green arches that would be like a splendid cathedral, we would be married.'

Marilla sniffed scornfully and Mrs Lynde looked shocked.

'But that would be terrible queer, Anne. Why, it wouldn't really seem legal. And what would Mrs Harmon Andrews say?'

'Ah, there's the rub,' sighed Anne. 'There are so many things in life we cannot do because of the fear of what Mrs Harmon Andrews would say. " 'Tis true, 'tis pity, and pity 'tis, 'tis true." What delightful things we might do were it not for Mrs Harmon Andrews!'

'By times, Anne, I don't feel quite sure that I understand

you altogether,' complained Mrs Lynde.

'Anne was always romantic, you know,' said Marilla apologetically.

'Well, married life will most likely cure her of that,' Mrs Rachel responded comfortingly.

Anne laughed and slipped away to Lovers' Lane, where Gilbert found her; and neither of them seemed to entertain much fear, or hope, that their married life would cure them of romance.

The Echo Lodge people came over the next week, and Green Gables buzzed with the delight of them. Miss Lavendar had changed so little that the three years since her last Island visit might have been a watch in the night; but Anne gasped with amazement over Paul. Could this splendid six feet of manhood be the little Paul of Avonlea schooldays?

'You really make me feel old, Paul,' said Anne. 'Why, I have to look up to you!'

'You'll never grow old, Teacher,' said Paul. 'You are one of the fortunate mortals who have found and drunk from the Fountain of Youth – you and Mother Lavendar. See here! When you're married I *won't* call you Mrs Blythe. To me you'll always be "Teacher" – the teacher of the best lessons I ever learned. I want to show you something.'

The 'something' was a pocket-book full of poems. Paul had put some of his beautiful fancies into verse, and magazine editors had not been as unappreciative as they are sometimes supposed to be. Anne read Paul's poems with real delight. They were full of charm and promise.

'You'll be famous yet, Paul. I always dreamed of having one famous pupil. He was to be a college president – but a great poet would be even better. Some day I'll be able to boast that I whipped the distinguished Paul Irving. But then I never did whip you, did I, Paul? What an opportunity lost! I think I kept you in at recess, however.'

'You may be famous yourself, Teacher. I've seen a good deal of your work these last three years.'

'No. I know what I can do. I can write poetry, fanciful little sketches that children love and editors send welcome cheques for. But I can do nothing big. My only chance for earthly immortality is a corner in your Memoirs.'

Charlotta the Fourth had discarded the blue bows, but her freckles were not noticeably less.

'I never did think I'd come down to marrying a Yankee, Miss Shirley, ma'am,' she said. 'But you never know what's before you, and it isn't his fault. He was born that way.'

'You're a Yankee yourself, Charlotta, since you've married one.'

'Miss Shirley, ma'am, I'm *not*! And I wouldn't be if I was to marry a dozen Yankees! Tom's kind of nice. And besides, I thought I'd better not be too hard to please, for I mightn't get another chance. Tom don't drink and he don't growl because he has to work between meals, and when all's said and done I'm satisfied, Miss Shirley, ma'am.'

'Does he call you Leonora?' asked Anne.

'Goodness, no, Miss Shirley, ma'am. I wouldn't know who he meant if he did. Of course, when we got married he had to say, "I take thee, Leonora," and I declare to you, Miss Shirley, ma'am, I've had the most dreadful feeling ever since that it wasn't me he was talking to and I haven't been rightly married at all. And so you're going to be married yourself, Miss Shirley, ma'am? I always thought I'd like to marry a doctor. It would be so handy when the children had measles and croup. Tom is only a bricklayer, but he's real good-tempered. When I said to him, says I, "Tom, can I go to Miss Shirley's wedding? I mean to go anyhow, but I'd like to have your consent," he just says, "Suit yourself, Charlotta, and you'll suit me." That's a real pleasant kind of husband to have, Miss Shirley, ma'am.'

Philippa and her Reverend Jo arrived at Green Gables the day before the wedding. Anne and Phil had a rapturous meeting which presently simmered down to a cosy, confidential chat over all that had been and was about to be.

'Queen Anne, you're as queenly as ever. I've got fearfully thin since the babies came. I'm not half so good-looking; but I think Jo likes it. There's not such a contrast between us, you see. And oh, it's perfectly magnificent that you're going to marry Gilbert. Roy Gardner wouldn't have done at all, at all. I can see that now, though I was horribly disappointed at the time. You know, Anne, you did treat Roy very badly.'

'He has recovered, I understand,' smiled Anne.

'Oh, yes. He is married and his wife is a sweet little thing and they're perfectly happy. Everything works together for good. Jo and the Bible say that, and they are pretty good authorities.'

'Are Alec and Alonzo married yet?'

'Alec is, but Alonzo isn't. How those dear old days at Patty's Place come back when I'm talking to you, Anne! What fun we had!'

'Have you been to Patty's Place lately?'

'Oh, yes, I go often. Miss Patty and Miss Maria still sit by the fireplace and knit. And that reminds me – we've brought you a wedding gift from them, Anne. Guess what it is.'

'I never could. How did they know I was going to be married?'

'Oh, I told them. I was there last week. And they were so interested. Two days ago Miss Patty wrote me a note asking me to call; and then she asked if I would take her gift to you. What would you wish most from Patty's Place, Anne?'

'You can't mean that Miss Patty has sent me her china dogs?'

'Go up head. They're in my trunk this very moment. And I've a letter for you. Wait a moment and I'll get it.'

'Dear Miss Shirley,' Miss Patty had written, 'Maria and I were very much interested in hearing of your approaching nuptials. We send you our best wishes. Maria and I have never married, but we have no objection to other people doing so. We are sending you the china dogs. I intended to leave them to you in my will, because you seemed to have a sincere affection for them. But Maria and I expect to live a good while yet (D.V.), so I have decided to give you the dogs while you are young. You will not have forgotten that Gog looks to the right and Magog to the left.'

'Just fancy those lovely old dogs sitting by the fireplace in my house of dreams,' said Anne rapturously. 'I never expected anything so delightful.'

That evening Green Gables hummed with preparations for the following day; but in the twilight Anne slipped away. She had a little pilgrimage to make on this last day of her girlhood and she must make it alone. She went to Matthew's grave, in the little poplar-shaded Avonlea graveyard, and there kept a silent tryst with old memories and immortal loves.

'How glad Matthew would be tomorrow if he were here,'

29

she whispered. 'But I believe he does know and is glad of it – somewhere else. I've read somewhere that "our dead are never dead until we have forgotten them". Matthew will never be dead to me, for I can never forget him.'

She left on his grave the flowers she had brought and walked slowly down the long hill. It was a gracious evening, full of delectable lights and shadows. In the west was a sky of mackerel clouds – crimson and amber-tinted, with long strips of apple-green sky between. Beyond was the glimmering radiance of a sunset sea, and the ceaseless voice of many waters came up from the tawny shore. All around her, lying in the fine, beautiful country silence, were the hills and fields and woods she had known and loved so long.

'History repeats itself,' said Gilbert, joining her as she passed the Blythe gate. 'Do you remember our first walk down this hill, Anne – our first walk together anywhere, for that matter?'

'I was coming home in the twilight from Matthew's grave – and you came out of the gate; and I swallowed the pride of years and spoke to you.'

'And all heaven opened before me,' supplemented Gilbert. 'From that moment I looked forward to tomorrow. When I left you at your gate that night and walked home I was the happiest boy in the world. Anne had forgiven me.'

'I think you had the most to forgive. I was an ungrateful little wretch – and after you had really saved my life that day on the pond, too. How I loathed that load of obligation at first! I don't deserve the happiness that has come to me.'

Gilbert laughed and clasped tighter the girlish hand that wore his ring. Anne's engagement ring was a circlet of pearls. She had refused to wear a diamond.

'I've never really liked diamonds since I found out they weren't the lovely purple I had dreamed. They will always suggest my old disappointment.'

'But pearls are for tears, the old legend says,' Gilbert had objected.

'I'm not afraid of that. And tears can be happy as well as sad. My very happiest moments have been when I had tears in my eyes – when Marilla told me I might stay at Green Gables – when Matthew gave me the first pretty dress I ever had – when I heard that you were going to recover from the fever. So give me pearls for our troth ring, Gilbert, and I'll willingly accept the sorrow of life with its joy.'

But tonight our lovers thought only of joy and never of sorrow. For the morrow was their wedding day, and their house of dreams awaited them on the misty purple shore of Four Winds Harbour.

CHAPTER 4

The First Bride of Green Gables

ANNE WAKENED on the morning of her wedding day to find the sunshine winking in at the window of the little porch-gable and a September breeze frolicking with her curtains.

'I'm so glad the sun will shine on me,' she thought happily.

She recalled the first morning she had wakened in that little porch-room, when the sunshine had crept in on her through the blossom-drift of the old Snow Queen. That had not been a happy wakening, for it brought with it the bitter disappointment of the preceding night. But since then the little room had been endeared and consecrated by years of happy childhood dreams and maiden visions. To it she had come back joyfully after all her absences; at its window she had knelt through that night of bitter agony, when she believed Gilbert dying, and by it she had sat in speechless happiness the night of her betrothal. Many vigils of joy and some of sorrow had been kept there; and today she must leave it for ever. Henceforth it would be hers no more; fifteen-year-old Dora was to inherit it when she had gone. Nor did Anne wish it otherwise; the little room was sacred to youth and girlhood – to the past that was to close today before the chapter of wifehood opened.

Green Gables was a busy and joyous house that forenoon. Diana arrived early, with little Fred and Small Anne Cordelia, to lend a hand. Davy and Dora, the Green Gable twins, whisked the babies off to the garden.

'Don't let Small Anne Cordelia spoil her clothes,' warned Diana anxiously.

'You needn't be afraid to trust her with Dora,' said Marilla. 'That child is more sensible and careful than most of the mothers I've known. She's really a wonder in some ways. Not much like that other harum-scarum I brought up.'

Marilla smiled across her chicken salad at Anne. It might even be suspected that she liked the harum-scarum best after all.

'Those twins are real nice children,' said Mrs Rachel, when she was sure they were out of earshot. 'Dora is so womanly and helpful, and Davy is developing into a very smart boy. He isn't the holy terror for mischief he used to be.'

'I never was so distracted in my life as I was the first six months he was here,' acknowledged Marilla. 'After that I suppose I got used to him. He's taken a great notion to farming lately, and wants me to let him try running the farm next year. I may, for Mr Barry doesn't think he'll want to rent it much longer, and some new arrangement will have to be made.'

'Well, you certainly have a lovely day for your wedding, Anne,' said Diana, as she slipped a voluminous apron over her silken array. 'You couldn't have had a finer one if you'd ordered it from Eaton's.'

'Indeed, there's too much money going out of this Island to that same Eaton's,' said Mrs Lynde indignantly. She had strong views on the subject of octopus-like department stores, and never lost an opportunity of airing them. 'And as

33

for those catalogues of theirs, they're the Avonlea girls' Bible now, that's what. They pore over them on Sundays instead of studying the Holy Scriptures.'

'Well, they're splendid to amuse children with,' said Diana. 'Fred and Small Anne look at the pictures by the hour.'

'*I* amused ten children without the aid of Eaton's catalogue,' said Mrs Rachel severely.

'Come, you two, don't quarrel over Eaton's catalogue,' said Anne gaily. 'This is my day of days, you know. I'm so happy I want everyone else to be happy, too.'

'I'm sure I hope your happiness will last, child,' sighed Mrs Rachel. She did hope it truly, and believed it, but she was afraid it was in the nature of a challenge to Providence to flaunt your happiness too openly. Anne, for her own good, must be toned down a trifle.

But it was a happy and beautiful bride who came down the old, homespun-carpeted stairs that September noon – the first bride of Green Gables, slender and shining-eyed, in the mist of her maiden veil, with her arms full of roses. Gilbert, waiting for her in the hall below, looked up at her with adoring eyes. She was his at last, this evasive, long-sought Anne, won after years of patient waiting. It was to him she was coming in the sweet surrender of the bride. Was he worthy of her? Could he make her as happy as he hoped? If he failed her – if he could not measure up to her standard of manhood – then, as she held out her hand, their eyes met and all doubt was swept away in a glad certainty. They belonged to each other; and, no matter what life might hold for them, it could never alter that. Their happiness was in each other's keeping and both were unafraid.

They were married in the sunshine of the old orchard, circled by the loving and kindly faces of long-familiar friends. Mr Allan married them, and the Reverend Jo made what Mrs Rachel Lynde afterwards pronounced to be the 'most beautiful wedding prayer' she had ever heard. Birds do not often sing in September, but one sang sweetly from some hidden bough while Gilbert and Anne repeated their deathless vows. Anne heard it, and thrilled to it; Gilbert heard it, and wondered only that all the birds in the world had not burst into jubilant song; Paul heard it and later wrote a lyric about it which was one of the most admired in his first volume of verse; Charlotta the Fourth heard it and was blissfully sure it meant good luck for her adored Miss Shirley. The bird sang until the ceremony was ended and then it wound up with one mad little, glad little trill. Never had the old grey-green house among its enfolding orchards known a blither, merrier afternoon. All the old jests and quips, that must have done duty at weddings since Eden, were served up, and seemed as new and brilliant and mirth-provoking as if they had never been uttered before. Laughter and joy had their way; and when Anne and Gilbert left to catch the Carmody train, with Paul as driver, the twins were ready with rice and old shoes, in the throwing of which Charlotta the Fourth and Mr Harrison bore a valiant part. Marilla stood at the gate and watched the carriage out of sight down the long lane with its banks of golden-rod. Anne turned at its end to wave her last good-bye. She was gone – Green Gables was her home no more; Marilla's face looked very grey and old as she turned to the house which Anne had filled for fourteen years, and even in her absence, with light and life.

But Diana and her small fry, the Echo Lodge people and the Allans, had stayed to help the two old ladies over the loneliness of the first evening; and they contrived to have a quietly pleasant little supper-time, sitting long around the table and chatting over all the details of the day. While they were sitting there Anne and Gilbert were alighting from the train at Glen St Mary.

CHAPTER 5

The Home-coming

DR DAVID BLYTHE had sent his horse and buggy to meet them, and the urchin who had brought it slipped away with a sympathetic grin, leaving them to the delight of driving alone to their new home through the radiant evening.

Anne never forgot the loveliness of the view that broke upon them when they had driven over the hill behind the village. Her new home could not yet be seen; but before her lay Four Winds Harbour like a great, shining mirror of rose and silver. Far down, she saw its entrance between the bar of sand-dunes on one side and a steep, high, grim, red-sandstone cliff on the other. Beyond the bar the sea, calm and austere, dreamed in the afterlight. The little fishing village, nestled in the cove where the sand-dunes met the harbour shore, looked like a great opal in the haze. The sky over them was like a jewelled cup from which the dusk was pouring; the air was crisp with the compelling tang of the sea, and the whole landscape was infused with the subtleties of a sea evening. A few dim sails drifted along the darkening, fir-clad harbour shores. A bell was ringing from the tower of a little white church on the far side; mellowly and dreamily sweet, the chime floated across the water blent with the moan of the sea. The great revolving light on the cliff at the channel flashed warm and golden against the clear northern sky, a trembling, quivering star of good hope. Far out along the horizon was the crinkled grey ribbon of a passing steamer's smoke.

'Oh, beautiful, beautiful,' murmured Anne. 'I shall love Four Winds, Gilbert. Where is our house?'

'We can't see it yet – the belt of birch running up from that little cove hides it. It's about two miles from Glen St Mary, and there's another mile between it and the lighthouse. We won't have many neighbours, Anne. There's only one house near us and I don't know who lives in it. Shall you be lonely when I'm away?'

'Not with that light and that loveliness for company. Who lives in that house, Gilbert?'

'I don't know. It doesn't look – exactly – as if the occupants would be kindred spirits, Anne, does it?'

The house was a large, substantial affair, painted such a vivid green that the landscape seemed quite faded by contrast. There was an orchard behind it, and a nicely kept lawn before it, but, somehow, there was a certain bareness about it. Perhaps its neatness was responsible for this; the whole establishment, house, barns, orchard, garden, lawn, and lane, was so starkly neat.

'It doesn't seem probable that anyone with that taste in paint could be *very* kindred,' acknowledged Anne, 'unless it were an accident – like our blue hall. I feel certain there are no children there, at least. It's even neater than the old Copp place on the Tory road, and I never expected to see anything neater than that.'

They had not met anybody on the moist red road that wound along the harbour shore. But just before they came to the belt of birch which hid their home Anne saw a girl who was driving a flock of snow-white geese along the crest of a velvety green hill on the right. Great, scattered firs grew along it. Between their trunks one saw glimpses of yellow harvest fields, gleams of golden sand-hills, and bits of blue sea. The girl was tall and wore a dress of pale blue print. She walked with a certain springiness of step and erectness of bearing. She and her geese came out of the gate at the foot of the hill as Anne and Gilbert passed. She stood with her hand on the fastening of the gate, and looked steadily at them, with an expression that hardly attained to interest, but did not descend to curiosity. It seemed to Anne, for a fleeting moment, that there was even a veiled hint of hostility in it. But it was the girl's beauty which made Anne give a little gasp – a beauty so marked that it must have attracted attention anywhere. She was hatless, but heavy braids of burnished hair, the hue of ripe wheat, were twisted about her head like a coronet; her eyes were blue and star-like; her figure, in its plain print gown, was magnificent; and her lips were as crimson as the bunch of blood-red poppies she wore at her belt.

'Gilbert, who is the girl we have just passed?' asked Anne, in a low voice.

'I didn't notice any girl,' said Gilbert, who had eyes only for his bride.

'She was standing by that gate – no, don't look back. She is still watching us. I never saw such a beautiful face.'

'I don't remember seeing any very handsome girls while I was here. There are some pretty girls up at the Glen, but I hardly think they could be called beautiful.'

'This girl is. You can't have seen her, or you would remember her. Nobody could forget her. I never saw such a face except in pictures. And her hair! It made me think of

Browning's "cord of gold" and "gorgeous snake"!'

'Probably she's some visitor in Four Winds — likely some-one from that big summer hotel over the harbour.'

'She wore a white apron and she was driving geese.'

'She might do that for amusement. Look, Anne — there's our house.'

Anne looked and forgot for a time the girl with the splendid, resentful eyes. The first glimpse of her new home was a delight to eye and spirit — it looked so like a big, creamy sea-shell stranded on the harbour shore. The rows of tall Lombardy poplars down its lane stood out in stately purple silhouette against the sky. Behind it, sheltering its garden from the too keen breath of sea winds, was a cloudy fir-wood, in which the winds might make all kinds of weird and haunting music. Like all woods, it seemed to be holding and enfolding secrets in its recesses — secrets whose charm is only to be won by entering in and patiently seeking. Out-wardly, dark green arms keep them inviolate from curious or indifferent eyes.

The night winds were beginning their wild dances beyond the bar and the fishing hamlet across the harbour was gemmed with lights as Anne and Gilbert drove up the poplar lane. The door of the little house opened, and a warm glow of fire-light flickered out into the dusk. Gilbert lifted Anne from the buggy and led her into the garden, through the little gate between the ruddy-tipped firs, up the trim red path to the sandstone step.

'Welcome home,' he whispered, and hand in hand they stepped over the threshold of their house of dreams.

CHAPTER 6

Captain Jim

'OLD DOCTOR DAVE' and 'Mrs Doctor Dave' had come down to the little house to greet the bride and groom. Doctor Dave was a big, jolly, white-whiskered old fellow, and Mrs Doctor was a trim, rosy-cheeked, silver-haired little lady who took Anne at once to her heart, literally and figuratively.

'I'm so glad to see you, dear. You must be real tired. We've got a bite of supper ready, and Captain Jim brought up some trout for you. Captain Jim – where are you? Oh, he's slipped out to see to the horse, I suppose. Come upstairs and take your things off.'

Anne looked about her with bright, appreciative eyes as she followed Mrs Doctor Dave upstairs. She liked the appearance of her new home very much. It seemed to have the atmosphere of Green Gables and the flavour of her old traditions.

'I think I would have found Miss Elizabeth Russell a "kindred spirit",' she murmured when she was alone in her room. There were two windows in it; the dormer one looked out on the lower harbour and the sand-bar and the Four Winds light.

'A magic casement opening on the foam
Of perilous seas in fairy lands forlorn,'

quoted Anne softly. The gable window gave a view of a little harvest-hued valley through which a brook ran. Half a mile up the brook was the only house in sight – an old, rambling grey one surrounded by huge willows through which its windows peered, like shy, seeking eyes, into the dusk. Anne wondered who lived there; they would be her nearest neighbours and she hoped they would be nice. She suddenly found herself thinking of the beautiful girl with the white geese.

'Gilbert thought she didn't belong here,' mused Anne, 'but I feel sure she does. There was something about her that made her part of the sea and the sky and the harbour. Four Winds is in her blood.'

When Anne went downstairs Gilbert was standing before the fireplace talking to a stranger. Both turned as Anne entered.

'Anne, this is Captain Boyd. Captain Boyd, my wife.'

It was the first time Gilbert had said 'my wife' to anybody but Anne, and he narrowly escaped bursting with the pride of it. The old captain held out a sinewy hand to Anne; they smiled at each other and were friends from that moment. Kindred spirit flashed recognition to kindred spirit.

'I'm right down pleased to meet you, Mistress Blythe; and I hope you'll be as happy as the first bride was who came here. I can't wish you no better than *that*. But your husband doesn't introduce me jest exactly right. "Captain Jim" is my week-a-day name and you might as well begin as you're sartain to end up – calling me that. You sartainly are a nice little bride, Mistress Blythe. Looking at you sorter makes me feel that I've jest been married myself.'

Amid the laughter that followed Mrs Doctor Dave urged Captain Jim to stay and have supper with them.

'Thank you kindly. 'Twill be a real treat, Mistress Doctor. I mostly has to eat my meals alone, with the reflection of my ugly old phiz in a looking-glass opposite for company. 'Tisn't often I have a chance to sit down with two such sweet, purty ladies.'

Captain Jim's compliments may look very bald on paper, but he paid them with such a gracious, gentle deference of tone and look that the woman upon whom they were bestowed felt that she was being offered a queen's tribute in a kingly fashion.

Captain Jim was a high-souled, simple-minded old man, with eternal youth in his eyes and heart. He had a tall, rather ungainly figure, somewhat stooped, yet suggestive of great strength and endurance; a clean-shaven face deeply lined and bronzed; a thick mane of iron-grey hair falling quite to his shoulders, and a pair of remarkably blue, deep-set eyes, which sometimes twinkled and sometimes dreamed, and sometimes looked out seaward with a wistful quest in them, as of one seeking something precious and lost. Anne was to learn one day what it was for which Captain Jim looked.

It could not be denied that Captain Jim was a homely man. His spare jaws, rugged mouth, and square brow were not fashioned on the lines of beauty; and he had passed through many hardships and sorrows which had marked his body as well as his soul; but though at first sight Anne thought him plain, she never thought anything more about it – the spirit shining through that rugged tenement beautified it so wholly.

They gathered gaily around the supper table. The hearth-fire banished the chill of the September evening, but the window of the dining-room was open and sea breezes entered at their own sweet will. The view was magnificent, taking in the harbour and the sweep of low purple hills beyond. The table was heaped with Mrs Doctor's delicacies, but the *pièce de résistance* was undoubtedly the big platter of sea-trout.

'Thought they'd be sorter tasty after travelling,' said Captain Jim. 'They're fresh as trout can be, Mistress Blythe. Two hours ago they were swimming in the Glen Pond.'

'Who is attending to the light tonight, Captain Jim?' asked Doctor Dave.

'Nephew Alec. He understands it as well as I do. Well, now, I'm real glad you asked me to stay to supper. I'm proper hungry – didn't have much of a dinner today.'

'I believe you half-starve yourself most of the time down at that light,' said Mrs Doctor Dave severely. 'You won't take the trouble to get up a decent meal.'

'Oh, I do, Mistress Doctor, I do,' protested Captain Jim. 'Why, I live like a king gen'rally. Last night I was up to the Glen and took home two pounds of steak. I meant to have a spanking good dinner today.'

'And what happened to the steak?' asked Mrs Doctor Dave. 'Did you lose it on the way home?'

'No.' Captain Jim looked sheepish. 'Just at bedtime a poor, ornery sort of dog came along and asked for a night's lodging. Guess he belonged to some of the fishermen 'long shore. I couldn't turn the poor cur out – he had a sore foot. So I shut him in the porch, with an old bag to lie on, and went to bed. But somehow I couldn't sleep. Come to think it over, I sorter remembered that the dog looked hungry.'

'And you got up and gave him that steak – *all* that steak,' said Mrs Doctor Dave, with a kind of triumphant reproof.

'Well, there wasn't anything else *to* give him,' said Captain Jim deprecatingly. 'Nothing a dog'd care for, that is. I reckon he *was* hungry, for he made about two bites of it. I had a fine sleep the rest of the night but my dinner had to be sorter scanty – potatoes and point, as you might say. The dog, he lit out for home this morning. I reckon *he* weren't a vegetarian.'

'The idea of starving yourself for a worthless dog!' sniffed Mrs Doctor.

'You don't know but he may be worth a lot to somebody,' protested Captain Jim. 'He didn't *look* of much account, but you can't go by looks in jedging a dog. Like meself, he might be a real beauty inside. The First Mate didn't approve of him, I'll allow. His language was right down forcible. But the First Mate is prejudiced. No use in taking a cat's opinion of a dog. 'Tennyrate, I lost my dinner, so this nice spread in this dee-lightful company is real pleasant. It's a great thing to have good neighbours.'

'Who lives in the house among the willows up the brook?' asked Anne.

'Mrs Dick Moore,' said Captain Jim – 'and her husband,' he added, as if by way of an afterthought.

Anne smiled, and deduced a mental picture of Mrs Dick Moore from Captain Jim's way of putting it; evidently a second Mrs Rachel Lynde.

'You haven't many neighbours, Mistress Blythe,' Captain Jim went on. 'This side of the harbour is mighty thinly settled. Most of the land belongs to Mr Howard up yander past the Glen, and he rents it out for pasture. The other side of the harbour, now, is thick with folks – 'specially Mac-Allisters. There's a whole colony of MacAllisters – you can't

45

throw a stone but you hit one. I was talking to old Leon Blacquiere the other day. He's been working on the harbour all summer. "They're nearly all MacAllisters over thar," he told me. "Dare's Neil MacAllister and Sandy MacAllister and William MacAllister and Alec MacAllister and Angus MacAllister – and I believe dare's de Devil MacAllister." '

'There are nearly as many Elliotts and Crawfords,' said Doctor Dave, after the laughter had subsided. 'You know, Gilbert, we folk on this side of Four Winds have an old saying – "From the conceit of the Elliotts, the pride of the MacAllisters, and the vainglory of the Crawfords, good Lord deliver us." '

'There's a plenty of fine people among them, though,' said Captain Jim. 'I sailed with William Crawford for many a year, and for courage and endurance and truth that man hadn't an equal. They've got brains over on that side of Four Winds. Mebbe that's why this side is sorter inclined to pick on 'em. Strange, ain't it, how folks seem to resent anyone being born a mite cleverer than they be.'

Doctor Dave, who had a forty years' feud with the over-harbour people, laughed and subsided.

'Who lives in that brilliant emerald house about half a mile up the road?' asked Gilbert.

Captain Jim smiled delightedly.

'Miss Cornelia Bryant. She'll likely be over to see you soon, seeing you're Presbyterians. If you were Methodists she wouldn't come at all. Cornelia has a holy horror of Methodists.'

'She's quite a character,' chuckled Doctor Dave. 'A most inveterate man-hater!'

'Sour grapes?' queried Gilbert, laughing.

'No, 'tisn't sour grapes,' answered Captain Jim seriously. 'Cornelia could have had her pick when she was young. Even yet she's only to say the word to see the old widowers jump. She jest seems to have been born with a sort of chronic spite agin men and Methodists. She's got the bitterest tongue and the kindest heart in Four Winds. Wherever there's any trouble, that woman is there, doing everything to help in the tenderest way. She never says a harsh word about another woman, and if she likes to card us poor scallawags of men down I reckon our tough old hides can stand it.'

'She always speaks well of you, Captain Jim,' said Mrs Doctor.

'Yes, I'm afraid so. I don't half-like it. It makes me feel as if there must be something sorter unnatteral about me.'

CHAPTER 7

The Schoolmaster's Bride

'WHO WAS the first bride who came to this house, Captain Jim?' Anne asked, as they sat around the fireplace after supper.

'Was she a part of the story I've heard was connected with this house?' asked Gilbert. 'Somebody told me you could tell it, Captain Jim.'

'Well, yes, I know it. I reckon I'm the only person living in Four Winds now that can remember the schoolmaster's bride as she was when she came to the Island. She's been dead this thirty year, but she was one of them women you never forget.'

'Tell us the story,' pleaded Anne. 'I want to find out all about the women who have lived in this house before me.'

'Well, there's jest been three – Elizabeth Russell, and Mrs Ned Russell, and the schoolmaster's bride. Elizabeth Russell was a nice, clever little critter, and Mrs Ned was a nice woman, too. But they weren't ever like the schoolmaster's bride.

'The schoolmaster's name was John Selwyn. He came out from the Old Country to teach school at the Glen when I was a boy of sixteen. He wasn't much like the usual run of derelicts who used to come out to P.E.I. to teach school in them days. Most of them were clever, drunken critters who taught the children the three Rs when they were sober, and lambasted them when they wasn't. But John Selwyn was a fine, handsome young fellow. He boarded at my father's, and he and me were cronies, though he was ten years older'n me. We read and walked and talked a heap together. He knew about all the poetry that was ever written, I reckon, and he used to quote it to me along shore in the evenings. Dad thought it an awful waste of time, but he sorter endured it, hoping it'd put me off the notion of going to sea. Well, nothing could do *that* – mother come of a race of sea-going folk and it was born in me. But I loved to hear John read and recite. It's almost sixty years ago, but I could repeat yards of poetry I learned from him. Nearly sixty years!'

Captain Jim was silent for a space, gazing into the glowing fire in a quest of the bygones. Then, with a sigh, he resumed his story.

'I remember one spring evening I met him on the sand-hills. He looked sorter uplifted – jest like you did, Dr Blythe, when you brought Mistress Blythe in tonight. I thought of him the minute I seen you. And he told me that he had a sweetheart back home and that she was coming out to him. I wasn't more'n half pleased, ornery young lump of selfishness that I was; I thought he wouldn't be as much my friend after she came. But I'd enough decency not to let him see it. He told me all about her. Her name was Persis Leigh, and she would have come out with him if it hadn't been for her old uncle. He was sick, and he'd looked after her when her parents died and she wouldn't leave him. And now he was dead and she was coming out to marry John Selwyn. 'Twasn't no easy journey for a woman in them days. There weren't no steamers, you must ricollect.

' "When do you expect her?" says I.

' "She sails on the *Royal William*, the 20th June," says he, "and so she should be here by mid-July. I must set Carpenter Johnson to building me a home for her. Her letter come today. I know before I opened it that it had good news for me. I saw her a few nights ago."

'I didn't understand him, and then he explained – though I didn't understand *that* much better. He said he had a gift – or a curse. Them was his words, Mistress Blythe – a gift or a curse. He didn't know which it was. He said a great-great-grandmother of his had had it, and they burned her for a witch on account of it. He said queer spells – trances, I think was the name he given 'em – come over him now and again. Are there such things, doctor?'

'There are people who are certainly subject to trances,' answered Gilbert. 'The matter is more in the line of psychical research than medical. What were the trances of this John Selwyn like?'

'Like dreams,' said the old doctor sceptically.

'He said he could see things in them,' said Captain Jim slowly. 'Mind you, I'm telling you jest what *he* said – things that were happening – things that were *going* to happen. He said they were sometimes a comfort to him and sometimes a horror. Four nights before this he'd been in one – went into it while he was sitting looking at the fire. And he saw an old room he knew well in England, and Persis Leigh in it, holding out her hands to him and looking glad and happy. So he knew he was going to hear good news of her.'

'A dream – a dream,' scoffed the old doctor.

'Likely – likely,' conceded Captain Jim. 'That's what *I* said to him at the time. It was a vast more comfortable to think so. I didn't like the idea of him seeing things like that – it was real uncanny.

' "No," says he, "I didn't dream it. But we won't talk of this again. You won't be so much my friend if you think much about it."

'I told him nothing could make me any less his friend. But he jest shook his head and says, says he:

' "Lad, I know. I've lost friends before because of this. I don't blame them. There are times when I feel hardly friendly to myself because of it. Such a power has a bit of divinity in it – whether of a good or an evil divinity who shall say? And we mortals all shrink from too close contact with God or devil."

'Them was his words. I remember them as if 'twas yesterday, though I didn't know jest what he meant. What do you s'pose he *did* mean, doctor?'

'I doubt if he knew what he meant himself,' said Doctor Dave testily.

'I think I understand,' whispered Anne. She was listening in her old attitude of clasped lips and shining eyes. Captain Jim treated himself to an admiring smile before he went on with his story.

'Well, purty soon all the Glen and Four Winds people knew the schoolmaster's bride was coming, and they were all glad because they thought so much of him. And everybody took an interest in his new house – *this* house. He picked this site for it, because you could see the harbour and hear the sea from it. He made the garden out there for his bride, but he didn't plant the Lombardies. Mrs Ned Russell planted *them*. But there's a double row of rose-bushes in the garden that the little girls who went to the Glen school set out there, for the schoolmaster's bride. He said they were pink for her cheeks and white for her brow and red for her lips. He'd quoted poetry so much that he sorter got into the habit of talking it, too, I reckon.

'Almost everybody sent him some little present to help out the furnishing of the house. When the Russells came into it they were well-to-do and furnished it real handsome, as you can see; but the first furniture that went into it was plain enough. This little house was rich in love, though. The women sent in quilts and table-cloths and towels, and one man made a chest for her, and another a table and so on. Even blind old Aunt Margaret Boyd wove a little basket for her out of the sweet-scented sand-hill grass. The schoolmaster's wife used it for years to keep her handkerchiefs in.

'Well, at last everything was ready – even to the logs in the big fireplace ready for lighting. 'Twasn't exactly *this* fireplace, though 'twas in the same place. Miss Elizabeth had this put in when she made the house over fifteen years ago. It was a big, old-fashioned fireplace where you could have roasted an ox. Many's the time I've sat here and spun yarns, same's I'm doing tonight.'

Again there was a silence, while Captain Jim kept a passing tryst with visitants Anne and Gilbert could not see – the folks who had sat with him around that fireplace in the vanished years, with mirth and bridal joy shining in eyes long since closed for ever, under churchyard sod or heaving leagues of sea. Here on olden nights children had tossed laughter lightly to and fro. Here on winter evenings friends had gathered. Dance and music and jest had been here. Here youths and maidens had dreamed. For Captain Jim the little house was tenanted with shapes entreating remembrance.

'It was the first of July when the house was finished. The schoolmaster began to count the days then. We used to see him walking along the shore, and we'd say to each other, "She'll soon be with him now."

'She was expected the middle of July, but she didn't come then. Nobody felt anxious. Vessels were often delayed for days and mebbe weeks. The *Royal William* was a week overdue – and then two – and then three. And at last we began to be frightened, and it got worse and worse. Fin'lly I couldn't bear to look into John Selwyn's eyes. D'ye know, Mistress Blythe' – Captain Jim lowered his voice – 'I used to think that they looked just like what his old great-great-grandmother's must have been when they were burning her to death. He never said much, but he taught school like a man in a dream and then hurried to the shore. Many a night he walked there from dark to dawn. People said he was losing his mind. Everybody had given up hope – the *Royal William* was eight weeks overdue. It was the middle of September and the schoolmaster's bride hadn't come – never would come, we thought.

'There was a big storm then that lasted three days, and on the evening after it died away I went to the shore. I found the schoolmaster there, leaning with his arms folded against a big rock, gazing out to sea.

'I spoke to him but he didn't answer. His eyes seemed to be looking at something I couldn't see. His face was set, like a dead man's.

' "John – John," I called out – jest like that – jest like a frightened child, "wake up – wake up."

'That strange, awful look seemed to sorter fade out of his eyes. He turned his head and looked at me. I've never forgot his face – never will forget it till I ships for my last voyage.

' "All is well, lad," he says. "I've seen the *Royal William* coming around East Point. She will be here by dawn. Tomorrow night I shall sit with my bride by my own hearth-fire."

'Do you think he did see it?' demanded Captain Jim abruptly.

'God knows,' said Gilbert softly. 'Great love and great pain might compass we know not what marvels.'

'I am sure he did see it,' said Anne earnestly.

'Fol-de-rol,' said Doctor Dave, but he spoke with less conviction than usual.

'Because, you know,' said Captain Jim solemnly, 'the *Royal William* came into Four Winds Harbour at daylight the next morning. Every soul in the Glen and along the shore was at the old wharf to meet her. The schoolmaster had been watching there all night. How we cheered as she sailed up the channel.'

Captain Jim's eyes were shining. They were looking at the Four Winds Harbour of sixty years agone, with a battered old ship sailing through the sunrise splendour.

'And Persis Leigh was on board?' asked Anne.

'Yes – her and the captain's wife. They'd had an awful passage – storm after storm – and their provisions give out, too. But there they were at last. When Persis Leigh stepped on to the old wharf John Selwyn took her in his arms – and folks stopped cheering and begun to cry. I cried myself, though 'twas years, mind you, afore I'd admit it. Ain't it funny how ashamed boys are of tears?'

'Was Persis Leigh beautiful?' asked Anne.

'Well, I don't know that you'd call her beautiful exactly –

54

I – don't – know,' said Captain Jim slowly. 'Somehow, you never got so far along as to wonder if she was handsome or not. It jest didn't matter. There was something so sweet and winsome about her that you had to love her, that was all. But she was pleasant to look at – big, clear hazel eyes and heaps of glossy brown hair, and an English skin. John and her were married at our house that night at early candle-lighting; everybody from far and near was there to see it and we all brought them down here afterwards. Mistress Selwyn lighted the fire, and we went away and left them sitting here, jest as John had seen in that vision of his. A strange thing – a strange thing! But I've seen a turrible lot of strange things in my time.'

Captain Jim shook his head sagely.

'It's a dear story,' said Anne, feeling that for once she had got enough romance to satisfy her. 'How long did they live here?'

'Fifteen years. I ran off to sea soon after they were married, like the young scallawag I was. But every time I come back from a voyage I'd head for here, even before I went home, and tell Mistress Selwyn all about it. Fifteen happy years! They had a sort of talent for happiness, them two. Some folks are like that, if you've noticed. They *couldn't* be unhappy for long, no matter what happened. They quarrelled once or twice, for they was both high-sperrited. But Mistress Selwyn says to me once, says she, laughing in that pretty way of hers, "I felt dreadful when John and I quarrelled, but underneath it all I was very happy because I had such a nice husband to quarrel with and make it up with." Then they moved to Charlottetown, and Ned Russell bought this house and brought his bride here. They were a gay young pair, as I remember them. Miss Elizabeth Russell was Alec's sister. She came to live with them a year or so later, and she was a creature of mirth, too. The walls of this house must be sorter *soaked* with laughing and good times. You're the third bride I've seen come here, Mistress Blythe – and the handsomest.'

Captain Jim contrived to give his sunflower compliment the delicacy of a violet, and Anne wore it proudly. She was looking her best that night, with the bridal rose on her cheeks and the love-light in her eyes; even gruff old Doctor Dave gave her an approving glance, and told his wife, as they drove home together, that that red-headed wife of the boy's was something of a beauty.

'I must be getting back to the light,' announced Captain Jim. 'I've enj'yed this evening something tremenjus.'

'You must come often to see us,' said Anne.

'I wonder if you'd give that invitation if you knew how likely I'll be to accept it,' Captain Jim remarked whimsically.

'Which is another way of saying you wonder if I mean it,' smiled Anne. 'I do, "cross my heart", as we used to say at school.'

'Then I'll come. You're likely to be pestered with me at any hour. And I'll be proud to have you drop down and visit me now and then, too. Gin'rally I haven't anyone to talk to but the First Mate, bless his sociable heart. He's a mighty good listener, and has forgot more'n any MacAllister of them all ever knew, but he isn't much of a conversationalist. You're young and I'm old, but our souls are about the same age, I reckon. We both belong to the race that knows Joseph, as Cornelia Bryant would say.'

'The race that knows Joseph?' puzzled Anne.

'Yes. Cornelia divides all the folks in the world into two kinds – the race that knows Joseph and the race that don't. If a person sorter sees eye to eye with you, and has pretty much the same ideas about things, and the same taste in jokes – why, then he belongs to the race that knows Joseph.'

'Oh, I understand,' exclaimed Anne, light breaking in upon her. 'It's what I used to call – and still call in quotation marks – "kindred spirits".'

'Jest so – jest so,' agreed Captain Jim. 'We're *it*, whatever it is. When you come in tonight, Mistress Blythe, I says to myself, says I, "Yes, she's of the race that knows Joseph." And mighty glad I was, for if it wasn't so we couldn't have had any real satisfaction in each other's company. The race that knows Joseph is the salt of the airth, I reckon.'

The moon had just risen when Anne and Gilbert went to the door with their guests. Four Winds Harbour was beginning to be a thing of dream and glamour and enchantment – a spellbound haven where no tempest might ever ravin. The Lombardies down the lane, tall and sombre as the priestly forms of some mystic band, were tipped with silver.

'Always like Lombardies,' said Captain Jim, waving a long arm at them. 'They're the trees of princesses. They're out of fashion now. Folks complain that they die at the top and get ragged-looking. So they do – so they do, if you don't risk your neck every spring climbing up a light ladder to trim them out. I always did it for Miss Elizabeth, so her Lombardies never got out-at-elbows. She was especially fond of them. She liked their dignity and stand-offishness. *They* don't hob-nob with every Tom, Dick, and Harry. If it's maples for company, Mistress Blythe, it's Lombardies for society.'

'What a beautiful night,' said Mrs Doctor Dave, as she climbed into the Doctor's buggy.

'Most nights are beautiful,' said Captain Jim. 'But I 'low that moonlight over Four Winds makes me sorter wonder what's left for heaven. The moon's a great friend of mine, Mistress Blythe. I've loved her ever since I can remember. When I was a little chap of eight I fell asleep in the garden one evening and wasn't missed. I woke up alone in the night and I was most scared to death. What shadows and queer noises there was! I dursn't move. Jest crouched there quaking, poor small mite. Seemed 'sif there weren't anyone in the world but meself and it was mighty big. Then all at once I saw the moon looking down at me through the apple boughs, jest like an old friend. I was comforted right off. Got up and walked to the house as brave as a lion, looking at her. Many's the night I've watched her from the deck of my vessel, on seas far away from here. Why don't you folks tell me to take in the slack of my jaw and go home?'

The laughter of the good-nights died away. Anne and Gilbert walked hand in hand around their garden. The brook that ran across the corner dimpled pellucidly in the shadows of the birches. The poppies along its banks were like shallow cups of moonlight. Flowers that had been planted by the hands of the schoolmaster's bride flung their sweetness on the shadowy air, like the beauty and blessing of sacred yesterdays. Anne paused in the gloom to gather a spray.

'I love to smell flowers in the dark,' she said. 'You get hold of their soul then. Oh, Gilbert, this little house is all I've dreamed it. And I'm so glad that we are not the first who have kept bridal tryst here!'

CHAPTER 8

Miss Cornelia Bryant Comes to Call

THAT SEPTEMBER was a month of golden mists and purple hazes at Four Winds Harbour – a month of sun-stepped days and of nights that were swimming in moonlight, or pulsating with stars. No storm marred it, no rough wind blew. Anne and Gilbert put their nest in order, rambled on the shores, sailed on the harbour, drove about Four Winds and the Glen, or through the ferny, sequestered roads of the woods around the harbour head; in short, had such a honeymoon as any lovers in the world might have envied them.

'If life were to stop short just now it would still have been richly worth while, just for the sake of these past four weeks, wouldn't it?' said Anne. 'I don't suppose we will ever have four such perfect weeks again – but we've *had* them. Everything – wind, weather, folks, house of dreams – has conspired to make our honeymoon delightful. There hasn't even been a rainy day since we came here.'

'And we haven't quarrelled once,' teased Gilbert.

'Well, "that's a pleasure all the greater for being deferred",' quoted Anne. 'I'm so glad we decided to spend our honeymoon here. Our memories of it will always belong here, in our house of dreams, instead of being scattered about in strange places.'

There was a certain tang of romance and adventure in the

59

atmosphere of their new home which Anne had never found in Avonlea. There, although she had lived in sight of the sea, it had not entered intimately into her life. In Four Winds it surrounded her and called to her constantly. From every window of her new home she saw some varying aspect of it. Its haunting murmur was ever in her ears. Vessels sailed up the harbour every day to the wharf at the Glen, or sailed out again through the sunset, bound for ports that might be halfway round the globe. Fishing boats went white-winged down the channel in the mornings, and returned laden in the evenings. Sailors and fisher-folk travelled the red, winding harbour roads, light-hearted and content. There was always a certain sense of things going to happen – of adventures and farings-forth. The ways of Four Winds were less staid and settled and grooved than those of Avonlea; winds of change blew over them; the sea called ever to the dwellers on shore, and even those who might not answer its call felt the thrill and unrest and mystery and possibilities of it.

'I understand now why some men must go to sea,' said Anne. 'That desire which comes to us all at times – "to sail beyond the bourne of sunset" – must be very imperious when it is born in you. I don't wonder Captain Jim ran away because of it. I never see a ship sailing out of the channel, or a gull soaring over the sand-bar, without wishing I were on board the ship or had wings, not like a dove "to fly away and be at rest", but like a gull, to sweep out into the very heart of a storm.'

'You'll stay right here with me, Anne-girl,' said Gilbert lazily. 'I won't have you flying away from me into the hearts of storms.'

They were sitting on their red sandstone doorstep in the

late afternoon. Great tranquillities were all about them in land and sea and sky. Silvery gulls were soaring over them. The horizons were laced with long trails of frail, pinkish clouds. The hushed air was threaded with a murmurous refrain of minstrel winds and waves. Pale asters were blowing in the sere and misty meadows between them and the harbour.

'Doctors who have to be up all night waiting on sick folk don't feel very adventurous, I suppose,' Anne said indulgently. 'If you had had a good sleep last night, Gilbert, you'd be as ready as I am for a flight of imagination.'

'I did good work last night, Anne,' said Gilbert quietly, 'Under God, I saved a life. This is the first time I could ever really claim that. In other cases I may have helped; but, Anne, if I had not stayed at Allonby's last night and fought death hand to hand that woman would have died before morning. I tried an experiment that was certainly never tried in Four Winds before. I doubt if it was ever tried anywhere before outside of a hospital. It was a new thing in Kingsport hospital last winter. I could never have dared try it here if I had not been absolutely certain that there was no other chance. I risked it – and it succeeded. As a result, a good wife and mother is saved for long years of happiness and usefulness. As I drove home this morning, while the sun was rising over the harbour, I thanked God that I had chosen the profession I did. I had fought a good fight and won – think of it, Anne, *won*, against the Great Destroyer. It's what I dreamed of doing long ago when we talked together of what we wanted to do in life. That dream of mine came true this morning.'

'Was that the only one of your dreams that has come

true?' asked Anne, who knew perfectly well what the substance of his answer would be, but wanted to hear it again.

'*You* know, Anne-girl,' said Gilbert, smiling into her eyes. At that moment there were certainly two perfectly happy people sitting on the doorstep of a little white house on the Four Winds Harbour shore.

Presently Gilbert said, with a change of tone, 'Do I or do I not see a full-rigged ship sailing up our lane?'

Anne looked and sprang up.

'That must be either Miss Cornelia Bryant or Mrs Moore coming to call,' she said.

'I'm going into the office, and if it is Miss Cornelia I warn you that I'll eavesdrop,' said Gilbert. 'From all I've heard regarding Miss Cornelia I conclude that her conversation will not be dull, to say the least.'

'It may be Mrs Moore.'

'I don't think Mrs Moore is built on those lines. I saw her working in her garden the other day, and, though I was too far away to see clearly, I thought she was rather slender. She doesn't seem very socially inclined when she has never called on you yet, although she's your nearest neighbour.'

'She can't be like Mrs Lynde, after all, or curiosity would have brought her,' said Anne. 'This caller is, I think, Miss Cornelia.'

Miss Cornelia it was; moreover, Miss Cornelia had not come to make any brief and fashionable wedding call. She had her work under her arm in a substantial parcel, and when Anne asked her to stay she promptly took off her capacious sun-hat, which had been held on her head, despite irreverent September breezes, by a tight elastic band under her hard little knob of fair hair. No hat-pins for Miss

Cornelia, an it please ye! Elastic bands had been good enough for her mother and they were good enough for *her*. She had a fresh, round, pink-and-white face, and jolly brown eyes. She did not look in the least like the traditional old maid, and there was something in her expression which won Anne instantly. With her old instinctive quickness to discern kindred spirits she knew she was going to like Miss Cornelia, in spite of uncertain oddities of opinion, and certain oddities of attire.

Nobody but Miss Cornelia would have come to make a call arrayed in a striped blue-and-white apron and a wrapper of chocolate print, with a design of huge pink roses scattered over it. And nobody but Miss Cornelia could have looked dignified and suitably garbed in it. Had Miss Cornelia been entering a palace to call on a prince's bride she would have been just as dignified and just as wholly mistress of the situation. She would have trailed her rose-spattered flounce over the marble floors just as unconcernedly, and she would have proceeded just as calmly to disabuse the mind of the princess of any idea that the possession of a mere man, be he prince or peasant, was anything to brag of.

'I've brought my work, Mrs Blythe, dearie,' she remarked, unrolling some dainty material. 'I'm in a hurry to get this done, and there isn't any time to lose.'

Anne looked in some surprise at the white garment spread over Miss Cornelia's ample lap. It was certainly a baby's dress, and it was most beautifully made, with tiny frills and tucks. Miss Cornelia adjusted her glasses, and fell to embroidering with exquisite stitches.

'This is for Mrs Fred Proctor up at the Glen,' she announced. 'She's expecting her eighth baby any day now, and not a stitch has she ready for it. The other seven have wore out all she made for the first, and she's never had time or strength or spirit to make any more. That woman is a martyr, Mrs Blythe, believe *me*. When she married Fred Proctor *I* knew how it would turn out. He was one of your wicked, fascinating men. After he got married he left off being fascinating and just kept on being wicked. He drinks and he neglects his family. Isn't that like a man? I don't know how Mrs Proctor would ever keep her children decently clothed if her neighbours didn't help her out.'

As Anne was afterwards to learn, Miss Cornelia was the only neighbour who troubled herself much about the decency of the young Proctors.

'When I heard this eighth baby was coming I decided to make some things for it,' Miss Cornelia went on. 'This is the last and I want to finish it today.'

'It's certainly very pretty,' said Anne. 'I'll get my sewing and we'll have a little thimble party of two. You are a beautiful sewer, Miss Bryant.'

'Yes, I'm the best sewer in these parts,' said Miss Cornelia in a matter-of-fact tone. 'I ought to be! Lord, I've done more of it than if I'd had a hundred children of my own, believe *me*! I s'pose I'm a fool, to be putting hand embroidery on this dress for an eighth baby. But, Lord, Mrs Blythe, dearie, it isn't to blame for being the eighth, and I kind of wished it to have one real pretty dress, just as if it *was* wanted. Nobody's wanting the poor mite – so I put some extra fuss on its little things just on that account.'

'Any baby might be proud of that dress,' said Anne, feeling still more strongly that she was going to like Miss Cornelia.

'I s'pose you've been thinking I was never coming to call on you,' resumed Miss Cornelia. 'But this is harvest month, you know, and I've been busy – and a lot of extra hands hanging round, eating more'n they work, just like the men. I'd have come yesterday, but I went to Mrs Roderick MacAllister's funeral. At first I thought my head was aching so badly I couldn't enjoy myself if I did go. But she was a hundred years old, and I'd always promised myself that I'd go to her funeral.'

'Was it a successful function?' asked Anne, noticing that the office door was ajar.

'What's that? Oh, yes, it was a tremendous funeral. She had a very large connection. There was over one hundred and twenty carriages in the procession. There was one or two funny things happened. I thought that die I would to see old Joe Bradshaw, who is an infidel and never darkens the door of a church, singing "Safe in the Arms of Jesus" with great gusto and fervour. He glories in singing – that's why he never misses a funeral. Poor Mrs Bradshaw didn't look much like singing – all wore out slaving. Old Joe starts out once in a while to buy her a present and brings home some new kind of farm machinery. Isn't that like a man? But what else would you expect of a man who never goes to church, even a Methodist one? I was real thankful to see you and the young Doctor in the Presbyterian church your first Sunday. No doctor for me who isn't a Presbyterian.'

'We were in the Methodist church last Sunday evening,' said Anne wickedly.

'Oh, I s'pose Dr Blythe has to go to the Methodist church once in a while or he wouldn't get the Methodist practice.'

'We liked the sermon very much,' declared Anne boldly. 'And I thought the Methodist minister's prayer was one of the most beautiful I ever heard.'

'Oh, I've no doubt he can pray. I never heard anyone make more beautiful prayers than old Simon Bentley, who was always drunk, or hoping to be, and the drunker he was the better he prayed.'

'The Methodist minister is very fine-looking,' said Anne, for the benefit of the office door.

'Yes, he's quite ornamental,' agreed Miss Cornelia. 'Oh, and *very* ladylike. And he thinks that every girl who looks at him falls in love with him – as if a Methodist minister, wandering about like any Jew, was such a prize! If you and the young doctor take *my* advice you won't have much to do with the Methodists. My motto is – if you *are* a Presbyterian, *be* a Presbyterian.'

'Don't you think that Methodists go to heaven as well as Presbyterians?' asked Anne smilelessly.

'That isn't for *us* to decide. It's in higher hands than ours,' said Miss Cornelia solemnly. 'But I ain't going to associate with them on earth whatever I may have to do in heaven. *This* Methodist minister isn't married. The last one they had was, and his wife was the silliest, flightiest little thing I ever saw. I told her husband once that he should have waited till she was grown up before he married her. He said he wanted to have the training of her. Wasn't that like a man?'

'It's rather hard to decide just when people *are* grown up,' laughed Anne.

'That's a true word, dearie. Some are grown up when they're born, and others ain't grown up when they're eighty, believe *me*. That same Mrs Roderick I was speaking of never grew up. She was as foolish when she was a hundred as when she was ten.'

'Perhaps that was why she lived so long,' suggested Anne.

'Maybe 'twas. *I*'d rather live fifty sensible years than a hundred foolish ones.'

'But just think what a dull world it would be if everyone was sensible,' pleaded Anne.

Miss Cornelia disdained any skirmish of flippant epigram.

'Mrs Roderick was a Milgrave, and the Milgraves never had much sense. Her nephew, Ebenezer Milgrave, used to be insane for years. He believed he was dead and used to rage at his wife because she wouldn't bury him. *I*'d a-done it.'

Miss Cornelia looked so grimly determined that Anne could almost see her with a spade in her hand.

'Don't you know *any* good husbands, Miss Bryant?'

'Oh, yes, lots of them – over yonder,' said Miss Cornelia, waving her hand through the open window towards the little graveyard of the church across the harbour.

'But living – going about in the flesh?' persisted Anne.

'Oh, there's a few, just to show that with God all things are possible,' acknowledged Miss Cornelia reluctantly. 'I don't deny that an odd man here and there, if he's caught young and trained up proper, and if his mother has spanked him well beforehand, may turn out a decent being. *Your* husband, now, isn't so bad, as men go, from all I hear. I s'pose' – Miss Cornelia looked sharply at Anne over her glasses – 'you think there's nobody like him in the world.'

'There isn't,' said Anne promptly.

'Ah, well, I heard another bride say that once,' sighed Miss Cornelia. 'Jennie Dean thought when she married that there wasn't anybody like *her* husband in the world. And she was right – there wasn't! And a good thing, too, believe *me*! He led her an awful life – and he was courting his second wife while Jennie was dying. Wasn't that like a man? However, I hope *your* confidence will be better justified, dearie. The young doctor is taking real well. I was afraid at first he mightn't, for folks hereabouts have always thought old Doctor Dave the only doctor in the world. Doctor Dave hadn't much tact, to be sure – he was always talking of ropes in houses where someone had hanged himself. But folks forgot their hurt feelings when they had a pain in their stomachs. If he'd been a minister instead of a doctor they'd never have forgiven him. Soul-ache doesn't worry folks near as much as stomach-ache. Seeing as we're both Presbyterians and no Methodists around, will you tell me your candid opinion of *our* minister?'

'Why – really – I – well,' hesitated Anne.

Miss Cornelia nodded.

'Exactly. I agree with you, dearie. We made a mistake when we called *him*. His face just looks like one of those long, narrow stones in the graveyard, doesn't it? "Sacred to the memory" ought to be written on his forehead. I shall never forget the first sermon he preached after he came. It was on the subject of everyone doing what they were best fitted for – a very good subject, of course; but such illustrations as he used! He said, "If you had a cow and an apple-tree, and if you tied the apple-tree in your stable and planted the cow in your orchard, with her legs up, how much milk would you get from the apple-tree, or how many apples from the cow?" Did you ever hear the like in your born days, dearie? I was so thankful there were no Methodists there that day – they'd never have been done hooting over it. But what I dislike most in him is his habit of agreeing with everybody, no matter what is said. If you said to him, "You're a scoundrel", he'd say, with that smooth smile of his, "Yes, that's so." A minister should have more backbone. The long and the short of it is, I consider him a reverend jackass. But, of course, this is just between you and me. When there are Methodists in hearing I praise him to the skies. Some folks think his wife dresses too gay, but *I* say when she has to live with a face like that she needs something to cheer her up. You'll never hear *me* condemning a woman for her dress. I'm only too thankful when her husband isn't too mean and miserly to allow it. Not that I bother much with dress myself. Women just dress to please the men, and I'd never stoop to *that*. I have had a real placid, comfortable life, dearie, and it's just because I never cared a cent what the men thought.'

'Why do you hate the men so, Miss Bryant?'

'Lord, dearie, I don't hate them. They aren't worth it. I just sort of despise them. I think I'll like *your* husband if he keeps on as he has begun. But apart from him, about the only men in the world I've much use for are the old doctor and Captain Jim.'

'Captain Jim is certainly splendid,' agreed Anne cordially.

'Captain Jim is a good man, but he's kind of vexing in one way. You *can't* make him mad. I've tried for twenty years and he just keeps on being placid. It does sort of rile me. And I s'pose the woman he should have married got a man who went into tantrums twice a day.'

'Who was she?'

'Oh, I don't know, dearie. I never remember of Captain

Jim making up to anybody. He was edging on old as far as my memory goes. He's seventy-six, you know. I never heard any reason for his staying a bachelor, but there must be one, believe *me*. He sailed all his life till five years ago, and there's no corner of the earth he hasn't poked his nose into. He and Elizabeth Russell were great cronies, all their lives, but they never had any notion of sweet-hearting. Elizabeth never married, though she had plenty of chances. She was a great beauty when she was young. The year the Prince of Wales came to the Island she was visiting her uncle in Charlotte-town and he was a Government official, and so she got invited to the great ball. She was the prettiest girl there, and the Prince danced with her, and all the other women he didn't dance with were furious about it, because their social standing was higher than hers and they said he shouldn't have passed them over. Elizabeth was always very proud of that dance. Mean folks said that was why she never married — she couldn't put up with an ordinary man after dancing with a prince. But that wasn't so. She told me the reason once — it was because she had such a temper that she was afraid she couldn't live peaceably with any man. She *had* an awful temper — she used to have to go upstairs and bite pieces out of her bureau to keep it down by times. But I told her that wasn't any reason for not marrying if she wanted to. There's no reason why we should let the men have a monopoly of temper, is there, Mrs Blythe, dearie?'

'I've a bit of temper myself,' sighed Anne.

'It's well you have, dearie. You won't be half so likely to be trodden on, believe *me*! My, how that golden glow of yours is blooming! Your garden looks fine. Poor Elizabeth always took such care of it.'

'I love it,' said Anne. 'I'm glad it's so full of old-fashioned flowers. Speaking of gardening, we want to get a man to dig up that little lot beyond the fir-grove and set it out with strawberry plants for us. Gilbert is so busy he will never get time for it this fall. Do you know anyone we can get?'

'Well, Henry Hammond up at the Glen goes out doing jobs like that. He'll do, maybe. He's always a heap more interested in his wages than in his work, just like a man, and he's so slow in the uptake that he stands still for five minutes before it dawns on him that he's stopped. His father threw a stump at him when he was small. Nice gentle missile, wasn't it? So like a man! Course, the boy never got over it. But he's the only one I can recommend at all. He painted my house for me last spring. It looks real nice now, don't you think?'

Anne was saved by the clock striking five.

'Lord, is it that late!' exclaimed Miss Cornelia. 'How time does slip by when you're enjoying yourself! Well, I must betake myself home.'

'No, indeed! You are going to stay and have tea with us,' said Anne eagerly.

'Are you asking me because you think you ought to, or because you really want to?' demanded Miss Cornelia.

'Because I really want to.'

'Then I'll stay. *You* belong to the race that knows Joseph.'

'I know we are going to be friends,' said Anne, with the smile that only they of the household of faith ever saw.

'Yes, we are, dearie. Thank goodness, we can choose our friends. We have to take our relatives as they are, and be thankful if there are no penitentiary birds among them. Not that I've many – none nearer than second cousins. I'm a kind of lonely soul, Mrs Blythe.'

There was a wistful note in Miss Cornelia's voice.

'I wish you would call me Anne,' exclaimed Anne impulsively. 'It would seem more *homey*. Every one in Four Winds, except my husband, calls me Mrs Blythe, and it makes me feel like a stranger. Do you know that your name is very near being the one I yearned after when I was a child? I hated "Anne" and I called myself "Cordelia" in imagination.'

'I like Anne. It was my mother's name. Old-fashioned names are the best and sweetest in my opinion. If you're going to get tea you might send the young doctor to talk to me. He's been lying on the sofa in that office ever since I came, laughing fit to kill over what I've been saying.'

'How did you know?' cried Anne, too aghast at this instance of Miss Cornelia's uncanny prescience to make a polite denial.

'I saw him sitting beside you when I came up the lane, and I know men's tricks,' retorted Miss Cornelia. 'There, I've finished my little dress, dearie, and the eighth baby can come as soon as it pleases.'

CHAPTER 9

An Evening at Four Winds Point

IT WAS late September when Anne and Gilbert were able to pay Four Winds light their promised visit. They had often planned to go, but something always occurred to prevent them. Captain Jim had 'dropped in' several times at the little house.

'I don't stand on ceremony, Mistress Blythe,' he told Anne. 'It's a real pleasure to me to come here, and I'm not going to deny myself jest because you haven't got down to see me. There oughtn't to be no bargaining like that among the race that knows Joseph. I'll come when I can, and you come when you can, and so long's we have our pleasant little chat it don't matter a mite what roof's over us.'

Captain Jim took a great fancy to Gog and Magog, who were presiding over the destinies of the hearth in the little house with as much dignity and aplomb as they had done at Patty's Place.

'Aren't they the cutest little cusses?' he would say delightedly; and he bade them greeting and farewell as gravely and invariably as he did his host and hostess. Captain Jim was not going to offend household deities by any lack of reverence and ceremony.

'You've made this little house just about perfect,' he told Anne. 'It never was so nice before. Mistress Selwyn had your taste and she did wonders; but folks in those days didn't have the pretty little curtains and pictures and nicknacks you have. As for Elizabeth, she lived in the past. You've kinder brought the future into it, so to speak. I'd be real happy even if we couldn't talk at all, when I come here – jest to sit and look at you and your pictures and your flowers would be enough of a treat. It's beautiful – beautiful.'

Captain Jim was a passionate worshipper of beauty. Every lovely thing heard or seen gave him a deep, subtle, inner joy that irradiated his life. He was quite keenly aware of his own lack of outward comeliness and lamented it.

'Folks say I'm good,' he remarked whimsically upon one occasion, 'but I sometimes wish the Lord had made me only half as good and put the rest of it into looks. But there, I reckon He knew what He was about, as a good Captain should. Some of us have to be homely, or the purty ones – like Mistress Blythe here – wouldn't show up so well.'

One evening Anne and Gilbert finally walked down to the Four Winds light. The day had begun sombrely in grey cloud and mist, but it had ended in a pomp of scarlet and gold. Over the western hills beyond the harbour were amber deeps and crystalline shallows, with the fire of sunset below. The north was a mackerel sky of little, fiery golden clouds. The red light flamed on the white sails of a vessel gliding down the channel, bound to a southern port in a land of palms. Beyond her, it smote upon and incarnadined the shining white grassless faces of the sand-dunes. To the right, it fell on the old house among the willows up the brook, and gave it for a fleeting space casements more splendid than those of an old cathedral. They glowed out of its quiet and greyness like the throbbing blood-red thoughts of a vivid soul imprisoned in a dull husk of environment.

'That old house up the brook always seems so lonely,' said Anne. 'I never see visitors there. Of course, its lane opens on the upper road – but I don't think there's much coming and going. It seems odd we've never met the Moores yet, when they live within fifteen minutes' walk of us. I may have seen them in church, of course, but if so I didn't know them. I'm sorry they are so unsociable, when they are our only near neighbours.'

'Evidently they don't belong to the race that knows Joseph,' laughed Gilbert. 'Have you ever found out who that girl was whom you thought so beautiful?'

'No. Somehow I have never remembered to ask about her. But I've never seen her anywhere, so I suppose she must have been a stranger. Oh, the sun has just vanished – and there's the light.'

As the dusk deepened, the great beacon cut swathes of light through it, sweeping in a circle over the fields and the harbour, the sand-bar and the gulf.

'I feel as if it might catch me and whisk me leagues out to sea,' said Anne, as one drenched them with radiance; and she felt rather relieved when they got so near the Point that they were inside the range of those dazzling, recurrent flashes.

As they turned into the little lane that led across the fields to the Point they met a man coming out of it – a man of such extraordinary appearance that for a moment they both frankly stared. He was a decidedly fine-looking person – tall, broad-shouldered, well featured, with a Roman nose and frank grey eyes; he was dressed in a prosperous farmer's Sunday best; in so far he might have been any inhabitant of Four Winds or the Glen. But flowing over his breast nearly to his knees was a river of crinkly brown beard; and adown his back, beneath his commonplace felt hat, was a corresponding cascade of thick, wavy brown hair.

'Anne,' murmured Gilbert, when they were out of earshot, 'you didn't put what Uncle Dave calls "a little of the Scott Act" in that lemonade you gave me just before we left home, did you?'

'No, I didn't,' said Anne, stifling her laughter, lest the retreating enigma should hear her. 'Who in the world can he be?'

'I don't know; but if Captain Jim keeps apparitions like that down at this Point I'm going to carry cold iron in my pocket when I come here. He wasn't a sailor, or one might pardon his eccentricity of appearance; he must belong to the over-harbour clans. Uncle Dave says they have several freaks over there.'

'Uncle Dave is a little prejudiced, I think. You know all the over-harbour people who come to the Glen Church seem very nice. Oh, Gilbert, isn't this beautiful?'

The Four Winds light was built on a spur of red sandstone cliff jutting out into the gulf. On one side, across the channel, stretched the silvery sand shore of the bar; on the other extended a long, curving beach of red cliffs, rising steeply from the pebbled coves. It was a shore that knew the magic and mystery of storm and star. There is a great solitude about such a shore. The woods are never solitary – they are full of whispering, beckoning, friendly life. But the sea is a mighty soul, for ever moaning of some great, unshareable sorrow, which shuts it up into itself for all eternity. We can never pierce its infinite mystery – we may only wander, awed and spellbound, on the outer fringe of it.

The woods call to us with a hundred voices, but the sea has one only – a mighty voice that drowns our souls in its majestic music. The woods are human, but the sea is of the company of the archangels.

Anne and Gilbert found Captain Jim sitting on a bench outside the lighthouse, putting the finishing touches to a wonderful, full-rigged toy schooner. He rose and welcomed them to his abode with the gentle, unconscious courtesy that became him so well.

'This has been a purty nice day all through, Mistress Blythe, and now, right at the last, it's brought its best. Would you like to sit down here outside a bit, while the light lasts? I've just finished this bit of a plaything for my little grand-nephew, Joe, up at the Glen. After I promised to make it for him I was kinder sorry, for his mother was vexed. She's afraid he'll be wanting to go to sea later on and she doesn't want the notion encouraged in him. But what could I do, Mistress Blythe? I'd *promised* him, and I think it's sorter real dastardly to break a promise you make to a child. Come, sit down. It won't take long to stay an hour.'

The wind was off shore, and only broke the sea's surface into long silvery ripples, and sent sheeny shadows flying out across it, from every point and headland, like transparent wings. The dusk was hanging a curtain of violet gloom over the sand-dunes and the headlands where gulls were huddling. The sky was faintly filmed over with scarfs of silken vapour. Cloud fleets rode at anchor along the horizons. An evening star was watching over the bar.

'Isn't that a view worth looking at?' said Captain Jim, with a loving, proprietary pride. 'Nice and far from the market-place, ain't it? No buying and selling and getting gain. You don't have to pay anything – all that sea and sky free – "without money and without price". There's going to be a moonrise purty soon, too – I'm never tired of finding out what a moonrise can be over them rocks and sea and harbour. There's a surprise in it every time.'

They had their moonrise, and watched its marvel and magic in a silence that asked nothing of the world or each other. Then they went up into the tower, and Captain Jim showed and explained the mechanism of the great light. Finally they found themselves in the dining-room, where a fire of driftwood was weaving flames of wavering, elusive, sea-born hues in the open fireplace.

'I put this fireplace in myself,' remarked Captain Jim. 'The Government don't give lighthouse-keepers such luxuries. Look at the colours that wood makes. If you'd like some driftwood for your fire, Mistress Blythe, I'll bring you up a load some day. Sit down. I'm going to make you a cup of tea.'

Captain Jim placed a chair for Anne, having first removed therefrom a huge, orange-coloured cat and a newspaper.

'Get down, Matey. The sofa is your place. I must put this paper away safe till I can find time to finish the story in it. It's called *A Mad Love*. 'Tisn't my favourite brand of fiction, but I'm reading it jest to see how long she can spin it out. It's at the sixty-second chapter now, and the wedding ain't any nearer than when it begun, far's I can see. When little Joe comes I have to read him pirate yarns. Ain't it strange how innocent little creatures like children like the blood-thirstiest stories?'

'Like my lad Davy at home,' said Anne. 'He wants tales that reek with gore.'

Captain Jim's tea proved to be nectar. He was pleased as a child with Anne's compliments, but he affected a fine indifference.

'The secret is I don't skimp the cream,' he remarked airily. Captain Jim had never heard of Oliver Wendell Holmes, but he evidently agreed with that writer's dictum that 'big heart never liked little cream pot'.

'We met an odd-looking personage coming out of your lane,' said Gilbert as they sipped. 'Who was he?'

Captain Jim grinned.

'That's Marshall Elliott – a mighty fine man with jest one streak of foolishness in him. I s'pose you wondered what his object was in turning himself into a sort of dime museum freak.'

'Is he a modern Nazarite or a Hebrew prophet left over from olden times?' asked Anne.

'Neither of them. It's politics that's at the bottom of his freak. All those Elliotts and Crawfords and MacAllisters are dyed-in-the-wool politicians. They're born Grit or Tory, as the case may be, and they live Grit or Tory, and they die Grit or Tory; and what they're going to do in heaven, where there's probably no politics, is more than I can fathom. This Marshall Elliott was born a Grit. I'm a Grit myself in moderation, but there's no moderation about Marshall. Fifteen years ago there was a specially bitter general election. Marshall fought for his party tooth and nail. He was dead sure the Liberals would win – so sure that he got up at a public meeting and vowed that he wouldn't shave his face or cut his hair until the Grits were in power. Well, they didn't go in – and they've never got in yet – and you saw the result tonight for yourselves. Marshall stuck to his word.'

'What does his wife think of it?' asked Anne.

'He's a bachelor. But if he had a wife I reckon she couldn't make him break that vow. That family of Elliotts has always been more stubborn than natteral. Marshall's brother Alexander had a dog he set great store by, and when it died the man actilly wanted to have it buried in the graveyard, "along with the other Christians," he said. Course, he wasn't allowed to; so he buried it just outside the graveyard fence, and never darkened the church door again. But Sundays he'd drive his family to church and sit by that dog's grave and read his Bible all the time service was going on. They say when he was dying he asked his wife to bury him beside the dog; she was a meek little soul but she fired up at *that*. She said *she* wasn't going to be buried beside no dog, and if he'd rather have his last resting-place beside the dog than beside her, jest to say so. Alexander Elliott was a stubborn mule, but he was fond of his wife, so he give in and said, "Well, durn it, bury me where you please. But when Gabriel's trump blows I expect my dog to rise with the rest of us, for he had as much soul as any durned Elliott or Crawford or MacAllister that ever strutted." Them was *his* parting words. As for Marshall, we're all used to him, but he must strike strangers as right down peculiar-looking. I've known him ever since he was ten – he's about fifty now – and I like him. Him and me was out cod-fishing today. That's about all I'm good for now – catching trout and cod occasional. But 'tweren't always so – not by no manner of means. I used to do other things, as you'd admit if you saw my life-book.'

Anne was just going to ask what his life-book was when the First Mate created a diversion by springing upon Captain Jim's knee. He was a gorgeous beastie, with a face as round as a full moon, vivid green eyes, and immense white double paws. Captain Jim stroked his velvet back gently.

'I never fancied cats much till I found the First Mate,' he remarked, to the accompaniment of the Mate's tremendous purrs. 'I saved his life, and when you've saved a creature's life you're bound to love it. It's next thing to giving life. There's some turrible thoughtless people in the world, Mistress Blythe. Some of them city folks who have summer homes over the harbour are so thoughtless that they're cruel. It's the worst kind of cruelty — the thoughtless kind. You can't cope with it. They keep cats there in the summer, and feed and pet 'em, and doll 'em up with ribbons and collars. And then in the fall they go off and leave 'em to starve or freeze. It makes my blood boil, Mistress Blythe. One day last winter I found a poor old mother cat dead on the shore, lying against the skin-and-bone bodies of her three little kittens. She'd died trying to shelter 'em. She had her poor stiff paws around 'em. Master, I cried. Then I swore. Then I carried them poor little kittens home and fed 'em up and found good homes for 'em. I knew the woman who left the cat and when she come back this summer I jest went over the harbour and told her my opinion of her. It was rank meddling, but I do love meddling in a good cause.'

'How did she take it?' asked Gilbert.

'Cried and said she "didn't think". I says to her, says I, "Do you s'pose that'll be held for a good excuse in the day of Jedgment, when you'll have to account for that poor old mother's life? The Lord'll ask you what He give you your brains for if it wasn't to think, I reckon." I don't fancy she'll leave cats to starve another time.'

81

'Was the First Mate one of the forsaken?' asked Anne, making advances to him which were responded to graciously, if condescendingly.

'Yes. I found *him* one bitter cold day in winter, caught in the branches of a tree by his durn-fool ribbon collar. He was almost starving. If you could have seen his eyes, Mistress Blythe! He was nothing but a kitten, and he'd got his living somehow since he'd been left until he got hung up. When I loosed him he give my hand a pitiful swipe with his little red tongue. He wasn't the able seaman you see now. He was meek as Moses. That was nine years ago. His life has been long in the land for a cat. He's a good old pal, the First Mate is.'

'I should have expected you to have a dog,' said Gilbert.

Captain Jim shook his head.

'I had a dog once. I thought so much of him that when he died I couldn't bear the thought of getting another in his place. He was a *friend* – you understand, Mistress Blythe? Matey's only a pal. I'm fond of Matey – all the fonder on account of the spice of devilment that's in him – like there is in all cats. But I *loved* my dog. I always had a sneaking sympathy for Alexander Elliott about *his* dog. There isn't any devil in a good dog. That's why they're more lovable than cats, I reckon. But I'm darned if they're as interesting. Here I am, talking too much. Why don't you check me? When I do get a chance to talk to anyone I run on turrible. If you've done your tea I've a few little things you might like to look at – picked 'em up in the queer corners I used to be poking my nose into.'

Captain Jim's 'few little things' turned out to be a most interesting collection of curios, hideous, quaint, and beautiful. And almost every one had some striking story attached to it.

Anne never forgot the delight with which she listened to those old tales that moonlit evening by that enchanted driftwood fire, while the silver sea called to them through the open window and sobbed against the rocks below them.

Captain Jim never said a boastful word, but it was impossible to help seeing what a hero the man had been – brave, true, resourceful, unselfish. He sat there in his little room and made those things live again for his hearers. By a lift of the eyebrow, a twist of the lip, a gesture, a word, he painted a whole scene or character so that they saw it as it was.

Some of Captain Jim's adventures had such a marvellous edge that Anne and Gilbert secretly wondered if he were not drawing a rather long bow at their credulous expense. But in this, as they found later, they did him injustice. His tales were all literally true. Captain Jim had the gift of the born story-teller, whereby 'unhappy, far-off things' can be brought vividly before the hearer in all their pristine poignancy.

Anne and Gilbert laughed and shivered over his tales, and once Anne found herself crying. Captain Jim surveyed her tears with pleasure shining from his face.

'I like to see folks cry that way,' he remarked. 'It's a compliment. But I can't do justice to the things I've seen or helped to do. I've 'em all jotted down in my life-book, but I haven't got the knack of writing them out properly. If I could hit on jest the right words and string 'em together proper on paper I could make a great book. It would beat *A Mad Love* holler, and I believe Joe'd like it as well as the pirate yarns. Yes, I've had some adventures in my time; and, do you know, Mistress Blythe, I still lust after 'em. Yes, old and useless as I be, there's an awful longing sweeps over me at times to sail out – out – out there – for ever and ever.'

'Like Ulysses, you would

> Sail beyond the sunset, and the baths
> Of all the western stars, until you die,'

said Anne dreamily.

'Ulysses? I've read of him. Yes, that's jest how I feel – jest how all us old sailors feel, I reckon. I'll die on land after all, I s'pose. Well, what is to be will be. There was old William Ford at the Glen who never went on the water in his life, 'cause he was afraid of being drowned. A fortune-teller had predicted he would be. And one day he fainted and fell with his face in the barn trough and was drowned. Must you go? Well, come soon and come often. The doctor is to do the talking next time. He knows a heap of things I want to find out. I'm sorter lonesome here by times. It's been worse since Elizabeth Russell died. Her and me was such cronies.'

Captain Jim spoke with the pathos of the aged, who see their old friends slipping from them one by one – friends whose place can never be quite filled by those of a younger generation, even of the race that knows Joseph. Anne and Gilbert promised to come soon and often.

'He's a rare old fellow, isn't he?' said Gilbert, as they walked home.

'Somehow, I can't reconcile his simple, kindly personality with the wild, adventurous life he has lived,' mused Anne.

'You wouldn't find it so hard if you had seen him the other day down at the fishing village. One of the men of Peter Gautier's boat made a nasty remark about some girl along the shore. Captain Jim fairly scorched the wretched fellow with the lightning of his eyes. He seemed a man transformed. He didn't say much – but the way he said it! You'd have thought it would strip the flesh from the fellow's bones. I understand that Captain Jim will never allow a word against any woman to be said in his presence.'

'I wonder why he never married,' said Anne. 'He should have sons with their ships at sea now, and grandchildren climbing over him to hear his stories – he's that kind of a man. Instead, he has nothing but a magnificent cat.'

But Anne was mistaken. Captain Jim had more than that. He had a memory.

CHAPTER 10

Leslie Moore

'I'M GOING for a walk to the outside shore tonight,' Anne told Gog and Magog one October evening. There was no one else to tell, for Gilbert had gone over the harbour. Anne had her little domain in the speckless order one would expect of anyone brought up by Marilla Cuthbert, and felt that she could gad shoreward with a clear conscience. Many and delightful had been her shore rambles, sometimes with Gilbert, sometimes with Captain Jim, sometimes alone with her own thoughts and new, poignantly-sweet dreams that were beginning to span life with their rainbows. She loved the gentle, misty harbour shore and the silvery, wind-haunted sand shore, but best of all she loved the rock shore, with its cliffs and caves and piles of surf-worn boulders, and its coves where the pebbles glittered under the pools; and it was to this shore she hied herself tonight.

There had been an autumn storm of wind and rain, lasting for three days. Thunderous had been the crash of billows on the rocks, wild the white spray and spume that blew over the bar, troubled and misty and tempest-torn the erstwhile blue peace of Four Winds Harbour. Now it was over, and the shore lay clean-washed after the storm; not a wind stirred, but there was still a fine surf on, dashing on sand and rock in a splendid white turmoil – the only restless thing in the great, pervading stillness and peace.

'Oh, this is a moment worth living through weeks of storm and stress for,' Anne exclaimed, delightedly sending her far gaze across the tossing waters from the top of the cliff where she stood. Presently she scrambled down the steep path to the little cove below, where she seemed shut in with rocks and sea and sky.

'I'm going to dance and sing,' she said. 'There's no one here to see me – the sea-gulls won't carry tales of the matter. I may be as crazy as I like.'

She caught up her skirt and pirouetted along the hard strip of sand just out of reach of the waves that almost lapped her feet with their spent foam. Whirling round and round, laughing like a child, she reached the little headland that ran out to the east of the cove; then she stopped suddenly, blushing crimson; she was not alone; there had been a witness to her dance and laughter.

The girl of the golden hair and sea-blue eyes was sitting on a boulder of the headland, half hidden by a jutting rock. She was looking straight at Anne with a strange expression – part wonder, part sympathy, part – could it be? – envy. She was bareheaded, and her splendid hair, more than ever like Browning's 'gorgeous snake', was bound about her head with a crimson ribbon. She wore a dress of some dark material, very plainly made; but swathed about her waist, outlining its fine curves, was a vivid girdle of red silk. Her hands, clasped over her knee, were brown and somewhat work-hardened; but the skin of her throat and cheeks was as white as cream. A flying gleam of sunset broke through a low-lying western cloud and fell across her hair. For a moment she seemed the spirit of the sea personified – all its mystery, all its passion, all its elusive charm.

'You – you must think me crazy,' stammered Anne, trying to recover her self-possession. To be seen by this stately girl in such an abandon of childishness – she, Mrs Dr Blythe, with all the dignity of the matron to keep up – it was too bad!

'No,' said the girl, 'I don't.'

She said nothing more; her voice was expressionless; her manner slightly repellent; but there was something in her eyes – eager yet shy, defiant yet pleading – which turned Anne from her purpose of walking away. Instead, she sat down on the boulder beside the girl.

'Let's introduce ourselves,' she said, with the smile that had never yet failed to win confidence and friendliness. 'I am Mrs Blythe – and I live in that little white house up the harbour shore.'

'Yes, I know,' said the girl. 'I am Leslie Moore – Mrs Dick Moore,' she added stiffly.

Anne was silent for a moment from sheer amazement. It had not occurred to her that this girl was married – there seemed nothing of the wife about her. And that she should be the neighbour whom Anne had pictured as a commonplace Four Winds housewife! Anne could not quickly adjust her mental focus to this astonishing change.

'Then – then you live in that grey house up the brook,' she stammered.

'Yes. I should have gone over to call on you long ago,' said the other. She did not offer any explanation or excuse for not having gone.

'I wish you *would* come,' said Anne, recovering herself somewhat. 'We're such near neighbours we ought to be friends. That is the sole fault of Four Winds – there aren't quite enough neighbours. Otherwise it is perfection.'

'You like it?'

'*Like* it! I love it. It is the most beautiful place I ever saw.'

'I've never seen many places,' said Leslie Moore, slowly, 'but I've always thought it was very lovely here. I – I love it, too.'

She spoke, as she looked, shyly, yet eagerly. Anne had an odd impression that this strange girl – the word 'girl' would persist – could say a good deal if she chose.

'I often come to the shore,' she added.

'So do I,' said Anne. 'It's a wonder we haven't met here before.'

'Probably you come earlier in the evening than I do. It is generally late – almost dark – when I come. And I love to come just after a storm – like this. I don't like the sea so well when it's calm and quiet. I like the struggle – and the crash – and the noise.'

'I love it in all its moods,' declared Anne. 'The sea at Four Winds is to me what Lovers' Lane was at home. Tonight it seemed so free – so untamed – something broke loose in me, too, out of sympathy. That was why I danced along the shore in that wild way. I didn't suppose anybody was looking, of course. If Miss Cornelia Bryant had seen me she would have foreboded a gloomy prospect for poor young Dr Blythe.'

'You know Miss Cornelia?' said Leslie, laughing. She had an exquisite laugh; it bubbled up suddenly and unexpectedly with something of the delicious quality of a baby's. Anne laughed, too.

'Oh, yes. She has been down to my house of dreams several times.'

'Your house of dreams?'

'Oh, that's a dear, foolish little name Gilbert and I have for our home. We just call it that between ourselves. It slipped out before I thought.'

'So Miss Russell's little white house is *your* house of dreams,' said Leslie wonderingly. '*I* had a house of dreams once – but it was a palace,' she added, with a laugh, the sweetness of which was marred by a little note of derision.

'Oh, I once dreamed of a palace, too,' said Anne. 'I suppose all girls do. And then we settle down contentedly in eight-room houses that seem to fulfil all the desires of our hearts – because our prince is there. *You* should have had your palace really, though – you are so beautiful. You *must* let me say it – it *has* to be said – I'm nearly bursting with admiration. You are the loveliest thing I ever saw, Mrs Moore.'

'If we are to be friends you must call me Leslie,' said the other with an odd passion.

'Of course I will. And *my* friends call me Anne.'

'I suppose I am beautiful,' Leslie went on, looking stormily out to sea. 'I hate my beauty. I wish I had always been as brown and plain as the brownest and plainest girl at the fishing village over there. Well, what do you think of Miss Cornelia?'

The abrupt change of subject shut the door on any further confidences.

'Miss Cornelia is a darling, isn't she?' said Anne. 'Gilbert and I were invited to her house to a state tea last week. You've heard of groaning tables.'

'I seem to recall seeing the expression in the newspaper reports of weddings,' said Leslie, smiling.

'Well, Miss Cornelia's groaned – at least, it creaked – positively. You couldn't have believed she would have cooked so much for two ordinary people. She had every kind of pie you could name, I think – except lemon pie. She said she had taken the prize for lemon pies at the Charlottetown Exhibition ten years ago and had never made any since for fear of losing her reputation for them.'

'Were you able to eat enough pie to please her?'

'*I* wasn't. Gilbert won her heart by eating – I won't tell you how much. She said she never knew a man who didn't like pie better than his Bible. Do you know, I love Miss Cornelia.'

'So do I,' said Leslie. 'She is the best friend I have in the world.'

Anne wondered secretly why, if this were so, Miss Cornelia had never mentioned Mrs Dick Moore to her. Miss Cornelia had certainly talked freely about every other individual in or near Four Winds.

'Isn't that beautiful?' said Leslie, after a brief silence, pointing to the exquisite effect of a shaft of light falling through a cleft in the rock behind them, across a dark green pool at its base. 'If I had come here – and seen nothing but just that – I would go home satisfied.'

'The effects of light and shadow all along these shores are wonderful,' agreed Anne. 'My little sewing-room looks out on the harbour, and I sit at its window and feast my eyes. The colours and shadows are never the same two minutes together.'

'And you are never lonely?' asked Leslie abruptly. 'Never – when you are alone?'

'No. I don't think I've ever been really lonely in my life,' answered Anne. 'Even when I'm alone I have real good company – dreams and imaginations and pretendings. I *like* to be alone now and then, just to think over things and *taste* them. But I love friendship – and nice, jolly little times with people. Oh, *won't* you come to see me – often? Please do. I believe,' Anne added, laughing, 'that you'd like me if you knew me.'

'I wonder if *you* would like *me*,' said Leslie seriously. She was not fishing for a compliment. She looked out across the waves that were beginning to be garlanded with blossoms of moonlit foam, and her eyes filled with shadows.

'I'm sure I would,' said Anne. 'And please don't think I'm utterly irresponsible because you saw me dancing on the shore at sunset. No doubt I shall be dignified after a time. You see, I haven't been married very long. I feel like a girl, and sometimes like a child, yet.'

'I have been married twelve years,' said Leslie.

Here was another unbelievable thing.

'Why, you can't be as old as I am!' exclaimed Anne. 'You must have been a child when you were married.'

'I was sixteen,' said Leslie, rising, and picking up the cap and jacket lying beside her. 'I am twenty-eight now. Well, I must go back.'

'So must I. Gilbert will probably be home. But I'm so glad we both came to the shore tonight and met each other.'

Leslie said nothing, and Anne was a little chilled. She had offered friendship frankly, but it had not been accepted very graciously, if it had not been absolutely repelled. In silence they climbed the cliffs and walked across a pasture-field of which the feathery, bleached, wild grasses were like a carpet of creamy velvet in the moonlight. When they reached the shore lane Leslie turned.

'I go this way, Mrs Blythe. You will come over and see me some time, won't you?'

Anne felt as if the invitation had been thrown at her. She got the impression that Leslie Moore gave it reluctantly.

'I will come if you really want me to,' she said a little coldly.

'Oh, I do – I do,' exclaimed Leslie, with an eagerness which seemed to burst forth and beat down some restraint that had been imposed on it.

'Then I'll come. Good night – Leslie.'

'Good night, Mrs Blythe.'

Anne walked home in a brown study and poured out her tale to Gilbert.

'So Mrs Dick Moore isn't one of the race that knows Joseph?' said Gilbert teasingly.

'No – o – o, not exactly. And yet – I think she *was* one of them once, but has gone or got into exile,' said Anne musingly. 'She is certainly very different from the other women about here. You can't talk about eggs and butter to *her*. To think I've been imagining her a second Mrs Rachel Lynde! Have you ever seen Dick Moore, Gilbert?'

'No. I've seen several men working about the fields of the farm, but I don't know which was Moore.'

'She never mentioned him. I *know* she isn't happy.'

'From what you tell me I suppose she was married before she was old enough to know her own mind or heart, and found out too late that she had made a mistake. It's a common tragedy enough, Anne. A fine woman would have made the best of it. Mrs Moore has evidently let it make her bitter and resentful.'

'Don't let us judge her till we know,' pleaded Anne. 'I don't believe her case is so ordinary. You will understand her fascination when you meet her, Gilbert. It is a thing quite apart from her beauty. I feel that she possesses a rich nature, into which a friend might enter as into a kingdom; but for some reason she bars everyone out and shuts all her possibilities up in herself, so that they cannot develop and blossom. There, I've been struggling to define her to myself ever since I left her, and that is the nearest I can get to it. I'm going to ask Miss Cornelia about her.'

CHAPTER 11

The Story of Leslie Moore

'YES, the eighth baby arrived a fortnight ago,' said Miss Cornelia, from a rocker before the fire of the little house one chilly October afternoon. 'It's a girl. Fred was ranting mad – said he wanted a boy – when the truth is he didn't want it at all. If it had been a boy he'd have ranted because it wasn't a girl. They had four girls and three boys before, so I can't see that it made much difference what this one was, but of course he'd have to be cantankerous, just like a man. The baby is real pretty, dressed up in its nice little clothes. It has black eyes and the dearest, tiny hands.'

'I must go and see it. I just love babies,' said Anne, smiling to herself over a thought too dear and sacred to be put into words.

'I don't say but what they're nice,' admitted Miss Cornelia. 'But some folks seem to have more than they really need, believe *me*. My poor cousin Flora up at the Glen had eleven, and such a slave as she is! Her husband suicided three years ago. Just like a man!'

'What made him do that?' asked Anne, rather shocked.

'Couldn't get his way over something, so he jumped into the well. A good riddance! He was a born tyrant. But of course it spoiled the well. Flora could never abide the thought of using it again, poor thing! So she had another dug and a frightful expense it was, and the water as hard as nails.

If he *had* to drown himself there was plenty of water in the harbour, wasn't there? I've no patience with a man like that. We've only had two suicides in Four Winds in my recollection. The other was Frank West – Leslie Moore's father. By the way, has Leslie ever been over to call on you yet?'

'No, but I met her on the shore a few nights ago and we scraped an acquaintance,' said Anne, pricking up her ears.

Miss Cornelia nodded.

'I'm glad, dearie. I was hoping you'd foregather with her. What do you think of her?'

'I thought her very beautiful.'

'Oh, of course. There was never anybody about Four Winds could touch her for looks. Did you ever see her hair? It reaches to her feet when she lets it down. But I meant how did you like her?'

'I think I could like her very much if she'd let me,' said Anne slowly.

'But she wouldn't let you – she pushed you off and kept you at arm's length. Poor Leslie! You wouldn't be much surprised if you knew what her life has been. It's been a tragedy – a tragedy!' repeated Miss Cornelia emphatically.

'I wish you would tell me all about her – that is, if you can do so without betraying any confidence.'

'Lord, dearie, everybody in Four Winds knows poor Leslie's story. It's no secret – the *outside*, that is. Nobody knows the *inside* but Leslie herself, and she doesn't take folks into her confidence. I'm about the best friend she has on earth, I reckon, and she's never uttered a word of complaint to me. Have you ever seen Dick Moore?'

'No.'

'Well, I may as well begin at the beginning and tell you

everything straight through, so you'll understand it. As I said, Leslie's father was Frank West. He was clever and shiftless – just like a man. Oh, he had heaps of brains – and much good they did him! He started to go to college, and he went for two years, and then his health broke down. The Wests were all inclined to be consumptive. So Frank came home and started farming. He married Rose Elliott from over harbour. Rose was reckoned the beauty of Four Winds – Leslie takes her looks from her mother, but she has ten times the spirit and go that Rose had, and a far better figure. Now you know, Anne, I always take the ground that us women ought to stand by each other. We've got enough to endure at the hands of the men, the Lord knows, so I hold we hadn't ought to clapper-claw one another, and it isn't often you'll find me running down another woman. But I never had much use for Rose Elliott. She was spoiled to begin with, believe *me*, and she was nothing but a lazy, selfish, whining creature. Frank was no hand to work, so they were poor as Job's turkey. Poor! They lived on potatoes and point, believe *me*. They had two children – Leslie and Kenneth. Leslie had her mother's looks and her father's brains, and something she didn't get from either of them. She took after her Grandmother West – a splendid old lady. She was the brightest, friendliest, merriest thing when she was a child, Anne. Everybody liked her. She was her father's favourite and she was awful fond of him. They were "chums", as she used to say. She couldn't see any of his faults – and he *was* a taking sort of man in some ways.

'Well, when Leslie was twelve years old the first dreadful thing happened. She worshipped little Kenneth – he was four years younger than her, and he *was* a dear little chap.

97

And he was killed one day – fell off a big load of hay just as it was going into the barn, and the wheel went right over his little body and crushed the life out of it. And mind you, Anne, Leslie saw it. She was looking down from the loft. She gave one screech – the hired man said he never heard such a sound in all his life – he said it would ring in his ears till Gabriel's trump drove it out. But she never screeched or cried again about it. She jumped from the loft on to the load and from the load to the floor, and caught up the little bleeding, warm, dead body, Anne – they had to tear it from her before she would let it go. They sent for me – I can't talk of it.'

Miss Cornelia wiped the tears from her kindly brown eyes and sewed in bitter silence for a few minutes.

'Well,' she resumed, 'it was all over – they buried little Kenneth in that graveyard over the harbour, and after a while Leslie went back to her school and her studies. She never mentioned Kenneth's name – I've never heard it cross her lips from that day to this. I reckon that old hurt still aches and burns at times; but she was only a child and time is real kind to children, Anne, dearie. After a while she began to laugh again – she had the prettiest laugh. You don't often hear it now.'

'I heard it once the other night,' said Anne. 'It *is* a beautiful laugh.'

'Frank West began to go down after Kenneth's death. He wasn't strong and it was a shock to him, because he was real fond of the child, though, as I've said, Leslie was his favourite. He got mopy and melancholy, and couldn't or wouldn't work. And one day, when Leslie was fourteen years of age, he hanged himself – and in the parlour, too, mind you, Anne, right in the middle of the parlour from the lamp-hook in the ceiling. Wasn't that like a man? It was the anniversary of his wedding day, too. Nice, tasty time to pick for it, wasn't it? And, of course, that poor Leslie had to be the one to find him. She went into the parlour that morning, singing, with some fresh flowers for the vases, and there she saw her father hanging from the ceiling, his face as black as a coal. It was something awful, believe *me*!'

'Oh, how horrible!' said Anne, shuddering. 'The poor, poor child!'

'Leslie didn't cry at her father's funeral any more than she had cried at Kenneth's. Rose whooped and howled for two, however, and Leslie had all she could do trying to calm and comfort her mother. I was disgusted with Rose and so was everyone else, but Leslie never got out of patience. She loved her mother. Leslie is clannish – her own could never do wrong in her eyes. Well, they buried Frank West beside Kenneth, and Rose put up a great big monument to him. It was bigger than his character, believe *me*! Anyhow, it was bigger than Rose could afford, for the farm was mortgaged for more than its value. But not long after Leslie's old Grandmother West died and she left Leslie a little money – enough to give her a year at Queen's Academy. Leslie had made up her mind to pass for a teacher if she could, and then earn enough to put herself through Redmond College. That had been her father's pet scheme – he wanted her to have what he had lost. Leslie was full of ambition and her head was chock full of brains. She went to Queen's, and she took two years' work in one year and got her First; and when she came home she got the Glen school. She was so happy and hopeful and full of life and eagerness. When I think of what

99

she was then and what she is now, I say – drat the men!'

Miss Cornelia snipped her thread off as viciously as if, Nero-like, she was severing the neck of mankind by the stroke.

'Dick Moore came into her life that summer. His father, Abner Moore, kept store at the Glen, but Dick had a sea-going streak in him from his mother; he used to sail in summer and clerk in his father's store in winter. He was a big, handsome fellow, with a little ugly soul. He was always wanting something till he got it, and then he stopped wanting it – just like a man. Oh, he didn't growl at the weather when it was fine, and he was mostly real pleasant and agreeable when everything went right. But he drank a good deal, and there were some nasty stories told of him and a girl down at the fishing village. He wasn't fit for Leslie to wipe her feet on, that's the long and short of it. And he was a Methodist! But he was clean mad about her – because of her good looks in the first place, and because she wouldn't have anything to say to him in the second. He vowed he'd have her – and he got her!'

'How did he bring it about?'

'Oh, it was an iniquitous thing! I'll never forgive Rose West. You see, dearie, Abner Moore held the mortgage on the West farm, and the interest was overdue some years, and Dick just went and told Mrs West that if Leslie wouldn't marry him he'd get his father to foreclose the mortgage. Rose carried on terrible – fainted and wept, and pleaded with Leslie not to let her be turned out of her home. She said it would break her heart to leave the home she'd come to as a bride. I wouldn't have blamed her for feeling dreadful bad over it – but you wouldn't have thought she'd be so selfish as to sacrifice her own flesh and blood because of it, would you? Well, she was. And Leslie gave in – she loved her mother so much she would have done anything to save her pain. She married Dick Moore. None of us knew why at the time. It wasn't till long afterwards that I found out how her mother had worried her into it. I was sure there was something wrong, though, because I knew how she had snubbed him time and again, and it wasn't like Leslie to turn face-about like that. Besides, I knew that Dick Moore wasn't the kind of man Leslie could ever fancy, in spite of his good looks and dashing ways. Of course, there was no wedding, but Rose asked me to go and see them married. I went, but I was sorry I did. I'd seen Leslie's face at her brother's funeral and at her father's funeral – and now it seemed to me I was seeing it at her own funeral. But Rose was smiling as a basket of chips, believe *me*!

'Leslie and Dick settled down on the West place – Rose couldn't bear to part with her dear daughter! – and lived there for the winter. In the spring Rose took pneumonia and died – a year too late! Leslie was heart-broken enough over it. Isn't it terrible the way some unworthy folks are loved, while others that deserve it far more, you'd think, never get much affection? As for Dick, he'd had enough of quiet married life – just like a man. He was for up and off. He went over to Nova Scotia to visit his relations – his father had come from Nova Scotia – and he wrote back to Leslie that his cousin, George Moore, was going on a voyage to Havana and he was going too. The name of the vessel was the *Four Sisters* and they were to be gone about nine weeks.

'It must have been a relief to Leslie. But she never said anything. From the day of her marriage she was just what she is now – cold and proud, and keeping everyone but me at a distance. I won't *be* kept at a distance, believe *me*! I've just stuck to Leslie as close as I knew how in spite of everything.'

'She told me you were the best friend she had,' said Anne.

'Did she?' exclaimed Miss Cornelia delightedly. 'Well, I'm real thankful to hear it. Sometimes I've wondered if she really did want me around at all – she never let me think so. You must have thawed her out more than you think, or she wouldn't have said that much itself to you. Oh, that poor, heart-broken girl! I never see Dick Moore but I want to run a knife clean through him.'

Miss Cornelia wiped her eyes again and having relieved her feelings by her blood-thirsty wish, took up her tale.

'Well, Leslie was left over there alone. Dick had put in the crop before he went, and old Abner looked after it. The summer went by and the *Four Sisters* didn't come back. The Nova Scotia Moores investigated, and found she had got to Havana and discharged her cargo and took on another and left for home; and that was all they ever found out about her. By degrees people began to talk of Dick Moore as one that was dead. Almost everyone believed that he was, though no one felt certain, for men have turned up here at the harbour after they'd been gone for years. Leslie never thought he was dead – and she was right. A thousand pities too! The next summer Captain Jim was in Havana – that was before he gave up the sea, of course. He thought he'd poke round a bit – Captain Jim was always meddlesome, just like a man – and he went to inquiring round among the sailors' boarding-houses and places like that, to see if he could find out anything about the crew of the *Four Sisters*. He'd better have let sleeping dogs lie, in my opinion! Well, he went to one out-of-the-way place, and there he found a man and he knew at first sight it was Dick Moore, though he had a big beard. Captain Jim got it shaved off and then there was no doubt – Dick Moore it was – his body at least. His mind wasn't there – as for his soul, in my opinion he never had one!'

'What had happened to him?'

'Nobody knows the rights of it. All the folks who kept the boarding-house could tell was that about a year before they had found him lying on their doorstep one morning in an awful condition – his head battered to a jelly almost. They supposed he'd got hurt in some drunken row, and likely that's the truth of it. They took him in, never thinking he could live. But he did – and he was just like a child when he got well. He hadn't memory or intellect or reason. They tried to find out who he was, but they never could. He couldn't even tell them his name – he could only say a few simple words. He had a letter on him beginning "Dear Dick" and signed "Leslie", but there was no address on it and the envelope was gone. They let him stay on – he learned to do a few odd jobs about the place – and there Captain Jim found him. He brought him home – and I've always said it was a bad day's work, though I s'pose there was nothing else he could do. He thought maybe when Dick got home and saw his old surroundings and familiar faces his memory would wake up. But it hadn't any effect. There he's been at the house up the brook ever since. He's just like a child, no more nor less. Takes fractious spells occasionally, but mostly he's just vacant and good-humoured and harmless. He's apt to run away if he isn't watched. That's the burden Leslie has had to carry for eleven years – and all alone. Old Abner Moore died soon after Dick was brought home and it was found he was almost bankrupt. When things were settled up there was nothing for Leslie and Dick but the old West farm. Leslie rented it to John Ward, and the rent is all she has to live on. Sometimes in summer she takes a boarder to help out. But most visitors prefer the other side of the harbour where the hotels and summer cottages are. Leslie's house is too far from the bathing shore. She's taken care of Dick and she's never been away from him for eleven years – she's tied to that imbecile for life. And after all the dreams and hopes she once had! You can imagine what it has been like for her, Anne, dearie – with her beauty and spirit and pride and cleverness. It's just been a living death.'

'Poor, poor girl!' said Anne again. Her own happiness seemed to reproach her. What right had she to be so happy when another human soul must be so miserable?

'Will you tell me just what Leslie said and how she acted the night you met her on the shore?' asked Miss Cornelia.

She listened intently and nodded her satisfaction.

'*You* thought she was stiff and cold, Anne, dearie, but I can tell you she thawed out wonderful for her. She must have taken to you real strong. I'm so glad. You may be able to help her a good deal. I was thankful when I heard that a young couple was coming to this house, for I hoped it would mean some friends for Leslie; especially if you belonged to the race that knows Joseph. You *will* be her friend, won't you, Anne, dearie?'

'Indeed I will, if she'll let me,' said Anne, with all her own sweet, impulsive earnestness.

'No, you must be her friend, whether she'll let you or not,' said Miss Cornelia resolutely. 'Don't you mind if she's stiff by times – don't notice it. Remember what her life has been – and is – and must always be, I suppose, for creatures like Dick Moore live for ever, I understand. You should see how fat he's got since he came home. He used to be lean enough. Just *make* her be friends – you can do it – you're one of those who have the knack. Only you mustn't be sensitive. And don't mind if she doesn't seem to want you to go over there much. She knows that some women don't like to be where Dick is – they complain he gives them the creeps. Just get her to come over here as often as she can. She can't get away so very much – she can't leave Dick long, for the Lord knows what he'd do – burn the house down most likely. At nights, after he's in bed and asleep, is about the only time she's free. He always goes to bed early and sleeps like the dead till next morning. That is how you came to meet her at the shore likely. She wanders there considerable.'

'I will do everything I can for her,' said Anne. Her interest in Leslie Moore, which had been vivid ever since she had seen her driving her geese down the hill, was intensified a thousand-fold by Miss Cornelia's narration. The girl's beauty and sorrow and loneliness drew her with an irresistible fascination. She had never known anyone like her; her friends had hitherto been wholesome, normal, merry girls like herself, with only the average trials of human care and bereavement to shadow their girlish dreams. Leslie Moore stood apart, a tragic, appealing figure of thwarted womanhood. Anne resolved that she would win entrance into the kingdom of that lonely soul and find there the comradeship it could so richly give, were it not for the cruel fetters that held it in a prison not of its own making.

'And mind you this, Anne, dearie,' said Miss Cornelia, who had not yet wholly relieved her mind, 'you mustn't think Leslie is an infidel because she hardly ever goes to church – or even that she's a Methodist. She can't take Dick to church, of course – not that he ever troubled church much in his best days. But you just remember that she's a real strong Presbyterian at heart, Anne, dearie.'

CHAPTER 12

Leslie Comes Over

LESLIE CAME OVER to the house of dreams one frosty night, when moonlit mists were hanging over the harbour and curling like silver ribbons along the seaward glens. She looked as if she repented coming when Gilbert answered her knock; but Anne flew past him, pounced on her, and drew her in.

'I'm so glad you picked tonight for a call,' she said gaily. 'I made up a lot of extra good fudge this afternoon and we want some one to help us eat it – before the fire – while we tell stories. Perhaps Captain Jim will drop in, too. This is his night.'

'No. Captain Jim is over home,' said Leslie. 'He – he made me come here,' she added, half defiantly.

'I'll say a thank-you to him for that when I see him,' said Anne, pulling easy chairs before the fire.

'Oh, I don't mean that I didn't want to come,' protested Leslie, flushing a little. 'I – I've been thinking of coming – but it isn't always easy for me to get away.'

'Of course it must be hard for you to leave Mr Moore,' said Anne, in a matter-of-fact tone. She had decided that it would be best to mention Dick Moore occasionally as an accepted fact, and not give undue morbidness to the subject by avoiding it. She was right, for Leslie's air of constraint suddenly vanished. Evidently she had been wondering how much Anne knew of the conditions of her life and was relieved that no explanations were needed. She allowed her cap and jacket to be taken, and sat down with a girlish snuggle in the big arm-chair by Magog. She was dressed prettily and carefully, with the customary touch of colour in the scarlet geranium at her white throat. Her beautiful hair gleamed like molten gold in the warm firelight. Her sea-blue eyes were full of soft laughter and allurement. For the moment, under the influence of the little house of dreams, she was a girl again – a girl forgetful of the past and its bitterness. The atmosphere of the many loves that had sanctified the little house was all about her; the companionship of two healthy, happy young folks of her own generation encircled her; she felt and yielded to the magic of her surroundings – Miss Cornelia and Captain Jim would scarcely have recognized her; Anne found it hard to believe that this was the cold, unresponsive woman she had met on the shore – this animated girl who talked and listened with the eagerness of a starved soul. And how hungrily Leslie's eyes looked at the bookcases between the windows!

'Our library isn't very extensive,' said Anne, 'but every book in it is a *friend*. We've picked our books up through the years, here and there, never buying one until we had first read it and knew that it belonged to the race of Joseph.'

Leslie laughed – beautiful laughter that seemed akin to all the mirth that had echoed through the little house in the vanished years.

'I have a few books of Father's – not many,' she said. 'I've read them until I know them almost by heart. I don't get many books. There's a circulating library at the Glen store – but I don't think the committee who pick the books for Mr

Parker know what books are of Joseph's race – or perhaps they don't care. It was so seldom I got one I really liked that I gave up getting any.'

'I hope you'll look on our bookshelves as your own,' said Anne. 'You are entirely and whole-heartedly welcome to the loan of any book on them.'

'You are setting a feast of fat things before me,' said Leslie, joyously. Then, as the clock struck ten, she rose, half unwillingly.

'I must go. I didn't realize it was so late. Captain Jim is always saying it doesn't take long to stay an hour. But I've stayed two – and oh, but I've enjoyed them,' she added frankly.

'Come often,' said Anne and Gilbert. They had risen and stood together in the firelight's glow. Leslie looked at them – youthful, hopeful, happy, typifying all she had missed and must for ever miss. The light went out of her face and eyes; the girl vanished; it was the sorrowful, cheated woman who answered the invitation almost coldly and got herself away with a pitiful haste.

Anne watched her until she was lost in the shadows of the chill and misty night. Then she turned slowly back to the glow of her own radiant hearthstone.

'Isn't she lovely, Gilbert? Her hair fascinates me. Miss Cornelia says it reaches to her feet. Ruby Gillis had beautiful hair – but Leslie's is *alive* – every thread of it is living gold.'

'She is very beautiful,' agreed Gilbert, so heartily that Anne almost wished he were a *little* less enthusiastic.

'Gilbert, would you like my hair better if it were like Leslie's?' she asked wistfully.

'I wouldn't have your hair any colour but just what it is

for the world,' said Gilbert, with one or two convincing accompaniments. 'You wouldn't be *Anne* if you had golden hair – or hair of any colour but –'

'Red,' said Anne, with gloomy satisfaction.

'Yes, red – to give warmth to that milk-white skin and those shining grey-green eyes of yours. Golden hair wouldn't suit you at all, Queen Anne – *my* Queen Anne – queen of my heart and life and home.'

'Then you may admire Leslie's all you like,' said Anne magnanimously.

CHAPTER 13

A Ghostly Evening

ONE EVENING, a week later, Anne decided to run over the fields to the house up the brook for an informal call. It was an evening of grey fog that had crept in from the gulf, swathed the harbour, filled the glens and valleys, and clung heavily to the autumnal meadows. Through it the sea sobbed and shuddered. Anne saw Four Winds in a new aspect, and found it weird and mysterious and fascinating; but it also gave her a little feeling of loneliness. Gilbert was away and would be away until the morrow, attending a medical pow-wow in Charlottetown. Anne longed for an hour of fellowship with some girl friend. Captain Jim and Miss Cornelia were 'good fellows' each, in their own way; but youth yearned to youth.

'If only Diana or Phil or Pris or Stella could drop in for a chat,' she said to herself, 'how delightful it would be! This is such a *ghostly* night. I'm sure all the ships that ever sailed out of Four Winds to their doom could be seen tonight sailing up the harbour with their drowned crews on their decks, if that shrouding fog could suddenly be drawn aside. I feel as if it concealed innumerable mysteries — as if I were surrounded by the wraiths of old generations of Four Winds people peering at me through that grey veil. If ever the dear dead ladies of this little house came back to revisit it they would come on just such a night as this. If I sit here any longer I'll see one of them there opposite me in Gilbert's chair. This place isn't exactly canny tonight. Even Gog and Magog have an air of pricking up their ears to hear the footsteps of unseen guests. I'll run over to see Leslie before I frighten myself with my own fancies, as I did long ago in the matter of the Haunted Wood. I'll leave my house of dreams to welcome back its old inhabitants. My fire will give them my good-will and greeting – they will be gone before I come back, and my house will be mine once more. Tonight I am sure it is keeping a tryst with the past.'

Laughing a little over her fancy, yet with something of a creepy sensation in the region of her spine, Anne kissed her hand to Gog and Magog and slipped out into the fog, with some of the new magazines under her arm for Leslie.

'Leslie's wild for books and magazines,' Miss Cornelia had told her, 'and she hardly ever sees one. She can't afford to buy them or subscribe for them. She's really pitifully poor, Anne. I don't see how she makes out to live at all on the little rent the farm brings in. She never even hints a complaint on the score of poverty, but I know what it must be. She's been handicapped by it all her life. She didn't mind it when she was free and ambitious, but it must gall now, believe *me*. I'm glad she seemed so bright and merry the evening she spent with you. Captain Jim told me he had fairly to put her cap and coat on and push her out of the door. Don't be too long going to see her either. If you are she'll think it's because you don't like the sight of Dick, and she'll crawl into her shell again. Dick's a great, big, harmless baby, but that silly grin and chuckle of his do get on some people's nerves. Thank goodness, I've no nerves myself. I like Dick Moore better now than I ever did when he was in his right senses – though the Lord knows that isn't saying much. I was down there one day in house-cleaning time helping Leslie a bit, and I was frying doughnuts. Dick was hanging round to get one, as usual, and all at once he picked up a scalding hot one I'd just fished out and dropped it on the back of my neck when I was bending over. Then he laughed and laughed. Believe *me*, Anne, it took all the grace of God in my heart to keep me from just whisking up that stew-pan of boiling fat and pouring it over his head.'

Anne laughed over Miss Cornelia's wrath as she sped through the darkness. But laughter accorded ill with that night. She was sober enough when she reached the house among the willows. Everything was very silent. The front part of the house seemed dark and deserted, so Anne slipped round to the side door, which opened from the veranda into a little sitting-room. There she halted noiselessly.

The door was open. Beyond, in the dimly lighted room, sat Leslie Moore, with her arms flung out on the table and her head bent upon them. She was weeping horribly – with low, fierce, choking sobs, as if some agony in her soul were trying to tear itself out. An old black dog was sitting by her, his nose resting on her lap, his big doggish eyes full of mute, imploring sympathy and devotion. Anne drew back in dismay. She felt that she could not intermeddle with this bitterness. Her heart ached with a sympathy she might not utter. To go in now would be to shut the door for ever on any possible help or friendship. Some instinct warned Anne that the proud, bitter girl would never forgive the one who thus surprised her in her abandonment of despair.

Anne slipped noiselessly from the veranda and found her way across the yard. Beyond, she heard voices in the gloom and saw the dim glow of a light. At the gate she met two men – Captain Jim with a lantern, and another who she knew must be Dick Moore – a big man, badly gone to fat, with a broad, round red face, and vacant eyes. Even in the dull light Anne got the impression that there was something unusual about his eyes.

'Is this you, Mistress Blythe?' said Captain Jim. 'Now, now, you hadn't oughter be roaming about alone on a night like this. You could get lost in this fog easier than not. Jest you wait till I see Dick safe inside the door and I'll come back and light you over the fields. I ain't going to have Dr Blythe coming home and finding that you walked clean over Cape Leforce in the fog. A woman did that once, forty years ago.

'So you've been over to see Leslie,' he said, when he rejoined her.

'I didn't go in,' said Anne, and told what she had seen. Captain Jim sighed.

'Poor, poor, little girl! She don't cry often, Mistress Blythe – she's too brave for that. She must feel terrible when she does cry. A night like this is hard on poor women who have sorrows. There's something about it that kinder brings up all we've suffered – or feared.'

'It's full of ghosts,' said Anne, with a shiver. 'That was why I came over – I wanted to clasp a human hand and hear a human voice. There seem to be so many *inhuman* presences about tonight. Even my own dear house was full of them. They fairly elbowed me out. So I fled over here for companionship of my kind.'

'You were right not to go in, though, Mistress Blythe. Leslie wouldn't have liked it. She wouldn't have liked me going in with Dick, as I'd have done if I hadn't met you. I had

114

Dick down with me all day. I keep him with me as much as I can to help Leslie a bit.'

'Isn't there something odd about his eyes?' asked Anne.

'You noticed that? Yes, one is blue and t'other is hazel – his father had the same. It's a Moore peculiarity. That was what told me he was Dick Moore when I saw him first down in Cuby. If it hadn't a-bin for his eyes I mightn't a-known him, what with his beard and fat. You know, I reckon, that it was me found him and brought him home. Miss Cornelia always says I shouldn't have done it, but I can't agree with her. It was the *right* thing to do – and so 'twas the only thing. There ain't no question in my mind about *that*. But my old heart aches for Leslie. She's only twenty-eight and she's eaten more bread with sorrow than most women do in eighty years.'

They walked on in silence for a little while. Presently Anne said, 'Do you know, Captain Jim, I never like walking with a lantern. I have always the strangest feeling that just outside the circle of light, just over its edge in the darkness, I am surrounded by a ring of furtive, sinister things, watching me from the shadows with hostile eyes. I've had that feeling from childhood. What is the reason? I never feel like that when I'm really in the darkness – when it is close all around me – I'm not the least frightened.'

'I've something of that feeling myself,' admitted Captain Jim. 'I reckon when the darkness is close to us it is a friend. But when we sorter push it away from us – divorce ourselves from it, so to speak, with lantern light – it becomes an enemy. But the fog is lifting. There's a smart west wind rising, if you notice. The stars will be out when you get home.'

They were out; and when Anne re-entered her house of dreams the red embers were still glowing on the hearth, and all the haunting presences were gone.

CHAPTER 14

November Days

THE SPLENDOUR of colour which had glowed for weeks along the shores of Four Winds Harbour had faded out into the soft grey-blue of late autumnal hills. There came many days when fields and shores were dim with misty rain, or shivering before the breath of a melancholy sea-wind — nights, too, of storm and tempest, when Anne sometimes wakened to pray that no ship might be beating up the grim north shore, for if it were so not even the great, faithful light, whirling through the darkness unafraid, could avail to guide it into safe haven.

'In November I sometimes feel as if spring could never come again,' she sighed, grieving over the hopeless unsightliness of her frosted and bedraggled flower-pots. The gay little garden of the schoolmaster's bride was rather a forlorn place now, and the Lombardies and birches were under bare poles, as Captain Jim said. But the fir-wood behind the little house was for ever green and staunch; and even in November and December there came gracious days of sunshine and purple hazes, when the harbour danced and sparkled as blithely as in midsummer, and the gulf was so softly blue and tender that the storm and the wild wind seemed only things of a long-past dream.

Anne and Gilbert spent many an autumn evening at the lighthouse. It was always a cheery place. Even when the east wind sang in minor and the sea was dead and grey, hints of sunshine seemed to be lurking all about it. Perhaps this was because the First Mate always paraded it in panoply of gold. He was so large and effulgent that one hardly missed the sun, and his resounding purrs formed a pleasant accompaniment to the laughter and conversation which went on around Captain Jim's fireplace. Captain Jim and Gilbert had many long discussions and high converse on matters beyond the ken of cat or kind.

'I like to ponder on all kinds of problems, though I can't solve 'em,' said Captain Jim. 'My father held that we should never talk of things we couldn't understand, but if we didn't, Doctor, the subjects for conversation would be mighty few. I reckon the gods laugh many a time to hear us, but what matters so long as we remember that we're only men, and don't take to fancying that we're gods ourselves, really, knowing good and evil. I reckon our powwows won't do us or anyone much harm, so let's have another whack at the whence, why, and whither this evening, Doctor.'

While they 'whacked' Anne listened or dreamed. Sometimes Leslie went to the lighthouse with them, and she and Anne wandered along the shore in the eerie twilight, or sat on the rocks below the lighthouse until the darkness drove them back to the cheer of the driftwood fire. Then Captain Jim would brew them tea and tell them

> tales of land and sea
> And whatsoever might betide
> The great forgotten world outside.

Leslie seemed always to enjoy those lighthouse carousals very much, and bloomed out for the time being into ready wit and beautiful laughter, or glowing-eyed silence. There was a certain tang and savour in the conversation when Leslie was present which they missed when she was absent. Even when she did not talk she seemed to inspire others to brilliancy. Captain Jim told his stories better, Gilbert was quicker in argument and repartee, Anne felt little gushes and trickles of fancy and imagination bubbling to her lips under the influence of Leslie's personality.

'That girl was born to be a leader in social and intellectual circles, far away from Four Winds,' she said to Gilbert as they walked home one night. 'She's just wasted here – wasted.'

'Weren't you listening to Captain Jim and yours truly the other night when we discussed that subject generally? We came to the comforting conclusion that the Creator probably knew how to run His universe quite as well as we do, and that, after all, there are no such things as "wasted" lives, saving and except when an individual wilfully squanders and wastes his own life – which Leslie Moore certainly hasn't done. And some people might think that a Redmond B.A., whom editors were beginning to honour, was "wasted" as the wife of a struggling country doctor in the rural community of Four Winds.'

'Gilbert!'

'If you had married Roy Gardner, now,' continued Gilbert mercilessly, '*you* could have been "a leader in social and intellectual circles far away from Four Winds".'

'Gilbert *Blythe*!'

'You *know* you were in love with him at one time, Anne.'

'Gilbert, that's mean – "p'isen mean, just like all the men", as Miss Cornelia says. I *never* was in love with him. I only imagined I was. *You* know that. You *know* I'd rather be

119

your wife in our house of dreams and fulfilment than a queen in a palace.'

Gilbert's answer was not in words; but I am afraid that both of them forgot poor Leslie speeding her lonely way across the fields to a house that was neither a palace nor the fulfilment of a dream.

The moon was rising over the sad, dark sea behind them and transfiguring it. Her light had not yet reached the harbour, the farther side of which was shadowy and suggestive, with dim coves and rich glooms and jewelling lights.

'How the home lights shine out tonight through the dark!' said Anne. 'That string of them over the harbour looks like a necklace. And what a coruscation there is up at the Glen! Oh, look, Gilbert, there is ours. I'm so glad we left it burning. I hate to come home to a dark house. *Our* home-light, Gilbert! Isn't it lovely to see?'

'Just one of earth's millions of homes, Anne-girl – but ours – *ours* – our beacon in "a naughty world". When a fellow has a home and a dear little red-haired wife in it what more need he ask of life?'

'Well, he might ask *one* thing more,' whispered Anne happily. 'Oh, Gilbert, it seems as if I just *couldn't* wait for the spring.'

CHAPTER 15

Christmas at Four Winds

AT FIRST Anne and Gilbert talked of going home to Avonlea for Christmas; but eventually they decided to stay in Four Winds. 'I want to spend the first Christmas of our life together in our own home,' decreed Anne.

So it fell out that Marilla and Mrs Rachel Lynde and the twins came to Four Winds for Christmas. Marilla had the face of a woman who had circumnavigated the globe. She had never been sixty miles away from home before; and she had never eaten a Christmas dinner anywhere save at Green Gables.

Mrs Rachel had made and brought with her an enormous plum pudding. Nothing could have convinced Mrs Rachel that a college graduate of the younger generation could make a Christmas plum pudding properly; but she bestowed approval on Anne's house.

'Anne's a good housekeeper,' she said to Marilla in the spare room the night of their arrival. 'I've looked into her bread box and her scrap pail. I always judge a housekeeper by those, that's what. There's nothing in the pail that shouldn't have been thrown away, and no stale pieces in the bread box. Of course, she was trained up with you – but, then, she went to college afterwards. I notice she's got my tobacco stripe quilt on the bed here, and that big round braided mat of yours before her living-room fire. It makes me feel right at home.'

Anne's first Christmas in her own house was as delightful as she could have wished. The day was fine and bright; the first skim of snow had fallen on Christmas Eve and made the world beautiful; the harbour was still open and glittering.

Captain Jim and Miss Cornelia came to dinner. Leslie and Dick had been invited, but Leslie made excuse; they always went to her Uncle Isaac West's for Christmas, she said.

'She'd rather have it so,' Miss Cornelia told Anne. 'She can't bear taking Dick where there are strangers. Christmas is always a hard time for Leslie. She and her father used to make a lot of it.'

Miss Cornelia and Mrs Rachel did not take a very violent fancy to each other. 'Two suns held not their courses in one sphere.' But they did not clash at all, for Mrs Rachel was in the kitchen helping Anne and Marilla with the dinner, and it fell to Gilbert to entertain Captain Jim and Miss Cornelia – or rather to be entertained by them, for a dialogue between those two old friends and antagonists was assuredly never dull.

'It's many a year since there was a Christmas dinner here, Mistress Blythe,' said Captain Jim. 'Miss Russell always went to her friends in town for Christmas. But I was here to the first Christmas dinner that was ever eaten in this house – and the schoolmaster's bride cooked it. That was sixty years ago today, Mistress Blythe – and a day very like this – just enough snow to make the hills white, and the harbour as blue as June. I was only a lad, and I'd never been invited out to dinner before, and I was too shy to eat enough. I've got all over *that*.'

'Most men do,' said Miss Cornelia, sewing furiously. Miss Cornelia was not going to sit with idle hands, even on

Christmas. Babies come without any consideration for holidays, and there was one expected in a poverty-stricken household at Glen St Mary. Miss Cornelia had sent that household a substantial dinner for its little swarm, and so meant to eat her own with a comfortable conscience.

'Well, you know, the way to a man's heart is through his stomach, Cornelia,' explained Captain Jim.

'I believe you – when he *has* a heart,' retorted Miss Cornelia. 'I suppose that's why so many women kill themselves cooking – just as poor Amelia Baxter did. She died last Christmas morning, and she said it was the first Christmas since she was married that she didn't have to cook a big, twenty-plate dinner. It must have been a real pleasant change for her. Well, she's been dead a year, so you'll soon hear of Horace Baxter taking notice.'

'I heard he was taking notice already,' said Captain Jim, winking at Gilbert. 'Wasn't he up to your place one Sunday lately, with his funeral blacks on, and a boiled collar?'

'No, he wasn't. And he needn't come neither. I could have had him long ago when he was fresh. I don't want any second-hand goods, believe *me*. As for Horace Baxter, he was in financial difficulties a year ago last summer, and he prayed to the Lord for help; and when his wife died and he got her life insurance he said he believed it was the answer to his prayer. Wasn't that like a man?'

'Have you really proof that he said that, Cornelia?'

'I have the Methodist minister's word for it – if you call *that* proof. Robert Baxter told me the same thing too, but I admit *that* isn't evidence. Robert Baxter isn't often known to tell the truth.'

'Come, come, Cornelia, I think he generally tells the truth, but he changes his opinion so often it sometimes sounds as if he didn't.'

'It sounds like it mighty often, believe *me*. But trust one man to excuse another. I have no use for Robert Baxter. He turned Methodist just because the Presbyterian choir happened to be singing "Behold the bridegroom cometh" for a collection piece when him and Margaret walked up the aisle the Sunday after they were married. Served him right for being late! He always insisted the choir did it on purpose to insult him, as if he was of that much importance. But that family always thought they were much bigger potatoes than they really were. His brother Eliphalet imagined the devil was always at his elbow – but *I* never believed the devil wasted that much time on him.'

'I – don't – know,' said Captain Jim thoughtfully. 'Eliphalet Baxter lived too much alone – hadn't even a cat or dog to keep him human. When a man is alone he's mighty apt to be with the devil – if he ain't with God. He has to choose which company he'll keep, I reckon. If the devil always was at Life Baxter's elbow it must have been because Life liked to have him there.'

'Man-like,' said Miss Cornelia, and subsided into silence over a complicated arrangement of tucks until Captain Jim deliberately stirred her up again by remarking in a casual way:

'I was up to the Methodist church last Sunday morning.'

'You'd better have been home reading your Bible,' was Miss Cornelia's retort.

'Come, now, Cornelia, *I* can't see any harm in going to the Methodist church when there's no preaching in your own. I've been a Presbyterian for seventy-six years, and it isn't likely my theology will hoist anchor at this late day.'

'It's setting a bad example,' said Miss Cornelia grimly.

'Besides,' continued wicked Captain Jim, 'I wanted to hear some good singing. The Methodists have a good choir; and you can't deny, Cornelia, that the singing in our church is awful since the split in the choir?'

'What if the singing isn't good? They're doing their best, and God sees no difference between the voice of a crow and the voice of a nightingale.'

'Come, come, Cornelia,' said Captain Jim mildly, 'I've a better opinion of the Almighty's ear for music than *that*.'

'What caused the trouble in our choir?' asked Gilbert, who was suffering from suppressed laughter.

'It dates back to the new church, three years ago,' answered Captain Jim. 'We had a fearful time over the building of that church – fell out over the question of a new site. The two sites wasn't more'n two hundred yards apart, but you'd have thought they was a thousand by the bitterness of that fight. We was split up into three factions – one wanted the east site and one the south, and one held to the old. It was fought out in bed and at board, and in church and at market. All the old scandals of three generations were dragged out of their graves and aired. Three matches was broken up by it. And the meetings we had to try to settle the question! Cornelia, will you ever forget the one when old Luther Burns got up and made a speech? *He* stated his opinions forcibly.'

'Call a spade a spade, Captain. You mean he got red-mad and raked them all, fore and aft. They deserved it too – a pack of incapables. But what would you expect of a committee of men? That building committee held twenty-seven meetings, and at the end of the twenty-seventh weren't no nearer having a church than when they begun – not so near, for a fact, for in one fit of hurrying things along they'd gone to work and tore the old church down, so there we were, without a church, and no place but the hall to worship in.'

'The Methodists offered us their church, Cornelia.'

'The Glen St Mary church wouldn't have been built to this day,' went on Miss Cornelia, ignoring Captain Jim, 'if we women hadn't just started in and took charge. We said *we* meant to have a church, if the men meant to quarrel till doomsday, and we were tired of being a laughing-stock for the Methodists. We held *one* meeting and elected a committee and canvassed for subscriptions. We got them, too. When any of the men tried to sass us we told them they'd tried for two years to build a church and it was our turn now. We shut them up close, believe *me*, and in six months we had our church. Of course, when the men saw we were determined they stopped fighting and went to work, man-like, as soon as they saw they had to, or quit bossing. Oh, women can't preach or be elders; but they can build churches and scare up the money for them.'

'The Methodists allow women to preach,' said Captain Jim.

Miss Cornelia glared at him.

'I never said the Methodists hadn't common sense, Captain. What I say is, I doubt if they have much religion.'

'I suppose you are in favour of votes for women, Miss Cornelia,' said Gilbert.

'I'm not hankering after the vote, believe *me*,' said Miss Cornelia scornfully. '*I* know what it is to clean up after the men. But some of these days, when the men realize they've got the world into a mess they can't get it out of, they'll be glad to gives us the vote, and shoulder their troubles over on us. That's *their* scheme. Oh, it's well that women are patient, believe *me*!'

'What about Job?' suggested Captain Jim.

'Job! It was such a rare thing to find a patient man that when one was really discovered they were determined he shouldn't be forgotten,' retorted Miss Cornelia triumphantly. 'Anyhow, the virtue doesn't go with the name. There never was such an impatient man born as old Job Taylor over harbour.'

'Well, you know, he had a good deal to try him, Cornelia. Even you can't defend his wife. I always remember what old William MacAllister said of her at her funeral, "There's nae doot she was a Chreestian wumman, but she had the de'il's own temper."'

'I suppose she *was* trying,' admitted Miss Cornelia reluctantly, 'but that didn't justify what Job said when she died. He rode home from the graveyard the day of the funeral with my father. He never said a word till they got near home. Then he heaved a big sigh and said, "You may not believe it, Stephen, but this is the happiest day of my life!" Wasn't that like a man?'

'I s'pose poor old Mrs Job did make life kinder uneasy for him,' reflected Captain Jim.

'Well, there's such a thing as decency, isn't there? Even if a man is rejoicing in his heart over his wife being dead, he needn't proclaim it to the four winds of heaven. And happy day or not, Job Taylor wasn't long in marrying again, you might notice. His second wife could manage him. She made him walk Spanish, believe me! The first thing she did was to make him hustle round and put up a tombstone to the first Mrs Job – and she had a place left on it for her own name. She said there'd be nobody to make Job put up a monument to *her*.'

'Speaking of Taylors, how is Mrs Lewis Taylor up at the Glen, Doctor?' asked Captain Jim.

'She's getting better slowly – but she has to work too hard,' replied Gilbert.

'Her husband works hard too – raising prize pigs,' said Miss Cornelia. 'He's noted for his beautiful pigs. He's a heap prouder of his pigs than of his children. But then, to be sure, his pigs are the best pigs possible, while his children don't amount to much. He picked a poor mother for them, and starved her while she was bearing and rearing them. His pigs got the cream and his children got the skim milk.'

'There are times, Cornelia, when I have to agree with you, though it hurts me,' said Captain Jim. 'That's just exactly the truth about Lewis Taylor. When I see those poor, miserable children of his, robbed of all children ought to have, it p'isens my own bite and sup for days afterwards.'

Gilbert went out to the kitchen in response to Anne's beckoning. Anne shut the door and gave him a connubial lecture.

'Gilbert, you and Captain Jim must stop baiting Miss Cornelia. Oh, I've been listening to you – and I just won't allow it.'

'Anne, Miss Cornelia is enjoying herself hugely. You know she is.'

'Well, never mind. You two needn't egg her on like that. Dinner is ready now, and, Gilbert, *don't* let Mrs Rachel carve the geese. I know she means to offer to do it because she doesn't think you can do it properly. Show her you can.'

'I ought to be able to. I've been studying A-B-C-D diagrams of carving for the past month,' said Gilbert. 'Only don't talk to me while I'm doing it, Anne, for if you drive the letters out of my head I'll be in a worse predicament than you were in old geometry days when the teacher changed them.'

Gilbert carved the geese beautifully. Even Mrs Rachel had to admit that. And everybody ate of them and enjoyed them. Anne's first Christmas dinner was a great success and she beamed with housewifely pride. Merry was the feast and long; and when it was over they gathered around the cheer of the red hearth flame and Captain Jim told them stories until the red sun swung low over Four Winds Harbour, and the long blue shadows of the Lombardies fell across the snow in the lane.

'I must be getting back to the light,' he said finally. 'I'll jest have time to walk home before sun-down. Thank you for a beautiful Christmas, Mistress Blythe. Bring Master Davy down to the light some night before he goes home.'

'I want to see those stone gods,' said Davy with a relish.

CHAPTER 16

New Year's Eve at the Light

THE GREEN GABLES FOLK went home after Christmas, Marilla under solemn covenant to return for a month in the spring. More snow came before New Year's, and the harbour froze over, but the gulf still was free, beyond the white imprisoned fields. The last day of the old year was one of those bright, cold, dazzling winter days, which bombard us with their brilliancy and command our admiration but never our love. The sky was sharp and blue; the snow diamonds sparkled insistently; the stark trees were bare and shameless, with a kind of brazen beauty; the hills shot assaulting lances of crystal. Even the shadows were sharp and stiff and clear-cut, as no proper shadows should be. Everything that was handsome seemed ten times handsomer and less attractive in the glaring splendour; and everything that was ugly seemed ten times uglier, and everything was either handsome or ugly. There was no soft blending, or kind obscurity, or elusive mistiness in that searching glitter. The only things that held their own individuality were the firs — for the fir is the tree of mystery and shadow, and yields never to the encroachments of crude radiance.

But finally the day began to realize that she was growing old. Then a certain pensiveness fell over her beauty which dimmed yet intensified it; sharp angles, glittering points, melted away into curves and enticing gleams. The white

130

harbour put on soft greys and pinks; the far-away hills turned amethyst.

'The old year is going away beautifully,' said Anne.

She and Leslie and Gilbert were on their way to the Four Winds Point, having plotted with Captain Jim to watch the New Year in at the light. The sun had set and in the south-western sky hung Venus, glorious and golden, having drawn as near to her earth-sister as is possible for her. For the first time Anne and Gilbert saw the shadow cast by that brilliant star of evening, that faint, mysterious shadow, never seen save when there is white snow to reveal it, and then only with averted vision, vanishing when you gaze at it directly.

'It's like the spirit of a shadow, isn't it?' whispered Anne. 'You can see it so plainly haunting your side when you look ahead; but when you turn and look at it – it's gone.'

'I have heard that you can see the shadow of Venus only once in a lifetime, and that within a year of seeing it your life's most wonderful gift will come to you,' said Leslie. But she spoke rather hardly; perhaps she thought that even the shadow of Venus could bring her no gift of life. Anne smiled in the soft twilight; she felt quite sure what the mystic shadow promised her.

They found Marshall Elliott at the lighthouse. At first Anne felt inclined to resent the intrusion of this long-haired, long-bearded eccentric into the familiar little circle. But Marshall Elliott soon proved his legitimate claim to membership in the household of Joseph. He was a witty, intelligent, well-read man, rivalling Captain Jim himself in the knack of telling a good story. They were all glad when he agreed to watch the old year out with them.

Captain Jim's small nephew Joe had come down to spend New Year's with his great-uncle, and had fallen asleep on the sofa with the First Mate curled up in a huge golden ball at his feet.

'Ain't he a dear little man?' said Captain Jim gloatingly. 'I do love to watch a little child asleep, Mistress Blythe. It's the most beautiful sight in the world, I reckon. Joe does love to get down here for a night, because I have him sleep with me. At home he has to sleep with the other two boys, and he doesn't like it. "Why can't I sleep with Father, Uncle Jim?" say he. "Everybody in the Bible slept with their fathers." As for the questions he asks, the minister himself couldn't answer them. They fair swamp me. "Uncle Jim, if I wasn't *me* who'd I be?" and "Uncle Jim, what would happen if God died?" He fired them two off at me tonight, afore he went to sleep. As for his imagination, it sails away from everything. He makes up the most remarkable yarns – and then his mother shuts him up in the closet for telling stories. And he sits down and makes up another one, and has it ready to relate to her when she lets him out. He had one for me when he come down tonight. "Uncle Jim," says he, solemn as a tombstone, "I had a 'venture in the Glen today." "Yes, what was it?" says I, expecting something quite startling, but no-wise prepared for what I really got. "I met a wolf in the street," says he, "a 'normous wolf with a big red mouf and *awful* long teeth, Uncle Jim." "I didn't know there was any wolves up at the Glen," says I. "Oh, he comed there from far, far away," says Joe, "and I fought he was going to eat me up, Uncle Jim." "Were you scared?" says I. "No, 'cause I had a big gun," says Joe, "and I shot the wolf dead, Uncle Jim – solid dead – and then he went up to heaven and bit

God," says he. Well, I was fair staggered, Mistress Blythe.'

The hours bloomed into mirth around the driftwood fire. Captain Jim told tales, and Marshall Elliott sang old Scotch ballads in a fine tenor voice; finally Captain Jim took down his old brown fiddle from the wall and began to play. He had a tolerable knack of fiddling, which all appreciated save the First Mate, who sprang from the sofa as if he had been shot, emitted a shriek of protest, and fled wildly up the stairs.

'Can't cultivate an ear for music in that cat nohow,' said Captain Jim. 'He won't stay long enough to learn to like it. When we got the organ up at the Glen church old Elder Richards bounced up from his seat the minute the organist began to play and scuttled down the aisle and out of the church at the rate of no-man's-business. It reminded me so strong of the First Mate tearing loose as soon as I begin to fiddle that I come nearer to laughing out loud in church than I ever did before or since.'

There was something so infectious in the rollicking tunes which Captain Jim played that very soon Marshall Elliott's feet began to twitch. He had been a noted dancer in his youth. Presently he started up and held out his hands to Leslie. Instantly she responded. Round and round the firelit room they circled with a rhythmic grace that was wonderful. Leslie danced like one inspired; the wild, sweet abandon of the music seemed to have entered into and possessed her. Anne watched her in fascinated admiration. She had never seen her like this. All the innate richness and colour and charm of her nature seemed to have broken loose and overflowed in crimson cheek and glowing eye and grace of motion. Even the aspect of Marshall Elliott, with his long beard and hair, could not spoil the picture. On the contrary,

133

it seemed to enhance it. Marshall Elliott looked like a Viking of elder days, dancing with one of the blue-eyed, golden-haired daughters of the Northland.

'The purtiest dancing I ever saw, and I've seen some in my time,' declared Captain Jim, when at last the bow fell from his tired hand. Leslie dropped into her chair, laughing breathless.

'I love dancing,' she said apart to Anne. 'I haven't danced since I was sixteen – but I love it. The music seems to run through my veins like quicksilver and I forget everything – everything – except the delight of keeping time to it. There isn't any floor beneath me, or walls about me, or roof over me – I'm floating amid the stars.'

Captain Jim hung his fiddle up in its place, beside a large frame enclosing several banknotes.

'Is there anybody else of your acquaintance who can afford to hang his walls with banknotes for pictures?' he asked. 'There's twenty ten-dollar notes there, not worth the glass over them. They're old Bank of P.E. Island notes. Had them by me when the bank failed, and I had 'em framed and hung up, partly as a reminder not to put your trust in banks, and partly to give me a real luxurious, millionairy feeling. Hullo, Matey, don't be scared. You can come back now. The music and revelry is over for tonight. The old year has just another hour to stay with us. I've seen seventy-six New Years come in over that gulf yonder, Mistress Blythe.'

'You'll see a hundred,' said Marshall Elliott.

Captain Jim shook his head.

'No; and I don't want to – at least, I think I don't. Death grows friendlier as we grow older. Not that one of us really wants to die though, Marshall. Tennyson spoke the truth when he said that. There's old Mrs Wallace up at the Glen. She's had heaps of trouble all her life, poor soul, and she's lost almost everyone she cared about. She's always saying that she'll be glad when her time comes, and she doesn't want to sojourn any longer in this vale of tears. But when she takes a sick spell there's a fuss! Doctors from town, and a trained nurse, and enough medicine to kill a dog. Life may be a vale of tears, all right, but there are some folks who enjoy weeping, I reckon.'

They spent the old year's last hour quietly around the fire. A few minutes before twelve Captain Jim rose and opened the door.

'We must let the New Year in,' he said.

Outside was a fine blue night. A sparkling ribbon of moonlight garlanded the gulf. Inside the bar the harbour shone like a pavement of pearl. They stood before the door and waited – Captain Jim with his ripe, full experience, Marshall Elliott in his vigorous but empty middle life, Gilbert and Anne with their precious memories and exquisite hopes, Leslie with her record of starved years and her hopeless future. The clock on the little shelf above the fireplace struck twelve.

'Welcome, New Year,' said Captain Jim, bowing low as the last stroke died away. 'I wish you all the best year of your lives, mates. I reckon that whatever the New Year brings us will be the best the Great Captain has for us – and somehow or other we'll all make port in a good harbour.'

CHAPTER 17

A Four Winds Winter

WINTER SET IN vigorously after New Year's. Big white drifts heaped themselves about the little house, and palms of frost covered its windows. The harbour ice grew harder and thicker, until the Four Winds people began their usual winter travelling over it. The safe ways were 'bushed' by a benevolent Government, and night and day the gay tinkle of the sleigh-bells sounded on it. On moonlit nights Anne heard them in her house of dreams like fairy chimes. The gulf froze over, and the Four Winds light flashed no more. During the months when navigation was closed Captain Jim's office was a sinecure.

'The First Mate and I will have nothing to do till spring, except keep warm and amuse ourselves. The last lighthouse keeper always used to move up to the Glen in winter; but I'd rather stay at the Point. The First Mate might get poisoned or chewed up by dogs at the Glen. It's a mite lonely, to be sure, with neither the light nor the water for company, but if our friends come to see us often we'll weather it through.'

Captain Jim had an ice boat, and many a wild, glorious spin Gilbert and Anne and Leslie had over the glib harbour ice with him. Anne and Leslie took long snowshoe tramps together, too, over the fields, or across the harbour after storms, or through the woods beyond the Glen. They were very good comrades in their rambles and their fireside communings. Each had something to give the other – each felt life the richer for friendly exchange of thought and friendly silence; each looked across the white fields between their homes with a pleasant consciousness of a friend beyond. But, in spite of all this, Anne felt that there was always a barrier between Leslie and herself – a constraint that never wholly vanished.

'I don't know why I can't get closer to her,' Anne said one evening to Captain Jim. 'I like her so much – I admire her so much – I *want* to take her right into my heart and creep right into hers. But I can never cross the barrier.'

'You've been too happy all your life, Mistress Blythe,' said Captain Jim thoughtfully. 'I reckon that's why you and Leslie can't get real close together in your souls. The barrier between you is her experience of sorrow and trouble. She ain't responsible for it and you ain't; but it's there and neither of you can cross it.'

'My childhood wasn't very happy before I came to Green Gables,' said Anne, gazing soberly out of the window at the still, sad, dead beauty of the leafless tree-shadows on the moonlit snow.

'Mebbe not – but it was just the usual unhappiness of a child who hasn't anyone to look after it properly. There hasn't been any *tragedy* in your life, Mistress Blythe. And poor Leslie's has been almost *all* tragedy. She feels, I reckon, though mebbe she hardly knows she feels it, that there's a vast deal in her life you can't enter nor understand -- and so she has to keep you back from it – hold you off, so to speak, from hurting her. You know if we've got anything about us that hurts we shrink from anyone's touch on or near it. It holds good with our souls as well as our bodies, I reckon.

Leslie's soul must be near raw – it's no wonder she hides it away.'

'If that were really all, I wouldn't mind, Captain Jim. I would understand. But there are times – not always, but now and again – when I almost have to believe that Leslie doesn't – doesn't like me. Sometimes I surprise a look in her eyes that seems to show resentment and dislike – it goes so quickly – but I've seen it, I'm sure of that. And it hurts me, Captain Jim. I'm not used to being disliked – and I've tried so hard to win Leslie's friendship.'

'You have won it, Mistress Blythe. Don't you go cherishing any foolish notion that Leslie don't like you. If she didn't she wouldn't have anything to do with you, much less chumming with you as she does. I know Leslie Moore too well not to be sure of that.'

'The first time I ever saw her, driving her geese down the hill on the day I came to Four Winds, she looked at me with the same expression,' persisted Anne. 'I felt it, even in the midst of my admiration of her beauty. She looked at me resentfully – she did, indeed, Captain Jim.'

'The resentment must have been about something else, Mistress Blythe, and you jest come in for a share of it because you happened past. Leslie *does* take sullen spells now and again, poor girl. I can't blame her, when I know what she has to put up with. I don't know why it's permitted. The doctor and I have talked a lot about the origin of evil, but we haven't quite found out all about it yet. There's a vast of onunderstandable things in life, ain't there, Mistress Blythe? Sometimes things seem to work out real proper-like, same as with you and the doctor. And then again they all seem to go catawampus. There's Leslie, so clever and beautiful you'd think she was meant for a queen, and instead she's cooped up over there, robbed of almost everything a woman'd value, with no prospect except waiting on Dick Moore all her life. Though, mind you, Mistress Blythe, I dare say she'd choose her life now, such as it is, rather than the life she lived with Dick before he went away. *That's* something a clumsy old sailor's tongue mustn't meddle with. But you've helped Leslie a lot – she's a different creature since you come to Four Winds. Us old friends see the difference in her, as you can't. Miss Cornelia and me was talking it over the other day, and it's one of the mighty few p'ints that we see eye to eye on. So jest you throw overboard any idea of her not liking you.'

Anne could hardly discard it completely, for there were undoubtedly times when she felt, with an instinct that was not to be combated by reason, that Leslie harboured a queer, indefinable resentment towards her. At times this secret consciousness marred the delight of their comradeship; at others it was almost forgotten; but Anne always felt the hidden thorn was there, and might prick her at any moment. She felt a cruel sting from it on the day when she told Leslie of what she hoped the spring would bring to the little house of dreams. Leslie looked at her with hard, bitter, unfriendly eyes.

'So you are to have *that*, too,' she said in a choked voice. And without another word she had turned and gone across the fields homeward. Anne was deeply hurt; for the moment she felt as if she could never like Leslie again. But when Leslie came over a few evenings later she was so pleasant, so friendly, so frank, and witty, and winsome, that Anne was charmed into forgiveness and forgetfulness. Only, she never mentioned her darling hope to Leslie again; nor did Leslie ever refer to it. But one evening, when late winter was listening for the word of spring, she came over to the little house for a twilight chat; and when she went away she left a small white box on the table. Anne found it after she was gone and opened it wonderingly. In it was a tiny white dress of exquisite workmanship – delicate embroidery, wonderful tucking, sheer loveliness. Every stitch in it was handwork; and the little frills of lace at neck and sleeves were of real Valenciennes. Lying on it was a card – 'with Leslie's love'.

'What hours of work she must have put on it,' said Anne. 'And the material must have cost more than she could really afford. It is very sweet of her.'

But Leslie was brusque and curt when Anne thanked her, and again the latter felt thrown back upon herself.

Leslie's gift was not alone in the little house. Miss Cornelia had, for the time being, given up sewing for unwanted, unwelcome eighth babies, and fallen to sewing for a very much wanted first one, whose welcome would leave nothing to be desired. Philippa Blake and Diana Wright each sent a marvellous garment; and Mrs Rachel Lynde sent several, in which good material and honest stitches took the place of embroidery and frills. Anne herself made many, desecrated by no touch of machinery, spending over them the happiest hours of that happy winter.

Captain Jim was the most frequent guest of the little house, and none was more welcome. Every day Anne loved the simple-souled, true-hearted old sailor more and more. He was as refreshing as a sea-breeze, as interesting as some ancient chronicle. She was never tired of listening to his stories, and his quaint remarks and comments were a continual delight to her. Captain Jim was one of those rare and interesting people who 'never speak but they say something'. The milk of human kindness and the wisdom of the serpent were mingled in his composition in delightful proportions.

Nothing ever seemed to put Captain Jim out or depress him in any way.

'I've kind of contracted a habit of enj'ying things,' he remarked once, when Anne had commented on his invariable cheerfulness. 'It's got so chronic that I believe I even enj'y the disagreeable things. It's great fun thinking they can't last. "Old rheumatiz," says I, when it grips me hard, "you've *got* to stop aching sometime. The worse you are the sooner you'll stop, mebbe. I'm bound to get the better of you in the long run, whether in the body or out of the body."'

One night, by the fireside at the light, Anne saw Captain Jim's 'life-book'. He needed no coaxing to show it and proudly gave it to her to read.

'I writ it to leave to little Joe,' he said. 'I don't like the idea of everything I've done and seen being clean forgot after I've shipped for my last v'yage. Joe, he'll remember it, and tell the yarns to his children.'

It was an old leather-bound book filled with the record of his voyages and adventures. Anne thought what a treasure trove it would be to a writer. Every sentence was a nugget. In itself the book had no literary merit; Captain Jim's charm of story-telling failed him when he came to pen and ink; he could only jot roughly down the outline of his famous tales, and both spelling and grammar were sadly askew. But Anne felt that if anyone possessed of the gift could take that simple record of a brave, adventurous life, reading between the bald lines the tales of dangers staunchly faced and duty manfully done, a wonderful story might be made from it. Rich comedy and thrilling tragedy were both lying hidden in Captain Jim's 'life-book', waiting for the touch of the master hand to waken the laughter and grief and horror of thousands.

Anne said something of this to Gilbert as they walked home.

'Why don't you try your hand at it yourself, Anne?'

Anne shook her head.

'No. I only wish I could. But it's not in the power of my gift. You know what my forte is, Gilbert – the fanciful, the fairylike, the pretty. To write Captain Jim's life-book as it should be written one should be a master of vigorous yet subtle style, a keen psychologist, a born humorist and a born tragedian. A rare combination of gifts is needed. Paul might do it if he were older. Anyhow, I'm going to ask him to come down next summer and meet Captain Jim.'

'Come to this shore,' wrote Anne to Paul. 'I am afraid you cannot find here Nora or the Golden Lady or the Twin Sailors; but you will find one old sailor who can tell you wonderful stories.'

Paul, however, wrote back, saying regretfully that he could not come that year. He was going abroad for two years' study.

'When I return I'll come to Four Winds, dear Teacher,' he wrote.

'But meanwhile, Captain Jim is growing old,' said Anne, sorrowfully, 'and there is nobody to write his life-book.'

CHAPTER 18

Spring Days

THE ICE in the harbour grew black and rotten in the March suns; in April there were blue waters and a windy, white-capped gulf again; and again the Four Winds light begemmed the twilights.

'I'm so glad to see it once more,' said Anne, on the first evening of its reappearance. 'I've missed it so all winter. The north-western sky has seemed blank and lonely without it.'

The land was tender with brand-new, golden-green, baby leaves. There was an emerald mist on the woods beyond the Glen. The seaward valleys were full of fairy mists at dawn.

Vibrant winds came and went with salt foam in their breath. The sea laughed and flashed and preened and allured, like a beautiful, coquettish woman. The herring schooled and the fishing village woke to life. The harbour was alive with white sails making for the channel. The ships began to sail outward and inward again.

'On a spring day like this,' said Anne, 'I know exactly what my soul will feel like on the resurrection morning.'

'There are times in spring when I sorter feel that I might have been a poet if I'd been caught young,' remarked Captain Jim. 'I catch myself conning over old lines and verses I heard the schoolmaster reciting sixty years ago. They don't trouble me at other times. Now I feel as if I had to get out on the rocks or the fields or the water and spout them.'

Captain Jim had come up that afternoon to bring Anne a load of shells for her garden, and a little bunch of sweet-grass which he had found in a ramble over the sand-dunes.

'It's getting real scarce along this shore now,' he said. 'When I was a boy there was a-plenty of it. But now it's only once in a while you'll find a plot – and never when you're looking for it. You jest have to stumble on it – you're walking along on the sand-hills, never thinking of sweet-grass – and all at once the air is full of sweetness – and there's the grass under your feet. I favour the smell of sweet-grass. It always makes me think of my mother.'

'She was fond of it?' asked Anne.

'Not that I knows on. Dunno's she ever saw any sweet-grass. No, it's because it has a kind of motherly perfume – not too young, you understand – something kind of seasoned and wholesome and dependable – jest like a mother. The schoolmaster's bride always kept it among her handkerchiefs. You might put that little bunch among yours, Mistress Blythe. I don't like these boughten scents – but a whiff of sweet-grass belongs anywhere a lady does.'

Anne had not been especially enthusiastic over the idea of surrounding her flower-beds with quahog shells; as a decoration they did not appeal to her on first thought. But she would not have hurt Captain Jim's feelings for anything; so she assumed a virtue she did not at first feel, and thanked him heartily. And when Captain Jim had proudly encircled every bed with a rim of the big milk-white shells Anne found to her surprise that she liked the effect. On a town lawn, or even up at the Glen, they would not have been in keeping, but here, in the old-fashioned, sea-bound garden of the little house of dreams, they *belonged*.

'They *do* look nice,' she said sincerely.

'The schoolmaster's bride always had cow-hawks round her beds,' said Captain Jim. 'She was a master hand with flowers. She *looked* at 'em – and touched 'em – *so* – and they grew like mad. Some folks have that knack – I reckon you have it, too, Mistress Blythe.'

'Oh, I don't know – but I love my garden, and I love working in it. To potter with green, growing things, watching each day to see the dear, new sprouts come up, is like taking a hand in creation, I think. Just now my garden is like faith – the substance of things hoped for. But bide a wee.'

'It always amazes me to look at the little, wrinkled brown seeds and think of the rainbows in 'em,' said Captain Jim. 'When I ponder on them seeds I don't find it nowise hard to believe that we've got souls that'll live in other worlds. You couldn't hardly believe there was life in them tiny things, some no bigger than grains of dust, let alone colour and scent, if you hadn't seen the miracle, could you?'

Anne, who was counting her days like silver beads on a rosary, could not now take the long walk to the lighthouse or up the Glen road. But Miss Cornelia and Captain Jim came very often to the little house. Miss Cornelia was the joy of Anne's and Gilbert's existence. They laughed side-splittingly over her speeches after every visit. When Captain Jim and she happened to visit the little house at the same time there was much sport for the listening. They waged wordy warfare, she attacking, he defending. Anne once reproached the Captain for his baiting of Miss Cornelia.

'Oh, I do love to set her going, Mistress Blythe,' chuckled

the unrepentant sinner. 'It's the greatest amusement I have in life. That tongue of hers would blister a stone. And you and that young dog of a doctor enj'y listening to her as much as I do.'

Captain Jim came along another evening to bring Anne some mayflowers. The garden was full of the moist, scented air of a maritime spring evening. There was a milk-white mist on the edge of the sea, with a young moon kissing it, and a silver gladness of stars over the Glen. The bell of the church across the harbour was ringing dreamily sweet. The mellow chime drifted through the dusk to mingle with the soft spring-moan of the sea. Captain Jim's mayflowers added the last completing touch to the charm of the night.

'I haven't seen any this spring, and I've missed them,' said Anne, burying her face in them.

'They ain't to be found around Four Winds, only in the barrens away behind the Glen up yander. I took a little trip today to the Land-of-nothing-to-do, and hunted these up for you. I reckon they're the last you'll see this spring, for they're nearly done.'

'How kind and thoughtful you are, Captain Jim. Nobody else – not even Gilbert' – with a shake of her head at him – 'remembered that I always long for mayflowers in spring.'

'Well, I had another errand, too – I wanted to take Mr Howard back yander a mess of trout. He likes one occasional, and it's all I can do for a kindness he did me once. I stayed all the afternoon and talked to him. He likes to talk to me, though he's a highly eddicated man and I'm only an ignorant old sailor, because he's one of the folks that's *got* to talk or they're miserable, and he finds listeners scarce around here. The Glen folks fight shy of him because they think he's an infidel. He ain't that far gone exactly – few men is, I reckon – but he's what you might call a heretic. Heretics are wicked, but they're mighty int'resting. It's jest that they've got sorter lost looking for God, being under the impression that He's hard to find – which He ain't never. Most of 'em blunder to Him after a while, I guess. I don't think listening to Mr Howard's arguments is likely to do *me* much harm. Mind you, I believe what I was brought up to believe. It saves a vast of bother – and back of it all, God is good. The trouble with Mr Howard is that he's a leetle *too* clever. He thinks that he's bound to live up to his cleverness, and that it's smarter to thrash out some new way of getting to heaven than to go by the old track the common, ignorant folks is travelling. But he'll get there some time all right, and then he'll laugh at himself.'

'Mr Howard was a Methodist to begin with,' said Miss Cornelia, as if she thought he had not far to go from that to heresy.

'Do you know, Cornelia,' said Captain Jim gravely, 'I've often thought that if I wasn't a Presbyterian I'd be a Methodist.'

'Oh, well,' conceded Miss Cornelia, 'if you weren't a Presbyterian it wouldn't matter much what you were. Speaking of heresy, reminds me, doctor – I've brought back that book you lent me – that *Natural Law in the Spiritual World* – I didn't read more'n a third of it. I can read sense, and I can read nonsense, but that book is neither the one nor the other.'

It *is* considered rather heretical in some quarters,'

admitted Gilbert, 'but I told you that before you took it, Miss Cornelia.'

'Oh, I wouldn't have minded its being heretical. I can stand wickedness, but I can't stand foolishness,' said Miss Cornelia calmly, and with the air of having said the last thing there was to say about *Natural Law*.

'Speaking of books, *A Mad Love* come to an end at last two weeks ago,' remarked Captain Jim musingly. 'It run to one hundred and three chapters. When they got married the book stopped right off, so I reckon their troubles were all over. It's real nice that that's the way in books anyhow, isn't it, even if 'tisn't so anywhere else?'

'I never read novels,' said Miss Cornelia. 'Did you hear how Geordie Russell was today, Captain Jim?'

'Yes, I called in on my way home to see him. He's getting round all right – but stewing in a broth of trouble, as usual, poor man. 'Course he brews up most of it for himself, but I reckon that don't make it any easier to bear.'

'He's an awful pessimist,' said Miss Cornelia.

'Well, no, he ain't a pessimist exactly, Cornelia. He only jest never finds anything that suits him.'

'And isn't that a pessimist?'

'No, no. A pessimist is one who never expects to find anything to suit him. Geordie hain't got *that* far yet.'

'You'd find something good to say of the devil himself, Jim Boyd.'

'Well, you've heard the story of the old lady who said he was persevering. But no, Cornelia, I've nothing good to say of the devil.'

'Do you believe in him at all?' asked Miss Cornelia seriously.

148

'How can you ask that when you know what a good Presbyterian I am, Cornelia? How could a Presbyterian get along without a devil?'

'*Do* you?' persisted Miss Cornelia.

Captain Jim suddenly became grave.

'I believe in what I heard a minister once call "a mighty and malignant and *intelligent* power of evil working in the universe",' he said solemnly. 'I do *that*, Cornelia. You can call it the devil, or the "principle of evil", or the Old Scratch, or any name you like. It's *there*, and all the infidels and heretics in the world can't argue it away, any more'n they can argue God away. It's there, and it's working. But, mind you, Cornelia, I believe it's going to get the worst of it in the long run.'

'I am sure I hope so,' said Miss Cornelia, none too hopefully. 'But speaking of the devil, I am positive that Billy Booth is possessed by him now. Have you heard of Billy's latest performance?'

'No, what was that?'

'He's gone and burned up his wife's new brown broad-cloth suit, that she paid twenty-five dollars for in Charlotte-town, because he declares the men looked too admiring at her when she wore it to church the first time. Wasn't that like a man?'

'Mistress Booth *is* mighty pretty, and brown's her colour,' said Captain Jim reflectively.

'Is that any good reason why he should poke her new suit into the kitchen stove? Billy Booth is a jealous fool, and he makes his wife's life miserable. She's cried all the week about her suit. Oh, Anne, I wish I could write like you, believe *me*. Wouldn't I score some of the men round here!'

149

'Those Booths are all a mite queer,' said Captain Jim. 'Billy seemed the sanest of the lot till he got married and then this queer jealous streak cropped out in him. His brother Daniel, now, was always odd.'

'Took tantrums every few days or so and wouldn't get out of bed,' said Miss Cornelia with a relish. 'His wife would have to do all the barn work till he got over his spell. When he died people wrote her letters of condolence; if I'd written anything it would have been one of congratulation. Their father, old Abram Booth, was a disgusting old sot. He was drunk at his wife's funeral, and kept reeling round and hiccuping "I didn't dr – i – i – nk much but I feel a – a – awfully que – e – e – r." I gave him a good jab in the back with my umbrella when he came near me, and it sobered him up until they got the casket out of the house. Young Johnny Booth was to have been married yesterday, but he couldn't be because he's gone and got the mumps. Wasn't that like a man?'

'How could he help getting the mumps, poor fellow?'

'I'd poor fellow him, believe *me*, if I was Kate Sterns. I don't know how he could help getting the mumps, but I *do* know the wedding supper was all prepared and everything will be spoiled before he's well again. Such a waste! He should have had the mumps when he was a boy.'

'Come, come, Cornelia, don't you think you're a mite unreasonable?'

Miss Cornelia disdained to reply and turned instead to Susan Baker, a grim-faced, kind-hearted elderly spinster of the Glen, who had been installed as maid-of-all-work at the little house for some weeks. Susan had been up to the Glen to make a sick call, and had just returned.

'How is poor old Aunt Mandy tonight?' asked Miss Cornelia.

Susan sighed.

'Very poorly – very poorly, Cornelia. I am afraid she will soon be in heaven, poor thing!'

'Oh, surely it's not so bad as that!' exclaimed Miss Cornelia sympathetically.

Captain Jim and Gilbert looked at each other. Then they suddenly rose and went out.

'There are times,' said Captain Jim, between spasms, 'when it would be a sin *not* to laugh. Them two excellent women!'

CHAPTER 19

Dawn and Dusk

IN EARLY JUNE, when the sand-hills were a great glory of pink wild roses, and the Glen was smothered in apple-blossoms, Marilla arrived at the little house, accompanied by a black horse-hair trunk, patterned with brass nails, which had reposed undisturbed in the Green Gables garret for half a century. Susan Baker, who, during her few weeks' sojourn in the little house, had come to worship 'young Mrs Doctor', as she called Anne, with blind fervour, looked rather jealously askance at Marilla at first. But as Marilla did not try to interfere in kitchen matters, and showed no desire to interrupt Susan's ministrations to young Mrs Doctor, the good handmaiden became reconciled to her presence, and told her cronies at the Glen that Miss Cuthbert was a fine old lady and knew her place.

One evening, when the sky's limpid bowl was filled with a red glory, and the robins were thrilling the golden twilight with jubilant hymns to the stars of evening, there was a sudden commotion in the little house of dreams. Telephone messages were sent up to the Glen, Doctor Dave and a white-capped nurse came hastily down, Marilla paced the garden walks between the quahog shells, murmuring prayers between her set lips, and Susan sat in the kitchen with cotton wool in her ears and her apron over her head.

Leslie, looking out from the house up the brook, saw that every window of the little house was alight, and did not sleep that night.

The June night was short; but it seemed an eternity to those who waited and watched.

'Oh, will it *never* end?' said Marilla; then she saw how grave the nurse and Doctor Dave looked, and she dared ask no more questions. Suppose Anne – but Marilla could not suppose it.

'Do not tell me,' said Susan fiercely, answering the anguish in Marilla's eyes, 'that God could be so cruel as to take that darling lamb from us when we all love her so much.'

'He has taken others as well beloved,' said Marilla hoarsely.

But at dawn, when the rising sun rent apart the mists hanging over the sand-bar, and made rainbows of them, joy came to the little house. Anne was safe, and a wee white lady, with her mother's big eyes, was lying beside her. Gilbert, his face grey and haggard from his night's agony, came down to tell Marilla and Susan.

'Thank God,' shuddered Marilla.

Susan got up and took the cotton wool out of her ears.

'Now for breakfast,' she said briskly. 'I am of the opinion that we will all be glad of a bite and sup. You tell young Mrs Doctor not to worry about a single thing – Susan is at the helm. You tell her just to think of her baby.'

Gilbert smiled rather sadly as he went away. Anne, her pale face blanched with its baptism of pain, her eyes aglow with the holy passion of motherhood, did not need to be told to think of her baby. She thought of nothing else. For a few hours she tasted of happiness so rare and exquisite that she wondered if the angels in heaven did not envy her.

'Little Joyce,' she murmured, when Marilla came in to see the baby. 'We planned to call her that if she were a girlie. There were so many we would have liked to name her for; we couldn't choose between them, so we decided on Joyce – we can call her Joy for short – Joy – it suits so well. Oh, Marilla, I thought I was happy before. Now I know that I just dreamed a pleasant dream of happiness. *This* is the reality.'

'You mustn't talk, Anne – wait till you're stronger,' said Marilla warningly.

'You know how hard it is for me *not* to talk,' smiled Anne.

At first she was too weak and too happy to notice that Gilbert and the nurse looked grave and Marilla sorrowful. Then, as subtly, and coldly, and remorselessly as a sea-fog stealing landward, fear crept into her heart. Why was not Gilbert gladder? Why would he not talk about the baby? Why would they not let her have it with her after that first heavenly-happy hour? Was – was there anything wrong?

'Gilbert,' whispered Anne imploringly, 'the baby – is all right – isn't she? Tell me – tell me.'

Gilbert was a long while in turning round; then he bent over Anne and looked in her eyes. Marilla, listening fearfully outside the door, heard a pitiful, heartbroken moan, and fled to the kitchen where Susan was weeping.

'Oh, the poor lamb – the poor lamb! How can she bear it, Miss Cuthbert? I am afraid it will kill her. She has been that built up and happy, longing for that baby, and planning for it. Cannot anything be done nohow, Miss Cuthbert?'

154

'I'm afraid not, Susan. Gilbert says there is no hope. He knew from the first the little thing couldn't live.'

'And it is such a sweet baby,' sobbed Susan. 'I never saw one so white – they are mostly red or yellow. And it opened its big eyes as if it was months old. The little, little thing! Oh, the poor young Mrs Doctor!'

At sunset the little soul that had come with the dawning went away, leaving heartbreak behind it. Miss Cornelia took the wee white lady from the kindly but stranger hands of the nurse, and dressed the tiny waxen form in the beautiful dress Leslie had made for it. Leslie had asked her to do that. Then she took it back and laid it beside the poor, broken, tear-blinded little mother.

'The Lord has given and the Lord has taken away, dearie,' she said through her own tears. 'Blessed be the name of the Lord.'

Then she went away, leaving Anne and Gilbert alone together with their dead.

The next day the small white Joy was laid in a velvet casket which Leslie had lined with apple-blossoms, and taken to the graveyard of the church across the harbour. Miss Cornelia and Marilla put all the little love-made garments away, together with the ruffled basket which had been befrilled and belaced for dimpled limbs and downy head. Little Joy was never to sleep there; she had found a colder, narrower bed.

'This has been an awful disappointment to me,' sighed Miss Cornelia. 'I've looked forward to this baby – and I did want it to be a girl, too.'

'I can only be thankful that Anne's life was spared,' said Marilla, with a shiver, recalling those hours of darkness when the girl she loved was passing through the valley of the shadow.

'Poor, poor lamb! Her heart is broken,' said Susan.

'I *envy* Anne,' said Leslie suddenly and fiercely, 'and I'd envy her even if she had died! She was a mother for one beautiful day. I'd gladly give my life for *that*!'

'I wouldn't talk like that, Leslie, dearie,' said Miss Cornelia deprecatingly. She was afraid that the dignified Miss Cuthbert would think Leslie quite terrible.

Anne's convalescence was long, and made bitter for her by many things. The bloom and sunshine of the Four Winds world grated harshly on her; and yet, when the rain fell heavily, she pictured it beating so mercilessly down on that little grave across the harbour; and when the wind blew around the eaves she heard sad voices in it she had never heard before.

Kindly callers hurt her, too, with the well-meant platitudes with which they strove to cover the nakedness of bereavement. A letter from Phil Blake was an added sting. Phil had heard of the baby's birth, but not of its death, and she wrote Anne a congratulatory letter of sweet mirth which hurt her horribly.

'I would have laughed over it so happily if I had my baby,' she sobbed to Marilla. 'But when I haven't it just seems like wanton cruelty – though I know Phil wouldn't hurt me for the world. Oh, Marilla, I don't see how I can *ever* be happy again – *everything* will hurt me all the rest of my life.'

'Time will help you,' said Marilla, who was racked with sympathy but could never learn to express it in other than age-worn formulas.

'It doesn't seem *fair*,' said Anne rebelliously. 'Babies are born and live where they are not wanted – where they will be neglected – where they will have no chance. I would have loved my baby so – and cared for it so tenderly – and tried to give her every chance for good. And yet I wasn't allowed to keep her.'

'It was God's will, Anne,' said Marilla, helpless before the riddle of the universe – the *why* of undeserved pain. 'And little Joy is better off.'

'I can't believe *that*,' cried Anne bitterly. Then, seeing that Marilla looked shocked, she added passionately, 'Why should she be born at all – why should anyone be born at all – if she's better off dead? I *don't* believe it is better for a child to die at birth than to live its life out – and love and be loved – and enjoy and suffer – and do its work – and develop a character that would give it a personality in eternity. And how do you know it was God's will? Perhaps it was just a thwarting of His purpose by the Power of Evil. We can't be expected to be resigned to *that*.'

'Oh, Anne, don't talk so,' said Marilla, genuinely alarmed lest Anne were drifting into deep and dangerous waters. 'We can't understand – but we must have faith – we *must* believe that all is for the best. I know you find it hard to think so, just now. But try to be brave – for Gilbert's sake. He's so worried about you. You aren't getting strong as fast as you should.'

'Oh, I know I've been very selfish,' sighed Anne. 'I love Gilbert more than ever – and I want to live for his sake. But it seems as if part of me was buried over there in that little harbour graveyard – and it hurts so much that I'm afraid of life.'

'It won't hurt so much always, Anne.'

157

'The thought that it may stop hurting sometimes hurts me worse than all else, Marilla.'

'Yes, I know, I've felt that too, about other things. But we all love you, Anne. Captain Jim has been up every day to ask for you – and Mrs Moore haunts the place – and Miss Bryant spends most of her time, I think, cooking up nice things for you. Susan doesn't like it very well. She thinks she can cook as well as Miss Bryant.'

'Dear Susan! Oh, everybody has been so dear and good and lovely to me, Marilla. I'm not ungrateful – and perhaps – when this horrible ache grows a little less – I'll find that I can go on living.'

CHAPTER 20

Lost Margaret

ANNE FOUND that she could go on living; the day came
when she even smiled again over one of Miss Cornelia's
speeches. But there was something in the smile that had
never been in Anne's smile before and would never be absent
from it again.

On the first day she was able to go for a drive Gilbert took
her down to Four Winds Point, and left her there while he
rowed over the channel to see a patient at the fishing village.
A rollicking wind was scudding across the harbour and the
dunes, whipping the water into white-caps and washing the
sand shore with long lines of silvery breakers.

'I'm real proud to see you here again, Mistress Blythe,'
said Captain Jim. 'Sit down – sit down. I'm afeared it's
mighty dusty here today – but there's no need of looking at
dust when you can look at such scenery, is there?'

'I don't mind the dust,' said Anne, 'but Gilbert says I must
keep in the open air. I think I'll go and sit on the rocks down
there.'

'Would you like company or would you rather be alone?'

'If by company you mean yours I'd much rather have it
than be alone,' said Anne, smiling. Then she sighed. She had
never before minded being alone. Now she dreaded it. When
she was alone now she felt so dreadfully alone.

'Here's a nice little spot where the wind can't get at you,' said Captain Jim, when they reached the rocks. 'I often sit here. It's a great place jest to sit and dream.'

'Oh – dreams,' sighed Anne. 'I can't dream now, Captain Jim – I'm done with dreams.'

'Oh, no, you're not, Mistress Blythe – oh, no, you're not,' said Captain Jim meditatively. 'I know how you feel jest now – but if you keep on living you'll get glad again, and the first thing you know you'll be dreaming again – thank the good Lord for it! If it wasn't for our dreams they might as well bury us. How'd we stand living if it wasn't for our dream of immortality? And that's a dream that's *bound* to come true, Mistress Blythe. You'll see your little Joyce again some day.'

'But she won't be my baby,' said Anne, with trembling lips. 'Oh, she may be, as Longfellow says, "a fair maiden clothed with celestial grace" – but she'll be a stranger to me.'

'God will manage better'n *that*, I believe,' said Captain Jim.

They were both silent for a little time. Then Captain Jim said very softly:

'Mistress Blythe, may I tell you about lost Margaret?'

'Of course,' said Anne gently. She did not know who 'lost Margaret' was, but she felt that she was going to hear the romance of Captain Jim's life.

'I've often wanted to tell you about her,' Captain Jim went on. 'Do you know why, Mistress Blythe? It's because I want somebody to remember and think of her some time after I'm gone. I can't bear that her name should be forgotten by all living souls. And now nobody remembers lost Margaret but me.'

Then Captain Jim told the story – an old, old forgotten

story, for it was over fifty years since Margaret had fallen asleep one day in her father's dory and drifted – or so it was supposed, for nothing was ever certainly known as to her fate – out of the channel, beyond the bar, to perish in the black thunder-squall which had come up so suddenly that long-ago summer afternoon. But to Captain Jim those fifty years were but as yesterday when it is past.

'I walked the shore for months after that,' he said sadly, 'looking to find her dear, sweet little body; but the sea never give her back to me. But I'll find her some time, Mistress Blythe – I'll find her some time. She's waiting for me. I wish I could tell you jest how she looked, but I can't. I've seen a fine, silvery mist hanging over the bar at sunrise that seemed like her – and then again I've seen a white birch in the woods back yander that made me think of her. She had pale brown hair and a little white, sweet face, and long slender fingers like yours, Mistress Blythe, only browner, for she was a shore girl. Sometimes I wake up in the night and hear the sea calling to me in the old way, and it seems as if lost Margaret called in it. And when there's a storm and the waves are sobbing and moaning I hear her lamenting among them. And when they laugh on a gay day it's *her* laugh – lost Margaret's sweet, roguish little laugh. The sea took her from me, but some day I'll find her Mistress Blythe. It can't keep us apart for ever.'

'I am glad you have told me about her,' said Anne. 'I have often wondered why you had lived all your life alone.'

'I couldn't ever care for anyone else. Lost Margaret took my heart with her – out there,' said the old lover, who had been faithful for fifty years to his drowned sweetheart. 'You won't mind if I talk a good deal about her, will you, Mistress

Blythe? It's a pleasure to me – for all the pain went out of her memory years ago and jest left its blessing. I know you'll never forget her, Mistress Blythe. And if the years, as I hope, bring other little folks to your home, I want you to promise me that you'll tell *them* the story of lost Margaret, so that her name won't be forgotten among humankind.'

CHAPTER 21

Barriers Swept Away

'ANNE,' said Leslie, breaking abruptly a short silence, 'you don't know how *good* it is to be sitting here with you again – working – and talking – and being silent together.'

They were sitting among the blue-eyed grasses on the bank of the brook in Anne's garden. The water sparkled and crooned past them; the birches threw dappled shadows over them; roses bloomed along the walks. The sun was beginning to be low, and the air was full of woven music. There was one music of the wind in the firs behind the house, and another of the waves on the bar, and still another from the distant bell of the church near which the wee white lady slept. Anne loved that bell, though it brought sorrowful thoughts now.

She looked curiously at Leslie, who had thrown down her sewing and spoken with a lack of restraint that was very unusual with her.

'On that horrible night when you were so ill,' Leslie went on, 'I kept thinking that perhaps we'd have no more talks and walks and *works* together. And I realized just what your friendship had come to mean to me – just what *you* meant – and just what a hateful little beast I had been.'

'Leslie! Leslie! I never allow anyone to call my friends names.'

'It's true. That's exactly what I am – a hateful little beast. There's something I've *got* to tell you, Anne. I suppose it will make you despise me, but I *must* confess it. Anne, there have been times this past winter and spring when I have *hated* you.'

'I knew it,' said Anne calmly.

'You *knew* it?'

'Yes, I saw it in your eyes.'

'And yet you went on liking me and being my friend.'

'Well, it was only now and then you hated me, Leslie. Between times you loved me, I think.'

'I certainly did. But that other horrid feeling was always there, spoiling it, back in my heart. I kept it down – sometimes I forgot it – but sometimes it would surge up and take possession of me. I hated you because I *envied* you – oh, I was sick with envy of you at times. You had a dear little home – and love – and happiness – and glad dreams – everything I wanted – and never had – and never could have. Oh, never could have! *That* was what stung. I wouldn't have envied you if I had had any *hope* that life would ever be different for me. But I hadn't – I hadn't – and it didn't seem *fair*. It made me rebellious – and it hurt me – and so I hated you at times. Oh, I was so ashamed of it – I'm dying of shame now – but I couldn't conquer it. That night, when I was afraid you mightn't live – I thought I was going to be punished for my wickedness – and I loved you so then. Anne, Anne, I never had anything to love since my mother died, except Dick's old dog – and it's so dreadful to have nothing to love – life is so *empty* – and there's *nothing* worse than emptiness – and I might have loved you so much – and that horrible thing had spoiled it –'

Leslie was trembling and growing almost incoherent with the violence of her emotion.

'Don't, Leslie,' implored Anne, 'oh, don't. I understand – don't talk of it any more.'

'I must – I must. When I knew you were going to live I vowed that I would tell you as soon as you were well – that I wouldn't go on accepting your friendship and companionship without telling you how unworthy I was of it. And I've been so afraid – it would turn you against me.'

'You needn't fear that, Leslie.'

'Oh, I'm so glad – so glad, Anne.' Leslie clasped her brown, work-hardened hands tightly together to still their shaking. 'But I want to tell you everything, now I've begun. You don't remember the first time I saw you, I suppose – it wasn't that night on the shore –'

'No, it was the night Gilbert and I came home. You were driving your geese down the hill. I should think I *do* remember it! I thought you were so beautiful – I longed for weeks after to find out who you were.'

'I knew who *you* were, although I had never seen either of you before. I had heard of the new doctor and his bride who were coming to live in Miss Russell's little house. I – I hated you that very moment, Anne.'

'I felt the resentment in your eyes – then I doubted – I thought I must be mistaken – because *why* should it be?'

'It was because you looked so happy. Oh, you'll agree with me now that I *am* a hateful beast – to hate another woman just because she was happy – and when her happiness didn't take anything from me! That was why I never went to see you. I knew quite well I ought to go – even our simple Four Winds customs demanded that. But I couldn't. I used to watch you from my window – I could see you and your husband strolling about your garden in the evening – or you running down the poplar lane to meet him. And it hurt me. And yet in another way I wanted to go over. I felt that, if I were not so miserable, I could have liked you and found in you what I've never had in my life – an intimate, *real* friend of my own age. And then you remember that night at the shore? You were afraid I would think you crazy. You must have thought *I* was.'

'No, but I couldn't understand you, Leslie. One moment you drew me to you – the next you pushed me back.'

'I was very unhappy that evening. I had had a hard day. Dick had been very – very hard to manage that day. Generally he is quite good-natured and easily controlled, you know, Anne. But some days he is very different. I was so heartsick – I ran away to the shore as soon as he went to sleep. It was my only refuge. I sat there thinking of how my poor father had ended his life, and wondering if I wouldn't be driven to it some day. Oh, my heart was full of black thoughts! And then you came dancing along the cove like a glad, light-hearted child. I – I hated you more then than I've ever done since. And yet I craved your friendship. The one feeling swayed me one moment; the other feeling the next. When I got home that night I cried for shame of what you must think of me. But it's always been just the same when I came over here. Sometimes I'd be happy and enjoy my visit. And at other times that hideous feeling would mar it all. There were times when everything about you and your house hurt me. You had so many dear little things I couldn't have. Do you know – it's ridiculous – but I had an especial spite at those china dogs of yours. There were times when I wanted to catch up Gog and Magog and bang their pert black noses together! Oh, you smile, Anne – but it was never funny to me. I would come here and see you and Gilbert with your books and your flowers, and your household gods, and your little family jokes – and your love for each other showing in every look and word, even when you didn't know it – and I would go home to – you know what I went home to! Oh, Anne, I don't believe I'm jealous and envious by nature. When I was a girl I lacked many things my schoolmates had, but I never cared – I never disliked them for it. But I seem to have grown so hateful –'

'Leslie, dearest, stop blaming yourself. You are *not* hateful or jealous or envious. The life you have to live has warped you a little, perhaps – but it would have ruined a nature less fine and noble than yours. I'm letting you tell me all this because I believe it's better for you to talk it out and rid your soul of it. But don't blame yourself any more.'

'Well, I won't. I just wanted you to know me as I am. That time you told me of your darling hope for the spring was the worst of all, Anne. I shall never forgive myself for the way I behaved then. I repented it with tears. And I *did* put many a tender and loving thought of you into the little dress I made. But I might have known that anything I made could only be a shroud in the end.'

'Now, Leslie, that *is* bitter and morbid – put such thoughts away. I was so glad when you brought the little dress; and since I had to lose little Joyce I like to think that the dress she wore was the one you made for her when you let yourself love me.'

'Anne, do you know, I believe I shall always love you after this. I don't think I'll ever feel that dreadful way about you again. Talking it all out seems to have done away with it, somehow. It's very strange – and I thought it so real and bitter. It's like opening the door of a dark room to show some hideous creature you've believed to be there – and when the light streams in your monster turns out to have been just a shadow, vanishing when the light comes. It will never come between us again.'

'No, we are real friends now, Leslie, and I am very glad.'

'I hope you won't misunderstand me if I say something else. Anne, I was grieved to the core of my heart when you lost your baby; and if I could have saved her for you by cutting off one of my hands I would have done it. But your sorrow has brought us closer together. Your perfect happiness isn't a barrier any longer. Oh, don't misunderstand, dearest – I'm *not* glad that your happiness isn't perfect any longer – I can say that sincerely; but since it isn't, there isn't such a gulf between us.'

'I *do* understand that, too, Leslie. Now, we'll just shut up the past and forget what was unpleasant in it. It's all going to be different. We're both of the race of Joseph now. I think you've been wonderful – wonderful. And, Leslie, I can't help believing that life has something good and beautiful for you yet.'

Leslie shook her head.

'No,' she said dully. 'There isn't any hope. Dick will never be better – and even if his memory were to come back – oh, Anne, it would be worse, even worse, than it is now. *This* is something you can't understand, you happy bride. Anne, did Miss Cornelia ever tell you how I came to marry Dick?'

'Yes.'

'I'm glad – I wanted you to know – but I couldn't bring

myself to talk of it if you hadn't known. Anne, it seems to me that ever since I was twelve years old life has been bitter. Before that I had a happy childhood. We were very poor — but we didn't mind. Father was so splendid — so clever and loving and sympathetic. We were chums as far back as I can remember. And Mother was so sweet. She was very, very beautiful. I look like her, but I am not so beautiful as she was.'

'Miss Cornelia says you are far more beautiful.'

'She is mistaken — or prejudiced. I think my figure *is* better — Mother was slight and bent by hard work — but she had the face of an angel. I used just to look up at her in worship. We all worshipped her — Father and Kenneth and I.'

Anne remembered that Miss Cornelia had given her a very different impression of Leslie's mother. But had not love the truer vision? Still, it *was* selfish of Rose West to make her daughter marry Dick Moore.

'Kenneth was my brother,' went on Leslie. 'Oh, I can't tell you how I loved him. And he was cruelly killed. Do you know how?'

'Yes.'

'Anne, I saw his little face as the wheel went over him. He fell on his back. Anne — Anne — I can see it now. I shall always see it. Anne, all I ask of heaven is that that recollection shall be blotted out of my memory. O my God!'

'Leslie, don't speak of it. I know the story — don't go into details that only harrow your soul up unavailingly. It *will* be blotted out.'

After a moment's struggle Leslie regained a measure of self-control.

'Then Father's health got worse and he grew despondent

– his mind became unbalanced – you've heard all that, too?'

'Yes.'

'After that I had just Mother to live for. But I was very ambitious. I meant to teach and earn my way through college. I meant to climb to the very top – oh, I won't talk of that either. It's no use. You know what happened. I couldn't see my dear little broken-hearted mother, who had been such a slave all her life, turned out of her home. Of course, I could have earned enough for us to live on. But Mother *couldn't* leave her home. She had come there as a bride – and she had loved Father so – and all her memories were there. Even yet, Anne, when I think that I made her last year happy I'm not sorry for what I did. As for Dick – I didn't hate him when I married him – I just felt for him the indifferent, friendly feeling I had for most of my schoolmates. I knew he drank some – but I had never heard the story of the girl down at the fishing cove. If I had I *couldn't* have married him, even for Mother's sake. Afterwards – I *did* hate him – but Mother never knew. She died – and then I was alone. I was only seventeen and I was alone. Dick had gone off in the *Four Sisters*. I hoped he wouldn't be home very much more. The sea had always been in his blood. I had no other hope. Well, Captain Jim brought him home, as you know – and that's all there is to say. You know me now, Anne – the worst of me – the barriers are all down. And you still want to be my friend?'

Anne looked up through the birches, at the white paper-lantern of a half moon drifting downward to the gulf of sunset. Her face was very sweet.

'I am your friend and you are mine, for always,' she said. 'Such a friend as I never had before. I have had many dear and beloved friends – but there is a something in you, Leslie, that I never found in anyone else. You have more to offer me in that rich nature of yours, and I have more to give you than I had in my careless girlhood. We are both women -- and friends for ever.'

They clasped hands and smiled at each other through the tears that filled the grey eyes and the blue.

CHAPTER 22

Miss Cornelia Arranges Matters

GILBERT INSISTED that Susan should be kept on at the little house for the summer. Anne protested at first.

'Life here with just the two of us is so sweet, Gilbert. It spoils it a little to have anyone else. Susan is a dear soul, but she is an outsider. It won't hurt me to do the work here.'

'You must take your doctor's advice,' said Gilbert. 'There's an old proverb to the effect that shoemakers' wives go barefoot and doctor's wives die young. I don't mean that it shall be true in my household. You will keep Susan until the old spring comes back into your step, and those little hollows on your cheeks fill out.'

'You just take it easy, Mrs Doctor, dear,' said Susan, coming abruptly in. 'Have a good time and do not worry about the pantry. Susan is at the helm. There is no use in keeping a dog and doing your own barking. I am going to take your breakfast up to you every morning.'

'Indeed you are not,' laughed Anne. 'I agree with Miss Cornelia that it's a scandal for a woman who isn't sick to eat her breakfast in bed, and almost justifies the men in any enormities.'

'Oh, Cornelia!' said Susan, with ineffable contempt. 'I think you have better sense, Mrs Doctor, dear, than to heed what Cornelia Bryant says. I cannot see why she must be always running down the men, even if she is an old maid. *I* am an old maid, but you never hear *me* abusing the men. *I* like 'em. I would have married one if I could. Is it not funny nobody ever asked me to marry him, Mrs Doctor, dear? I am no beauty, but I am as good-looking as most of the married women you see. But I never had a beau. What do you suppose is the reason?'

'It may be predestination,' suggested Anne, with unearthly solemnity.

Susan nodded.

'That is what I have often thought, Mrs Doctor, dear, and a great comfort it is. I do not mind nobody wanting me if the Almighty decreed it so for His own wise purposes. But sometimes doubt creeps in, Mrs Doctor, dear, and I wonder if maybe the Old Scratch has not more to do with it than anyone else. I cannot feel resigned *then*. But maybe,' added Susan, brightening up, 'I will have a chance to get married yet. I often and often think of the old verse my aunt used to repeat:

There never was a goose so grey but some time soon or late
Some honest gander came her way and took her for his mate!

A woman cannot ever be sure of not being married till she is buried, Mrs Doctor, dear, and meanwhile I will make a batch of cherry pies. I notice the doctor favours 'em, and I *do* like cooking for a man who appreciates his victuals.'

Miss Cornelia dropped in that afternoon, puffing a little.

'I don't mind the world or the devil much, but the flesh *does* rather bother me,' she admitted. 'You always look as cool as a cucumber, Anne, dearie. Do I smell cherry pie? If I do, ask me to stay to tea. Haven't tasted a cherry pie this summer. My cherries have all been stolen by those scamps of Gilman boys from the Glen.'

173

'Now, now, Cornelia,' remonstrated Captain Jim, who had been reading a sea novel in a corner of the living-room, 'you shouldn't say that about those two poor, motherless little Gilman boys, unless you've got certain proof. Jest because their father ain't none too honest isn't any reason for calling them thieves. It's more likely it's been the robins took your cherries. They're turrible thick this year.'

'Robins!' said Miss Cornelia disdainfully. 'Humph! Two-legged robins, believe *me*!'

'Well, most of the Four Winds robins *are* constructed on that principle,' said Captain Jim gravely.

Miss Cornelia stared at him for a moment. Then she leaned back in her rocker and laughed long and ungrudgingly.

'Well, you *have* got one on me at last, Jim Boyd, I'll admit. Just look how pleased he is, Anne, dearie, grinning like a Chessy-cat. As for the robins' legs, if robins have great, big, bare, sunburned legs, with ragged trousers hanging on 'em, such as I saw up in my cherry-tree one morning at sunrise last week, I'll beg the Gilman boys' pardon. By the time I got down they were gone. I couldn't understand how they had disappeared so quick, but Captain Jim has enlightened me. They flew away, of course.'

Captain Jim laughed and went away, regretfully declining an invitation to stay to supper and partake of cherry pie.

'I'm on my way to see Leslie and ask her if she'll take a boarder,' Miss Cornelia resumed. 'I'd a letter yesterday from a Mrs Daly in Toronto, who boarded a spell with me two years ago. She wanted me to take a friend of hers for the summer. His name is Owen Ford, and he's a newspaper man, and it seems he's a grandson of the schoolmaster who built this house. John Selwyn's oldest daughter married an Ontario man named Ford, and this is her son. He wants to see the old place his grandparents lived in. He had a bad spell of typhoid in the spring and hasn't got rightly over it, so his doctor has ordered him to the sea. He doesn't want to go to the hotel – he just wants a quiet home place. I can't take him, for I have to be away in August. I've been appointed a delegate to the W.F.M.S. convention in Kingsport and I'm going. I don't know whether Leslie'll want to be bothered with him, either, but there's no one else. If she can't take him he'll have to go over the harbour.'

'When you've seen her come back and help us eat our cherry pies,' said Anne. 'Bring Leslie and Dick, too, if they can come. And so you're going to Kingsport? What a nice time you will have. I must give you a letter to a friend of mine there – Mrs Jonas Blake.'

'I've prevailed on Mrs Thomas Holt to go with me,' said Miss Cornelia complacently. 'It's time she had a little holiday, believe *me*. She has just about worked herself to death. Tom Holt can crochet beautifully, but he can't make a living for his family. He never seems to be able to get up early enough to do any work, but I notice he can always get up early to go fishing. Isn't that like a man?'

Anne smiled. She had learned to discount largely Miss Cornelia's opinions of the Four Winds men. Otherwise she must have believed them the most hopeless assortment of reprobates and ne'er-do-wells in the world, with veritable slaves and martyrs for wives. This particular Tom Holt, for example, she knew to be a kind husband, a much-loved father, and an excellent neighbour. If he were rather inclined to be lazy, liking better the fishing he had been born for than the farming he had not, and if he had a harmless eccentricity for doing fancy work, nobody save Miss Cornelia seemed to hold it against him. His wife was a 'hustler', who gloried in hustling; his family got a comfortable living off the farm; and his strapping sons and daughters, inheriting their mother's energy, were all in a fair way to do well in the world. There was not a happier household in Glen St Mary than the Holts.

Miss Cornelia returned satisfied from the house up the brook.

'Leslie's going to take him,' she announced. 'She jumped at the chance. She wants to make a little money to shingle the roof of her house this fall, and she didn't know how she was going to manage it. I expect Captain Jim'll be more than interested when he hears that a grandson of the Selwyns is coming here. Leslie said to tell you she hankered after cherry pie, but she couldn't come to tea because she has to go and hunt up her turkeys. They've strayed away. But she said, if there was a piece left, for you to put it in the pantry and she'd run over in the cat's light, when prowling's in order, to get it. You don't know, Anne, dearie, what good it did my heart to hear Leslie send you a message like that, laughing like she used to long ago. There's a great change come over her lately. She laughs and jokes like a girl, and from her talk I gather she's here real often.'

'Every day — or else I'm over there,' said Anne. 'I don't know what I'd do without Leslie, especially just now when Gilbert is so busy. He's hardly ever home except for a few hours in the wee sma's. He's really working himself to death. So many of the over-harbour people send for him now.'

'They might better be content with their own doctor,' said

Miss Cornelia. 'Though to be sure I can't blame them, for he's a Methodist. Ever since Dr Blythe brought Mrs Allonby round folks think he can raise the dead. I believe Dr Dave is a mite jealous – just like a man. He thinks Dr Blythe has too many new-fangled notions! "Well," I say to him, "it was a new-fangled notion saved Rhoda Allonby. If *you'd* been attending her she'd have died, and had a tombstone saying it had pleased God to take her away." Oh, I *do* like to speak my mind to Dr Dave! He's bossed the Glen for years, and he thinks he's forgotten more than other people ever knew. Speaking of doctors, I wish Dr Blythe'd run over and see to that boil on Dick Moore's neck. It's getting past Leslie's skill. I'm sure I don't know what Dick Moore wants to start in having boils for – as if he wasn't enough trouble without that!'

'Do you know, Dick has taken quite a fancy to me,' said Anne. 'He follows me round like a dog, and smiles like a pleased child when I notice him.'

'Does it make you creepy?'

'Not at all. I rather like poor Dick Moore. He seems so pitiful and appealing, somehow.'

'You wouldn't think him very appealing if you'd see him on his cantankerous days, believe *me*. But I'm glad you don't mind him – it's all the nicer for Leslie. She'll have more to do when her boarder comes. I hope he'll be a decent creature. You'll probably like him – he's a writer.'

'I wonder why people so commonly suppose that if two individuals are both writers they must therefore be hugely congenial,' said Anne, rather scornfully. 'Nobody would expect two blacksmiths to be violently attracted towards each other merely because they were both blacksmiths.'

Nevertheless, she looked forward to the advent of Owen Ford with a pleasant sense of expectation. If he were young and likeable he might prove a very pleasant addition to society in Four Winds. The latch-string of the little house was always out for the race of Joseph.

CHAPTER 23

Owen Ford Comes

ONE EVENING Miss Cornelia telephoned down to Anne.

'The writer man has just arrived here. I'm going to drive him down to your place, and you can show him the way over to Leslie's. It's shorter than driving round by the other road, and I'm in a mortal hurry. The Reese baby has gone and fallen into a pail of hot water at the Glen, and got nearly scalded to death, and they want me right off – to put a new skin on the child, I presume. Mrs Reese is always so careless, and then expects other people to mend her mistakes. You won't mind, will you, dearie? His trunk can go down tomorrow.'

'Very well,' said Anne. 'What is he like, Miss Cornelia?'

'You'll see what he's like outside when I take him down. As for what he's like inside only the Lord who made him knows *that*. I'm not going to say another word, for every receiver in the Glen is down.'

'Miss Cornelia evidently can't find much fault with Mr Ford's looks, or she would find it in spite of the receivers,' said Anne. 'I conclude therefore, Susan, that Mr Ford is rather handsome than otherwise.'

'Well, Mrs Doctor, dear, I *do* enjoy seeing a well-looking man,' said Susan candidly. 'Had I not better get up a snack for him? There is a strawberry pie that would melt in your mouth.'

'No, Leslie is expecting him and has his supper ready. Besides, I want that strawberry pie for my own poor man. He won't be home till late, so leave the pie and a glass of milk out for him, Susan.'

'That I will, Mrs Doctor, dear. Susan is at the helm. After all, it is better to give pie to your own men than to strangers, who may be only seeking to devour, and the doctor himself is as well-looking a man as you often come across.'

When Owen Ford came Anne secretly admitted, as Miss Cornelia towed him in, that he was very 'well-looking' indeed. He was tall and broad-shouldered, with thick brown hair, finely-cut nose and chin, large and brilliant dark-grey eyes.

'And did you notice his ears and his teeth, Mrs Doctor, dear?' queried Susan later on. 'He has got the nicest-shaped ears I ever saw on a man's head. I am choice about ears. When I was young I was scared that I might have to marry a man with ears like flaps. But I need not have worried, for never a chance did I have with any kind of ears.'

Anne had not noticed Owen Ford's ears, but she did see his teeth, as his lips parted over them in a frank and friendly smile. Unsmiling, his face was rather sad and absent in expression, not unlike the melancholy, inscrutable hero of Anne's own early dreams; but mirth and humour and charm lighted it up when he smiled. Certainly, on the outside, as Miss Cornelia said, Owen Ford was a very presentable fellow.

'You cannot realize how delighted I am to be here, Mrs Blythe,' he said, looking around him with eager, interested eyes. 'I have an odd feeling of coming home. My mother was born and spent her childhood here, you know. She used to

180

talk a great deal to me of her old home. I know the geography of it as well as of the one I lived in, and, of course, she told me the story of the building of the house, and of my grandfather's agonized watch for the *Royal William*. I had thought that so old a house must have vanished years ago, or I should have come to see it before this.'

'Old houses don't vanish easily on this enchanted coast,' smiled Anne. 'This is a "land where all things always seem the same" – nearly always, at least. John Selwyn's house hasn't even been much changed, and outside the rose-bushes your grandfather planted for his bride are blooming this very minute.'

'How the thought links me with them! With your leave I must explore the whole place soon.'

'Our latch-string will always be out for you,' promised Anne. 'And do you know that the old sea captain who keeps the Four Winds light knew John Selwyn and his bride well in his boyhood? He told me their story the night I came here – the third bride of the old house.'

'Can it be possible? This *is* a discovery. I must hunt him up.'

'It won't be difficult; we are all cronies of Captain Jim. He will be as eager to see you as you could be to see him. Your grandmother shines like a star in his memory. But I think Mrs Moore is expecting you. I'll show you our "cross-lots" road.'

Anne walked with him to the house up the brook, over a field that was as white as snow with daisies. A boat-load of people were singing far across the harbour. The sound drifted over the water like faint, unearthly music wind-blown across a starlit sea. The big light flashed and beaconed. Owen Ford looked around him with satisfaction.

'And so this is Four Winds,' he said. 'I wasn't prepared to find it quite so beautiful, in spite of all Mother's praises. What colours – what scenery – what charm! I shall get as strong as a horse in no time. And if inspiration comes from beauty, I should certainly be able to begin my great Canadian novel here.'

'You haven't begun it yet?' asked Anne.

'Alack-a-day, no. I've never been able to get the right idea for it. It lurks beyond me – it allures – and beckons – and recedes – I almost grasp it and it is gone. Perhaps amid this peace and loveliness I shall be able to capture it. Miss Bryant tells me that you write.'

'Oh, I do little things for children. I haven't done much since I was married. And I have no designs on a great Canadian novel,' laughed Anne. 'That is quite beyond me.'

Owen Ford laughed too.

'I dare say it is beyond me as well. All the same, I mean to have a try at it some day, if I can ever get time. A newspaper man doesn't have much chance for that sort of thing. I've done a good deal of short-story writing for the magazines, but I've never had the leisure that seems to be necessary for the writing of a book. With three months of liberty I ought to make a start, though – if I could only get the necessary *motif* for it – the *soul* of the book.'

An idea whisked through Anne's brain with a suddenness that made her jump. But she did not utter it, for they had reached the Moore house. As they entered the yard Leslie came out on the veranda from the side door, peering through the gloom for some sign of her expected guest. She stood just where the warm yellow light flooded her from the open door. She wore a plain dress of cheap, cream-tinted cotton voile, with the usual girdle of crimson. Leslie was never without her touch of crimson. She had told Anne that she never felt satisfied without a gleam of red somewhere about her, if it were only a flower. To Anne, it always seemed to symbolize Leslie's glowing, pent-up personality, denied all expression save in that flaming glint. Leslie's dress was cut a little away at the neck and had short sleeves. Her arms gleamed like ivory-tinted marble. Every exquisite curve of her form was outlined in soft darkness against the light. Her hair shone in it like flame. Beyond her was a purple sky, flowering with stars over the harbour.

Anne heard her companion give a gasp. Even in the dusk she could see the amazement and admiration on his face.

'Who is that beautiful creature?' he asked.

'That is Mrs Moore,' said Anne. 'She is very lovely, isn't she?'

'I – I never saw anything like her,' he answered, rather dazedly. 'I wasn't prepared – I didn't expect – good heavens, one *doesn't* expect a goddess for a landlady! Why, if she were clothed in a gown of sea-purple, with a rope of amethysts in her hair, she would be a veritable sea-queen. And she takes in boarders!'

'Even goddesses must live,' said Anne. 'And Leslie isn't a goddess. She's just a very beautiful woman, as human as the rest of us. Did Miss Bryant tell you about Mr Moore?'

'Yes – he's mentally deficient, or something of the sort, isn't he? But she said nothing about Mrs Moore, and I supposed she'd be the usual hustling country housewife who takes in boarders to earn an honest penny.'

'Well, that's just what Leslie is doing,' said Anne crisply.

'And it isn't altogether pleasant for her, either. I hope you won't mind Dick. If you do, please don't let Leslie see it. It would hurt her horribly. He's just a big baby, and sometimes a rather annoying one.'

'Oh, I won't mind him. I don't suppose I'll be much in the house, anyhow, except for meals. But what a shame it all is! Her life must be a hard one.'

'It is. But she doesn't like to be pitied.'

Leslie had gone back into the house and now met them at the front door. She greeted Owen Ford with cold civility, and told him in a business-like tone that his room and his supper were ready for him. Dick, with a pleased grin, shambled upstairs with the valise, and Owen Ford was installed as an inmate of the old house among the willows.

CHAPTER 24

The Life-book of Captain Jim

'I HAVE a little brown cocoon of an idea that may possibly expand into a magnificent moth of fulfilment,' Anne told Gilbert when she reached home. He had returned earlier than she had expected, and was enjoying Susan's cherry pie. Susan herself hovered in the background, like a rather grim but beneficent guardian spirit, and found as much pleasure in watching Gilbert eat pie as he did in eating it.

'What is your idea?' he asked.

'I shan't tell you just yet – not till I see if I can bring the thing about.'

'What sort of a chap is Ford?'

'Oh, very nice, and quite good-looking.'

'Such beautiful ears, doctor, dear,' interjected Susan with a relish.

'He is about thirty or thirty-five, I think, and he meditates writing a novel. His voice is pleasant and his smile delightful, and he knows how to dress. He looks as if life hadn't been altogether easy for him, somehow.'

Owen Ford came over the next evening with a note to Anne from Leslie; they spent the sunset-time in the garden and then went for a moonlit sail on the harbour, in the little boat Gilbert had set up for summer outings. They liked Owen immensely and had that feeling of having known him for many years which distinguishes the freemasonry of the house of Joseph. 'He is as nice as his ears, Mrs Doctor, dear,' said Susan, when he had gone. He had told Susan that he had never tasted anything like her strawberry shortcake, and Susan's susceptible heart was his for ever.

'He has got a way with him,' she reflected, as she cleared up the relics of the supper. 'It is real queer he is not married, for a man like that could have anybody for the asking. Well, maybe he is like me, and has not met the right one yet.'

Susan really grew quite romantic in her musings as she washed the supper dishes.

Two nights later Anne took Owen Ford down to Four Winds Point to introduce him to Captain Jim. The clover fields along the harbour shore were whitening in the western wind, and Captain Jim had one of his finest sunsets on exhibition. He himself had just returned from a trip over the harbour.

'I had to go over and tell Henry Pollock he was dying. Everybody else was afraid to tell him. They expected he'd take on turrible, for he's been dreadful determined to live, and been making no end of plans for the fall. His wife thought he oughter be told and that I'd be the best one to break it to him that he couldn't get better. Henry and me are old cronies – we sailed in the *Grey Gulf* for years together. Well, I went over and sat down by Henry's bed and I says to him, says I, jest right out plain and simple, for if a thing's got to be told it may as well be told first as last, says I, "Mate, I reckon you've got your sailing orders this time." I was sorter quaking inside, for it's an awful thing to have to tell a man who hain't any idea he's dying that he is. But lo and behold, Mistress Blythe, Henry looks up at me, with those bright old black eyes of his in his wizened face and says, says he, "Tell

186

me something I don't know, Jim Boyd, if you want to give me information. I've known *that* for a week." I was too astonished to speak, and Henry, he chuckled. "To see you coming in here," says he, "with your face as solemn as a tombstone and sitting down there with your hands clasped over your stomach, and passing me out a blue-mouldy old item of news like that! It'd make a cat laugh, Jim Boyd," says he. "Who told you?" says I, stupid like. "Nobody," says he. "A week ago Tuesday night I was lying here awake – and I jest knew. I'd suspicioned it before, but then I *knew*. I've been keeping up for the wife's sake. And I'd *like* to have got that barn built, for Eben'll never get it right. But anyhow, now that you've eased your mind, Jim, put on a smile and tell me something interesting." Well, there it was. They'd been so scared to tell him and he knew it all the time. Strange how nature looks out for us, ain't it, and lets us know what we should know when the time comes? Did I never tell you the yarn about Henry getting the fish-hook in his nose, Mistress Blythe?'

'No.'

'Well, him and me had a laugh over it today. It happened nigh unto thirty years ago. Him and me and several more was out mackerel-fishing one day. It was a great day – never saw such a school of mackerel in the gulf – and in the general excitement Henry got quite wild and contrived to stick a fish-hook clean through one side of his nose. Well, there he was; there was barb on one end and a big piece of lead on the other, so it couldn't be pulled out. We wanted to take him ashore at once, but Henry was game; he said he'd be jiggered if he'd leave a school like that for anything short of lockjaw; then he kept fishing away, hauling in hand over fist and groaning between times. Fin'lly the school passed and we come in with a load; I got a file and begun to try to file through that hook. I tried to be as easy as I could, but you should have heard Henry – no, you shouldn't either. It was well no ladies were around. Henry wasn't a swearing man, but he'd heard some few matters of that sort along shore in his time, and he fished 'em all out of his recollection and hurled 'em at me. Fin'lly he declared he couldn't stand it and I had no bowels of compassion. So we hitched up and I drove him to a doctor in Charlottetown, thirty-five miles – there weren't none nearer in them days – with that blessed hook still hanging from his nose. When we got there old Dr Crabb jest took a file and filed that hook jest the same as I'd tried to do, only he weren't a mite particular about doing it easy!'

Captain Jim's visit to his old friend had revived many recollections and he was now in the full tide of reminiscences.

'Henry was asking me today if I remembered the time old Father Chiniquy blessed Alexander MacAllister's boat. Another odd yarn – and true as gospel. I was in the boat myself. We went out, him and me, in Alexander MacAllister's boat one morning at sunrise. Besides, there was a French boy in the boat – Catholic of course. You know old Father Chiniquy had turned Protestant, so the Catholics hadn't much use for him. Well, we sat out in the gulf in the broiling sun till noon, and not a bite did we get. When we went ashore old Father Chiniquy had to go, so he said in that polite way of his, "I'm very sorry I cannot go out with you dis afternoon, Mr MacAllister, but I leave you my blessing. You will catch a t'ousand dis afternoon." Well, we did not catch a thousand, but we caught exactly nine hundred and ninety-nine – the biggest catch for a small boat on the whole north shore that summer. Curious, wasn't it? Alexander MacAllister, he says to Andrew Peters, "Well, and what do you think of Father Chiniquy now?" "Vell," growled Andrew, "I t'ink de old devil has got a blessing left yet." Laws, how Henry did laugh over that today!'

'Do you know who Mr Ford is, Captain Jim?' asked Anne, seeing that Captain Jim's fountain of reminiscence had run out for the present. 'I want you to guess.'

Captain Jim shook his head.

'I never was any hand at guessing, Mistress Blythe, and yet somehow when I come in I thought, "Where have I seen them eyes before?" – for I *have* seen 'em.'

'Think of a September morning many years ago,' said Anne, softly. 'Think of a ship sailing up the harbour – a ship long waited for and despaired of. Think of the day the *Royal William* came in and the first look you had at the schoolmaster's bride.'

Captain Jim sprang up.

'They're Persis Selwyn's eyes,' he almost shouted. 'You can't be her son – you must be her –'

'Grandson; yes, I am Alice Selwyn's son.'

Captain Jim swooped down on Owen Ford and shook his hand over again.

'Alice Selwyn's son! Lord, but you're welcome! Many's the time I've wondered where the descendants of the schoolmaster were living. I knew there was none on the Island. Alice – Alice – the first baby ever born in that little house. No baby ever brought more joy! I've dandled her a hundred times. It was from my knee she took her first steps alone. Can't I see her mother's face watching her – and it was near sixty years ago. Is she living yet?'

'No, she died when I was only a boy.'

'Oh, it doesn't seem right that I should be living to hear that,' sighed Captain Jim. 'But I'm heart-glad to see you. It's brought back my youth for a little while. You don't know yet what a boon *that* is. Mistress Blythe here has the trick – she does it quite often for me.'

Captain Jim was still more excited when he discovered that Owen Ford was what he called a 'real writing man'. He gazed at him as at a superior being. Captain Jim knew that Anne wrote, but he had never taken that fact very seriously. Captain Jim thought women were delightful creatures, who ought to have the vote, and everything else they wanted, bless their hearts; but he did not believe they could write.

'Jest look at *A Mad Love*,' he would protest. 'A woman wrote that and jest look at it – one hundred and three chapters when it could all have been told in ten. A writing woman never knows when to stop; that's the trouble. The p'int of good writing is to know when to stop.'

'Mr Ford wants to hear some of your stories, Captain Jim,' said Anne. 'Tell him the one about the captain who went crazy and imagined he was the Flying Dutchman.'

This was Captain Jim's best story. It was a compound of horror and humour, and though Anne had heard it several times she laughed as heartily and shivered as fearsomely over it as Mr Ford did. Other tales followed, for Captain Jim had an audience after his own heart. He told how his vessel had been run down by a steamer; how he had been boarded by Malay pirates; how his ship had caught fire; how he helped a political prisoner escape from a South African republic; how he had been wrecked one fall on the Magdalens and stranded there for the winter; how a tiger had broken loose on board ship; how his crew had mutinied and marooned him on a barren island – these and many other tales, tragic or humorous or grotesque, did Captain Jim relate. The mystery of the sea, the fascination of far lands, the lure of adventure, the laughter of the world – his hearers felt and realized them all. Owen Ford listened, with his head on his hand, and the First Mate purring on his knee, his brilliant eyes fastened on Captain Jim's rugged, eloquent face.

'Won't you let Mr Ford see your life-book, Captain Jim?' asked Anne, when Captain Jim finally declared that yarn-spinning must end for the time.

'Oh, he don't want to be bothered with *that*,' protested Captain Jim, who was secretly dying to show it.

'I should like nothing better than to see it, Captain Boyd,' said Owen. 'If it is half as wonderful as your tales it will be worth seeing.'

With pretended reluctance Captain Jim dug his life-book out of his old chest and handed it to Owen.

'I reckon you won't care to wrastle long with my old hand o' write. I never had much schooling,' he observed careless-ly. 'Just wrote that there to amuse my nephew Joe. He's always wanting stories. Comes here yesterday and says to me, reproachful-like, as I was lifting a twenty-pound codfish out of my boat, "Uncle Jim, ain't a codfish a dumb animal?" I'd been a-telling him, you see, that he must be real kind to dumb animals, and never hurt 'em in any way. I got out of the scrape by saying a codfish was dumb enough but it wasn't an animal, but Joe didn't look satisfied, and I wasn't satisfied myself. You've got to be mighty careful what you tell them little critters. *They* can see through you.'

While talking, Captain Jim watched Owen Ford from the corner of his eye as the latter examined the life-book; and presently observing that his guest was lost in its pages, he turned smilingly to his cupboard and proceeded to make a pot of tea. Owen Ford separated himself from the life-book, with as much reluctance as a miser wrenches himself from his gold, long enough to drink his tea, and then returned to it hungrily.

'Oh, you can take that thing home with you if you want to,' said Captain Jim, as if the 'thing' were not his most treasured possession. 'I must go down and pull my boat up a bit on the skids. There's a wind coming. Did you notice the sky tonight?

> Mackerel skies and mares' tails
> Make tall ships carry short sails.'

Owen Ford accepted the offer of the life-book gladly. On their way home Anne told him the story of lost Margaret.

'That old captain is a wonderful old fellow,' he said. 'What a life he has led! Why, the man had more adventures in one week of his life than most of us have in a lifetime. Do you really think his tales are all true?'

'I certainly do. I am sure Captain Jim could not tell a lie; and besides, all the people about here say that everything happened as he relates it. There used to be plenty of his old shipmates alive to corroborate him. He's one of the last of the old type of P.E. Island sea captains. They are almost extinct now.'

CHAPTER 25

The Writing of the Book

OWEN FORD came over to the little house the next morning in a state of great excitement.

'Mrs Blythe, this is a wonderful book — absolutely wonderful. If I could take it and use the material for a book I feel certain I could make the novel of the year out of it. Do you suppose Captain Jim would let me do it?'

'Let you! I'm sure he would be delighted,' cried Anne. 'I admit that it was what was in my head when I took you down last night. Captain Jim has always been wishing he could get somebody to write his life-book properly for him.'

'Will you go down to the Point with me this evening, Mrs Blythe? I'll ask him about the life-book myself, but I want you to tell him that you told me the story of lost Margaret and ask him if he will let me use it as a thread of romance with which to weave the stories of the life-book into a harmonious whole.'

Captain Jim was more excited than ever when Owen Ford told him of his plan. At last his cherished dream was to be realized and his 'life-book' given to the world. He was also pleased that the story of lost Margaret should be woven into it.

'It will keep her name from being forgotten,' he said wistfully. 'That's why I want it put in.'

'We'll collaborate,' cried Owen delightedly. 'You will give the soul and I the body. Oh, we'll write a famous book between us, Captain Jim. And we'll get right to work.'

'And to think my book is to be writ by the schoolmaster's grandson!' exclaimed Captain Jim. 'Lad, your grandfather was my dearest friend. I thought there was nobody like him. I see now why I had to wait so long. It couldn't be writ till the right man come. You *belong* here – you've got the soul of this old north shore in you – you're the only one who *could* write it.'

It was arranged that the tiny room off the living-room at the lighthouse should be given over to Owen for a workshop. It was necessary that Captain Jim should be near him as he wrote, for consultation upon many matters of seafaring and gulf lore of which Owen was quite ignorant.

He began work on the book the very next morning, and flung himself into it heart and soul. As for Captain Jim, he was a happy man that summer. He looked upon the little room where Owen worked as a sacred shrine. Owen talked everything over with Captain Jim, but he would not let him see the manuscript.

'You must wait until it is published,' he said. 'Then you'll get it all at once in its best shape.'

He delved into the treasures of the life-book and used them freely. He dreamed and brooded over lost Margaret until she became a vivid reality to him and lived in his pages. As the book progressed it took possession of him and he worked at it with feverish eagerness. He let Anne and Leslie read the manuscript and criticize it; and the concluding chapter of the book, which the critics, later on, were pleased to call idyllic, was modelled upon a suggestion of Leslie's.

Anne fairly hugged herself with delight over the success of her idea.

'I knew when I looked at Owen Ford that he was the very man for it,' she told Gilbert. 'Both humour and passion were in his face, and that, together with the art of expression, was just what was necessary for the writing of such a book. As Mrs Rachel would say, he was predestined for the part.'

Owen Ford wrote in the mornings. The afternoons were generally spent in some merry outing with the Blythes. Leslie often went, too, for Captain Jim took charge of Dick frequently, in order to set her free. They went boating on the harbour and up the three pretty rivers that flowed into it; they had clam-bakes on the bar and mussel-bakes on the rocks; they picked strawberries on the sand-dunes; they went out cod-fishing with Captain Jim; they shot plover in the shore fields and wild ducks in the cove – at least, the men did. In the evenings they rambled in the low-lying, daisied, shore fields under a golden moon, or they sat in the living-room at the little house where often the coolness of the sea-breeze justified a driftwood fire, and talked of the thousand and one things which happy, eager, clever young people can find to talk about.

Ever since the day on which she had made her confession to Anne, Leslie had been a changed creature. There was no trace of her old coldness and reserve, no shadow of her old bitterness. The girlhood of which she had been cheated seemed to come back to her with the ripeness of woman-hood; she expanded like a flower of flame and perfume; no laugh was readier than hers, no wit quicker, in the twilight circles of that enchanted summer. When she could not be with them all felt that some exquisite savour was lacking in their intercourse. Her beauty was illumined by the awakened soul within, as some rosy lamp might shine through a flawless vase of alabaster. There were hours when Anne's eyes seemed to ache with the splendour of her. As for Owen Ford, the 'Margaret' of his book, although she had the soft brown hair and elfin face of the real girl who had vanished so long ago, 'pillowed where lost Atlantis sleeps', had the personality of Leslie Moore, as it was revealed to him in those halcyon days at Four Winds Harbour.

And in all, it was a never-to-be-forgotten summer – one of those summers which come seldom into any life, but leave a rich heritage of beautiful memories in their going – one of those summers which, in a fortunate combination of delightful weather, delightful friends, and delightful doings, come as near to perfection as anything can come in this world.

'Too good to last,' Anne told herself with a little sigh, on the September day when a certain nip in the wind and a certain shade of intense blue on the gulf water said that autumn was hard by.

That evening Owen Ford told them that he had finished his book and that his vacation must come to an end.

'I have a good deal to do to it yet – revising and pruning and so forth,' he said, 'but in the main it's done. I wrote the last sentence this morning. If I can find a publisher for it it will probably be out next summer or fall.'

Owen had not much doubt that he would find a publisher. He knew that he had written a great book – a book that would score a wonderful success – a book that would *live*. He knew that it would bring him both fame and fortune; but when he had written the last line of it he had bowed his head on the manuscript, and so sat for a long time. And his thoughts were not of the good work he had done.

CHAPTER 26

Owen Ford's Confession

'I'M SO SORRY Gilbert is away,' said Anne. 'He had to go –
Allan Lyons at the Glen has met with a serious accident. He
will not likely be home till very late. But he told me to tell
you he'd be up and over early enough in the morning to see
you before you left. It's too provoking. Susan and I had
planned such a nice little jamboree for your last night here.'

She was sitting beside the garden brook on the little rustic
seat Gilbert had built. Owen Ford stood before her, leaning
against the bronze column of a yellow birch. He was very
pale and his face bore the marks of the preceding sleepless
night. Anne, glancing up at him, wondered if, after all, his
summer had brought him the strength it should. Had he
worked too hard over his book? She remembered that for a
week he had not been looking well.

'I'm rather glad the doctor is away,' said Owen slowly. 'I
wanted to see you alone, Mrs Blythe. There is something I
must tell somebody, or I think it will drive me mad. I've been
trying for a week to look it in the face – and I can't. I know I
can trust you – and, besides, you will understand. A woman
with eyes like yours always understands. You are one of the
folks people instinctively tell things to. Mrs Blythe, I love
Leslie. *Love* her! That seems too weak a word!'

His voice suddenly broke with the suppressed passion of
his utterance. He turned his head away and hid his face on

his arm. His whole form shook. Anne sat looking at him, pale and aghast. She had never thought of this! And yet – how was it she had never thought of it? It now seemed a natural and inevitable thing. She wondered at her own blindness. But – but – things like this did not happen in Four Winds. Elsewhere in the world human passions might set at defiance human conventions and laws – but not *here*, surely. Leslie had kept summer boarders off and on for ten years, and nothing like this had happened. But perhaps they had not been like Owen Ford; and the vivid, *living* Leslie of this summer was not the cold, sullen girl of other years. Oh, *somebody* should have thought of this! Why hadn't Miss Cornelia thought of it? Miss Cornelia was always ready enough to sound the alarum where men were concerned. Anne felt an unreasonable resentment against Miss Cornelia. Then she gave a little inward groan. No matter who was to blame, the mischief was done. And Leslie – what of Leslie? It was for Leslie Anne felt most concerned.

'Does Leslie know this, Mr Ford?' she asked quietly.

'No – no – unless she has guessed it. You surely don't think I'd be cad and scoundrel enough to tell her, Mrs Blythe. I couldn't help loving her – that's all – and my misery is greater than I can bear.'

'Does *she* care?' asked Anne. The moment the question crossed her lips she felt that she should not have asked it. Owen Ford answered it with over-eager protest.

'No – no, of course not. But I could make her care if she were free – I know I could.'

'She does care – and he knows it,' thought Anne. Aloud she said, sympathetically but decidedly:

'But she is not free, Mr Ford. And the only thing you can

do is to go away in silence and leave her to her own life.'

'I know – I know,' groaned Owen. He sat down on the grassy bank and stared moodily into the amber water beneath him. 'I know there's nothing to do – nothing but to say conventionally, "Good-bye, Mrs Moore. Thank you for all your kindness to me this summer," just as I would have said it to the sonsy, bustling, keen-eyed housewife I expected her to be when I came. Then I'll pay my board money like any honest boarder and go! Oh, it's very simple. No doubt – no perplexity – a straight road to the end of the world! And I'll walk it – you needn't fear that I won't, Mrs Blythe. But it would be easier to walk over red-hot ploughshares.'

Anne flinched with the pain of his voice. And there was so little she could say that would be adequate to the situation. Blame was out of the question – advice was not needed – sympathy was mocked by the man's stark agony. She could only feel with him in a maze of compassion and regret. Her heart ached for Leslie! Had not that poor girl suffered enough without this?

'It wouldn't be so hard to go and leave her if she were only happy,' resumed Owen passionately. 'But to think of her living death – to realize what it is to which I do leave her! *That* is the worst of all. I would give my life to make her happy – and I can do nothing even to help her – nothing. She is bound for ever to that poor wretch – with nothing to look forward to but growing old in a succession of empty, meaningless, barren years. It drives me mad to think of it. But I must go through my life, never seeing her, but always knowing what she is enduring. It's hideous – hideous!'

'It is very hard,' said Anne sorrowfully. 'We – her friends here – all know how hard it is for her.'

'And she is so richly fitted for life,' said Owen rebelliously. 'Her beauty is the least of her dower – and she is the most beautiful woman I've ever known. That laugh of hers! I've angled all summer to evoke that laugh, just for the delight of hearing it. And her eyes – they are as deep and blue as the gulf out there. I never saw such blueness – and gold! Did you ever see her hair down, Mrs Blythe?'

'No.'

'I did – once. I had gone down to the Point to go fishing with Captain Jim, but it was too rough to go out, so I came back. She had taken the opportunity of what she expected to be an afternoon alone to wash her hair, and she was standing on the veranda in the sunshine to dry it. It fell all about her to her feet in a fountain of living gold. When she saw me she hurried in, and the wind caught her hair and swirled it all around her – Danaë in her cloud. Somehow, just then the knowledge that I loved her came home to me – and I realized that I had loved her from the moment I first saw her standing against the darkness in that glow of light. And she must live on here – petting and soothing Dick, pinching and saving for a mere existence, while I spend my life longing vainly for her, and debarred, by that very fact, from even giving her the little help a friend might. I walked the shore last night, almost till dawn, and thrashed it all out over and over again. And yet, in spite of everything, I can't find it in my heart to be sorry that I came to Four Winds. It seems to me that, bad as everything is, it would be still worse never to have known Leslie. It's burning, searing pain to love her and leave her – but not to have loved her is unthinkable. I suppose all this sounds very crazy – all these terrible emotions always do sound foolish when we put them into our

201

inadequate words. They are not meant to be spoken – only felt and endured. I shouldn't have spoken – but it has helped – some. At least, it has given me strength to go away respectably tomorrow morning, without making a scene. You'll write me now and then, won't you, Mrs Blythe, and give me what news there is to give of her?'

'Yes,' said Anne. 'Oh, I'm so sorry you are going – we'll miss you so – we've all been such friends! If it were not for this you could come back other summers. Perhaps, even yet – by and by – when you've forgotten, perhaps –'

'I shall never forget – and I shall never come back to Four Winds,' said Owen briefly.

Silence and twilight fell over the garden. Far away the sea was lapping gently and monotonously on the bar. The wind of evening in the poplars sounded like some sad, weird, old rune – some broken dream of old memories. A slender shapely young aspen rose up before them against the fine maize and emerald and paling rose of the western sky, which brought out every leaf and twig in dark, tremulous, elfin loveliness.

'Isn't that beautiful?' said Owen, pointing to it with the air of a man who puts a certain conversation behind him.

'It's so beautiful that it hurts me,' said Anne softly. 'Perfect things like that always did hurt me – I remember I called it "the queer ache" when I was a child. What is the reason that pain like this seems inseparable from perfection? Is it the pain of finality – when we realize that there can be nothing beyond but retrogression?'

'Perhaps,' said Owen dreamily, 'it is the prisoned infinite in us calling out to its kindred infinite as expressed in that visible perfection.'

'You seem to have a cold in the head. Better rub some tallow on your nose when you go to bed,' said Miss Cornelia, who had come in through the little gate between the firs in time to catch Owen's last remark. Miss Cornelia liked Owen; but it was a matter of principle with her to visit any 'high-falutin' language from a man with a snub.

Miss Cornelia personated the comedy that ever peeps around the corner at the tragedy of life. Anne, whose nerves had been rather strained, laughed hysterically, and even Owen smiled. Certainly, sentiment and passion had a way of shrinking out of sight in Miss Cornelia's presence. And yet to Anne nothing seemed quite as hopeless and dark and painful as it had seemed a few moments before. But sleep was far from her eyes that night.

CHAPTER 27

On the Sand-bar

OWEN FORD left Four Winds the next morning. In the
evening Anne went over to see Leslie, but found nobody.
The house was locked and there was no light in any window.
It looked like a home left soulless. Leslie did not run over on
the following day – which Anne thought a bad sign.

Gilbert having occasion to go in the evening to the fishing
cove, Anne drove with him to the Point, intending to stay
awhile with Captain Jim. But the great light, cutting its
swathes through the fog of the autumn evening, was in care
of Alec Boyd and Captain Jim was away.

'What will you do?' asked Gilbert. 'Come with me?'

'I don't want to go to the cove – but I'll go over the
channel with you, and roam about on the sand shore till you
come back. The rock shore is too slippery and grim tonight.'

Alone on the sands of the bar, Anne gave herself up to the
eerie charm of the night. It was warm for September, and the
late afternoon had been very foggy; but a full moon had in
part lessened the fog and transformed the harbour and the
gulf and the surrounding shores into a strange, fantastic,
unreal world of pale silver mist, through which everything
loomed phantom-like. Captain Josiah Crawford's black
schooner sailing down the channel, laden with potatoes for
Bluenose ports, was a spectral ship bound for a far un-
charted land, ever receding, never to be reached. The calls of

unseen gulls overhead were the cries of the souls of doomed seamen. The little curls of foam that blew across the sand were elfin things stealing up from the sea-caves. The big, round-shouldered sand-dunes were the sleeping giants of some old northern tale. The lights that glimmered palely across the harbour were the delusive beacons on some coast of fairyland. Anne pleased herself with a hundred fancies as she wandered through the mist. It was delightful – romantic – mysterious to be roaming here alone on this enchanted shore.

But was she alone? Something loomed in the mist before her – took shape and form – suddenly moved towards her across the wave-rippled sand.

'Leslie!' exclaimed Anne in amazement. 'Whatever are you doing – *here* – tonight?'

'If it comes to that, whatever are *you* doing here?' said Leslie, trying to laugh. The effort was a failure. She looked very pale and tired; but the lovelocks under her scarlet cap were curling about her face and eyes like little sparkling rings of gold.

'I'm waiting for Gilbert – he's over at the cove. I intended to stay at the light, but Captain Jim is away.'

'Well, *I* came here because I wanted to walk – and walk – and *walk*,' said Leslie restlessly. 'I couldn't on the rock shore – the tide was too high and the rocks prisoned me. I had to come here – or I should have gone mad, I think. I rowed myself over the channel in Captain Jim's flat. I've been here for an hour. Come – come – let us walk. I can't stand still. Oh, Anne!'

'Leslie, dearest, what is the trouble?' asked Anne, though she knew too well already.

'I can't tell you – don't ask me. I wouldn't mind your knowing – I wish you did know – but I can't tell you – I can't tell anyone. I've been such a fool, Anne – and oh, it hurts so terribly to be a fool. There's nothing so painful in the world.'

She laughed bitterly. Anne slipped her arm around her.

'Leslie, is it that you have learned to care for Mr Ford?'

Leslie turned herself about passionately.

'How did you know?' she cried. 'Anne, how did you know? Oh, is it written in my face for everyone to see? Is it as plain as that?'

'No, no. I – I can't tell you how I knew. It just came into my mind, somehow. Leslie, don't look at me like that!'

'Do you despise me?' demanded Leslie in a fierce, low tone. 'Do you think I'm wicked – unwomanly? Or do you think I'm just plain fool?'

'I don't think you any of those things. Come, dear, let's just talk it over sensibly, as we might talk over any other of the great crises of life. You've been brooding over it and let yourself drift into a morbid view of it. You know you have a little tendency to do that about everything that goes wrong, and you promised me that you would fight against it.'

'But – oh, it's so – so shameful,' murmured Leslie. 'To love him – unsought – and when I'm not free to love anybody.'

'There's nothing shameful about it. But I'm very sorry that you have learned to care for Owen, because, as things are, it will only make you more unhappy.'

'I didn't *learn* to care,' said Leslie, walking on and speaking passionately. 'If it had been like that I could have prevented it. I never dreamed of such a thing until that day, a week ago, when he told me he had finished his book and must soon go away. Then – then I knew. I felt as if someone had struck me a terrible blow. I didn't say anything – I couldn't speak – but I don't know what I looked like. I'm so afraid my face betrayed me. Oh, I would die of shame if I thought he knew – or suspected.'

Anne was miserably silent, hampered by her deductions from her conversation with Owen. Leslie went on feverishly, as if she found relief in speech.

'I was so happy all this summer, Anne – happier than I ever was in my life. I thought it was because everything had been made clear between you and me, and that it was our friendship which made life seem so beautiful and full once more. And it *was*, in part – but not all – oh, not nearly all. I know now why everything was so different. And now it's all over – and he has gone. How can I live, Anne? When I turned back into the house this morning after he had gone the solitude struck me like a blow in the face.'

'It won't seem so hard by and by, dear,' said Anne, who always felt the pain of her friends so keenly that she could not speak easy, fluent words of comforting. Besides, she remembered how well-meant speeches had hurt her in her own sorrow and was afraid.

'Oh, it seems to me it will grow harder all the time,' said Leslie miserably. 'I've nothing to look forward to. Morning will come after morning – and he will not come back – he will never come back. Oh, when I think that I will never see him again I feel as if a great brutal hand had twisted itself among my heartstrings and was wrenching them. Once, long ago, I dreamed of love – and I thought it must be beautiful – and *now* – it's like *this*. When he went away yesterday morning he was so cold and indifferent. He said

"Good-bye, Mrs Moore," in the coldest tone in the world – as if we had not even been friends – as if I meant absolutely nothing to him. I know I don't – I didn't want him to care – but he *might* have been a little kinder.'

'Oh, I wish Gilbert would come,' thought Anne. She was racked between her sympathy for Leslie and the necessity of avoiding anything that would betray Owen's confidence. She knew why his good-bye had been so cold – why it could not have the cordiality that their good-comradeship demanded – but she could not tell Leslie.

'I couldn't help it, Anne – I couldn't help it,' said poor Leslie.

'I know that.'

'Do you blame me so very much?'

'I don't blame you at all.'

'And you won't – you won't tell Gilbert?'

'Leslie! Do you think I would do such a thing?'

'Oh, I don't know – you and Gilbert are such *chums*. I don't see how you could help telling him everything.'

'Everything about my own concerns – yes. But not my friends' secrets.'

'I couldn't have *him* know. But I'm glad *you* know. I would feel guilty if there were anything I was ashamed to tell you. I hope Miss Cornelia won't find out. Sometimes I feel as if those terrible, kind brown eyes of hers read my very soul. Oh, I wish this mist would never lift – I wish I could just stay in it for ever, hidden away from every living being. I don't see how I can go on with life. This summer has been so full. I never was lonely for a moment. Before Owen came there used to be horrible moments – when I had been with you and Gilbert – and then had to leave you. You two would walk away together and I would walk away *alone*. After Owen came he was always there to walk home with me – we would laugh and talk as you and Gilbert were doing – there were no more lonely, envious moments for me. And *now*! Oh, yes, I've been a fool. Let's have done talking about my folly. I'll never bore you with it again.'

'Here is Gilbert, and you are coming back with us,' said Anne, who had no intention of leaving Leslie to wander alone on the sand-bar on such a night and in such a mood. 'There's plenty of room in our boat for three, and we'll tie the flat on behind.'

'Oh, I suppose I must reconcile myself to being the odd one again,' said poor Leslie with another bitter laugh. 'Forgive me, Anne – that was hateful. I ought to be thankful – and I *am* – that I have two good friends who are glad to count me in as a third. Don't mind my hateful speeches. I just seem to be one great pain all over and everything hurts me.'

'Leslie seemed very quiet tonight, didn't she?' said Gilbert, when he and Anne reached home. 'What in the world was she doing over there on the bar alone?'

'Oh, she was tired – and you know she likes to go to the shore after one of Dick's bad days.'

'What a pity she hadn't met and married a fellow like Ford long ago,' ruminated Gilbert. 'They'd have made an ideal couple, wouldn't they?'

'For pity's sake, Gilbert, don't develop into a matchmaker. It's an abominable profession for a man,' cried Anne rather sharply, afraid that Gilbert might blunder on the truth if he kept on in this strain.

'Bless us, Anne-girl, I'm not matchmaking,' protested

Gilbert, rather surprised at her tone. 'I was only thinking of one of the might-have-beens.'

'Well, don't. It's a waste of time,' said Anne. Then she added suddenly:

'Oh, Gilbert, I wish everybody could be as happy as we are.'

CHAPTER 28

Odds and Ends

'I've been reading obituary notices,' said Miss Cornelia, laying down the *Daily Enterprise* and taking up her sewing.

The harbour was lying black and sullen under a dour November sky; the wet, dead leaves clung drenched and sodden to the window sills; but the little house was gay with firelight and spring-like with Anne's ferns and geraniums.

'It's always summer here, Anne,' Leslie had said one day; and all who were the guests of that house of dreams felt the same.

'The *Enterprise* seems to run to obituaries these days,' quoth Miss Cornelia. 'It always has a couple of columns of them, and I read every line. It's one of my forms of re-creation, especially when there's some original poetry attached to them. Here's a choice sample for you:

> She's gone to be with her Maker,
> Never more to roam.
> She used to play and sing with joy
> The song of Home, Sweet Home.

Who says we haven't any poetical talent on the Island! Have you ever noticed what heaps of good people die, Anne, dearie? It's kind of pitiful. Here's ten obituaries, and every one of them saints and models, even the men. Here's old Peter Stimson, who has "left a large circle of friends to mourn his untimely loss". Lord, Anne, dearie, that man was eighty, and everybody who knew him had been wishing him dead these thirty years. Read obituaries when you're blue, Anne, dearie – especially the ones of folks you know. If you've any sense of humour at all they'll cheer you up, believe *me*. I just wish *I* had the writing of the obituaries of some people. Isn't "obituary" an awful ugly word? This very Peter I've been speaking of had a face exactly like one. I never saw it but I thought of the word *obituary* then and there. There's only one uglier word that I know of, and that's *relict*. Lord, Anne, dearie, I may be an old maid, but there's this comfort in it – I'll never be any man's "relict".'

'It *is* an ugly word,' said Anne, laughing. 'Avonlea graveyard was full of old tombstones "sacred to the memory of So-and-so, *relict* of the late So-and-so". It always made me think of something worn-out and moth-eaten. Why is it that so many of the words connected with death are so disagreeable? I do wish that the custom of calling a dead body "the remains" could be abolished. I positively shiver when I hear the undertaker say at a funeral, "All who wish to see the remains please step this way." It always gives me the horrible impression that I am about to view the scene of a cannibal feast.'

'Well, all I hope,' said Miss Cornelia calmly, 'is that when I'm dead nobody will call me "our departed sister". I took a scunner at this sistering-and-brothering business five years ago when there was a travelling evangelist holding meetings at the Glen. I hadn't any use for him from the start. I felt in my bones that there was something wrong with him. And there was. Mind you, he was pretending to be a Presbyterian – Presby*tar*ian, *he* called it – and all the time he was a Methodist. He brothered and sistered everybody. He had a large circle of relations, that man had. He clutched my hand

212

fervently one night, and said imploringly, "My *dear* sister Bryant, are you a Christian?" I just looked him over a bit, and then I said calmly, "The only brother I ever had, *Mr* Fiske, was buried fifteen years ago, and I haven't adopted any since. As for being a Christian, I was that, I hope and believe, when you were crawling about the floor in petticoats." *That* squelched him, believe *me*. Mind you, Anne dearie, I'm not down on all evangelists. We've had some real fine, earnest men, who did a lot of good and made the old sinners squirm. But this Fiske-man wasn't one of them. I had a good laugh all to myself one evening. Fiske had asked all who were Christians to stand up. *I* didn't, believe *me*! I never had any use for that sort of thing. But most of them did, and then he asked all who wanted to be Christians to stand up. Nobody stirred for a spell, so Fiske started up a hymn at the top of his voice. Just in front of me poor little Ikey Baker was sitting in the Millison pew. He was a home boy, ten years old, and Millison just about worked him to death. The poor little creature was always so tired he fell asleep right off whenever he went to church or anywhere he could sit still for a few minutes. He'd been sleeping all through the meeting, and I was thankful to see the poor child getting a rest, believe *me*. Well, when Fiske's voice went soaring skyward and the rest joined in poor Ikey wakened with a start. He thought it was just an ordinary singing and that everybody ought to stand up, so he scrambled to his feet mighty quick, knowing he'd get a combing-down from Maria Millison for sleeping in meeting. Fiske saw him, stopped and shouted, "Another soul saved! Glory Hallelujah!" And there was poor, frightened Ikey, only half awake and yawning, never thinking about his soul at all. Poor child, he never had time to think of anything but his tired, overworked little body.

'Leslie went one night and the Fiske-man got right after her – oh, he was especially anxious about the souls of the nice-looking girls, believe me! – and he hurt her feelings so she never went again. And then he prayed every night after that, right in public, that the Lord would soften her hard heart. Finally I went to Mr Leavitt, our minister then, and told him if he didn't make Fiske stop that I'd just rise up the next night and throw my hymn-book at him when he mentioned that "beautiful but unrepentant young woman". I'd have done it too, believe *me*. Mr Leavitt did put a stop to it, but Fiske kept on with his meetings until Charley Douglas put an end to his career in the Glen. Mrs Charley had been out in California all winter. She'd been real melancholy in the fall – religious melancholy – it ran in her family. Her father worried so much over believing that he had committed the unpardonable sin that he died in the asylum. So when Rose Douglas got that way Charley packed her off to visit her sister in Los Angeles. She got perfectly well and came home just when the Fiske revival was in full swing. She stepped off the train at the Glen, real smiling and chipper, and the first thing she saw staring her in the face on the black gable-end of the freight shed was the question, in big white letters, two feet high, "Whither goest thou – to heaven or hell?" That had been one of Fiske's ideas, and he had got Henry Hammond to paint it. Rose just gave a shriek and fainted; and when they got her home she was worse than ever. Charley Douglas went to Mr Leavitt and told him that every Douglas would leave the church if Fiske was kept there any longer. Mr Leavitt had to give in, for the Douglases paid half his salary, so Fiske departed, and we had to depend on our Bibles once more for instructions on how to get to heaven. After he was gone Mr Leavitt found out he was just a masquerading Methodist, and he felt pretty sick, believe *me*. Mr Leavitt fell short in some ways, but he was a good, sound Presbyterian.'

'By the way, I had a letter from Mr Ford yesterday,' said Anne. 'He asked me to remember him kindly to you.'

'I don't want his remembrances,' said Miss Cornelia, curtly.

'Why?' said Anne, in astonishment. 'I thought you liked him.'

'Well, so I did, in a kind of way. But I'll never forgive him for what he done to Leslie. There's that poor child eating her heart out about him – as if she hadn't had trouble enough – and him ranting round Toronto, I've no doubt, enjoying himself same as ever. Just like a man.'

'Oh, Miss Cornelia, how did you find out?'

'Lord, Anne, dearie, I've got eyes, haven't I? And I've known Leslie since she was a baby. There's been a new kind of heartbreak in her eyes all the fall, and I know that writer-man was behind it somehow. I'll never forgive myself for being the means of bringing him here. But I never expected he'd be like he was. I thought he'd just be like the other men Leslie had boarded – conceited young asses, every one of them, that she never had any use for. One of them did try to flirt with her once and she froze him out – so bad, I feel sure he's never got himself thawed since. So I never thought of any danger.'

'Don't let Leslie suspect you know her secret,' said Anne hurriedly. 'I think it would hurt her.'

'Trust me, Anne, dearie. *I* wasn't born yesterday. Oh, a

plague on all the men! One of them ruined Leslie's life to begin with, and now another of the tribe comes and makes her still more wretched. Anne, this world is an awful place, believe *me*.'

'There's something in the world amiss
Will be unriddled by and by,'

quoted Anne dreamily.

'If it is, it'll be in a world where there aren't any men,' said Miss Cornelia gloomily.

'What have the men been doing now?' asked Gilbert, entering.

'Mischief – mischief! What else did they ever do?'

'It was Eve ate the apple, Miss Cornelia.'

' 'Twas a he-creature tempted her,' retorted Miss Cornelia triumphantly.

Leslie, after her first anguish was over, found it possible to go on with life after all, as most of us do, no matter what our particular form of torment has been. It is even possible that she enjoyed moments of it, when she was one of the gay circle in the little house of dreams. But if Anne ever hoped that she was forgetting Owen Ford she would have been undeceived by the furtive hunger in Leslie's eyes whenever his name was mentioned. Pitiful to that hunger, Anne always contrived to tell Captain Jim or Gilbert bits of news from Owen's letters when Leslie was with them. The girl's flush and pallor at such moments spoke all too eloquently of the emotion that filled her being. But she never spoke of him to Anne, or mentioned that night on the sand-bar.

One day her old dog died and she grieved bitterly over him.

'He's been my friend so long,' she said sorrowfully to Anne. 'He was Dick's old dog, you know – Dick had him for a year or so before we were married. He left him with me when he sailed on the *Four Sisters*. Carlo got very fond of me – and his dog-love helped me through that first dreadful year after Mother died, when I was all alone. When I heard that Dick was coming back I was afraid Carlo wouldn't be so much mine. But he never seemed to care for Dick, though he had been so fond of him once. He would snap and growl at him as if he were a stranger. I was glad. It was nice to have one thing whose love was all mine. That old dog has been such a comfort to me, Anne. He got so feeble in the fall that I was afraid he couldn't live long – but I hoped I could nurse him through the winter. He seemed pretty well this morning. He was lying on the rug before the fire; then, all at once, he got up and crept over to me; he put his head on my lap and gave me one loving look out of his big, soft, dog eyes – and then he just shivered and died. I shall miss him so.'

'Let me give you another dog, Leslie,' said Anne. 'I'm getting a lovely Gordon setter for a Christmas present for Gilbert. Let me give you one too.'

Leslie shook her head.

'Not just now, thank you, Anne. I don't feel like having another dog yet. I don't seem to have any affection left for another. Perhaps – in time – I'll let you give me one. I really need one as a kind of protection. But there was something almost human about Carlo – it wouldn't be *decent* to fill his place too hurriedly, dear old fellow.'

Anne went to Avonlea a week before Christmas and stayed until after the holidays. Gilbert came up for her, and there was a glad New Year celebration at Green Gables, when Barrys and Blythes and Wrights assembled to devour a dinner which had cost Mrs Rachel and Marilla much careful thought and preparation. When they went back to Four Winds the little house was almost drifted over, for the third storm of a winter that was to prove phenomenally stormy had whirled up the harbour and heaped huge snow mountains about everything it encountered. But Captain Jim had shovelled out doors and paths, and Miss Cornelia had come down and kindled the hearth-fire.

'It's good to see you back, Anne, dearie! But did you ever see such drifts? You can't see the Moore place at all unless you go upstairs. Leslie'll be so glad you're back. She's almost buried alive over there. Fortunately Dick can shovel snow and thinks it's great fun. Susan sent me word to tell you she would be on hand tomorrow. Where are you off to now, Captain?'

'I reckon I'll plough up to the Glen and sit a bit with old Martin Strong. He's not far from his end and he's lonesome. He hasn't many friends – been too busy all his life to make any. He's made heaps of money, though.'

'Well, he thought that since he couldn't serve God and Mammon he'd better stick to Mammon,' said Miss Cornelia crisply. 'So he shouldn't complain if he doesn't find Mammon very good company now.'

Captain Jim went out, but remembered something in the yard and turned back for a moment.

'I'd a letter from Mr Ford, Mistress Blythe, and he says the life-book is accepted and is going to be published next fall. I felt fair uplifted when I got the news. To think that I'm to see it in print at last.'

'That man is clean crazy on the subject of his life-book,' said Miss Cornelia compassionately. 'For my part, I think there's far too many books in the world now.'

CHAPTER 29

Gilbert and Anne Disagree

GILBERT LAID DOWN the ponderous medical tome over which he had been poring until the increasing dusk of the March evening made him desist. He leaned back in his chair and gazed meditatively out of the window. It was early spring – probably the ugliest time of the year. Not even the sunset could redeem the dead, sodden landscape and rotten-black harbour ice upon which he looked. No sign of life was visible, save a big black crow winging his solitary way across a leaden field. Gilbert speculated idly concerning that crow. Was he a family crow, with a black but comely crow wife awaiting him in the woods beyond the Glen? Or was he a glossy young buck of a crow on courting thoughts intent? Or was he a cynical bachelor crow, believing that he travels the fastest who travels alone? Whatever he was, he soon disappeared in congenial gloom and Gilbert turned to the cheerier view indoors.

The firelight flickered from point to point, gleaming on the white and green coats of Gog and Magog, on the sleek brown head of the beautiful setter basking on the rug, on the picture frames on the walls, on the vaseful of daffodils from the window garden, on Anne herself, sitting by her little table, with her sewing beside her and her hands clasped over her knee while she traced out pictures in the fire – Castles in Spain whose airy turrets pierced moonlit cloud and sunset bar – ships sailing from the Haven of Good Hopes straight to Four Winds Harbour with precious burthen. For Anne was again a dreamer of dreams, albeit a grim shape of fear went with her night and day to shadow and darken her visions.

Gilbert was accustomed to refer to himself as 'an old married man'. But he still looked upon Anne with the incredulous eyes of a lover. He couldn't wholly believe yet that she was really his. It *might* be only a dream after all, part and parcel of this magic house of dreams. His soul still went on tip-toe before her, lest the charm be shattered and the dream dispelled.

'Anne,' he said slowly, 'lend me your ears. I want to talk with you about something.'

Anne looked across at him through the fire-lit gloom.

'What is it?' she asked, gaily. 'You look fearfully solemn, Gilbert. I really haven't done anything naughty today. Ask Susan.'

'It's not of you – or ourselves – I want to talk. It's about Dick Moore.'

'Dick Moore?' echoed Anne, sitting up alertly. 'Why, what in the world have you to say about Dick Moore?'

'I've been thinking a great deal about him lately. Do you remember that time last summer I treated him for those carbuncles on his neck?'

'Yes – yes.'

'I took the opportunity to examine the scars on his head thoroughly. I've always thought Dick was a very interesting case from a medical point of view. Lately I've been studying the history of trephining and the cases where it has been employed. Anne, I have come to the conclusion that if Dick

221

Moore were taken to a good hospital and the operation of trephining performed on several places in his skull, his memory and faculties might be restored.'

'Gilbert!' Anne's voice was full of protest. 'Surely you don't mean it!'

'I do, indeed. And I have decided that it is my duty to broach the subject to Leslie.'

'Gilbert Blythe, you shall *not* do any such thing,' cried Anne vehemently. 'Oh, Gilbert, you won't – you won't. You couldn't be so cruel. Promise me you won't.'

'Why, Anne-girl, I didn't suppose you would take it like this. Be reasonable –'

'I won't be reasonable – I can't be reasonable – I *am* reasonable. It is you who are unreasonable. Gilbert, have you ever once thought what it would mean for Leslie if Dick Moore were to be restored to his right senses? Just stop and think! She's unhappy enough now; but life as Dick's nurse and attendant is a thousand times easier for her than life as Dick's wife. I know – I *know*! It's unthinkable. Don't you meddle with the matter. Leave well enough alone.'

'I *have* thought over that aspect of the case thoroughly, Anne. But I believe that a doctor is bound to set the sanctity of a patient's mind and body above all other considerations, no matter what the consequences may be. I believe it his duty to endeavour to restore health and sanity, if there is any hope whatever of it.'

'But Dick isn't your patient in that respect,' cried Anne, taking another tack. 'If Leslie had asked you if anything could be done for him, *then* it might be your duty to tell her what you really thought. But you've no right to meddle.'

222

'I don't call it meddling. Uncle Dave told Leslie twelve years ago that nothing could be done for Dick. She believes that, of course.'

'And why did Uncle Dave tell her that, if it wasn't true?' cried Anne, triumphantly. 'Doesn't he know as much about it as you?'

'I think not – though it may sound conceited and presumptuous to say it. And you know as well as I that he is rather prejudiced against what he calls "these new-fangled notions of cutting and carving". He's even opposed to operating for appendicitis.'

'He's right,' exclaimed Anne, with a complete change of front. 'I believe myself that you modern doctors are entirely too fond of making experiments with human flesh and blood.'

'Rhoda Allonby would not be a living woman today if I had been afraid of making a certain experiment,' argued Gilbert. 'I took the risk – and saved her life.'

'I'm sick and tired of hearing about Rhoda Allonby,' cried Anne – most unjustly, for Gilbert had never mentioned Mrs Allonby's name since the day he had told Anne of his success in regard to her. And he could not be blamed for other people's discussion of it.

Gilbert felt rather hurt.

'I had not expected you to look at the matter as you do, Anne,' he said a little stiffly, getting up and moving towards the office door. It was their first approach to a quarrel.

But Anne flew after him and dragged him back.

'Now, Gilbert, you are not "going off mad". Sit down here and I'll apologize bee-*yew*-ti-fully. I shouldn't have said that. But – oh, if you knew –'

Anne checked herself just in time. She had been on the very verge of betraying Leslie's secret.

'Knew what a woman feels about it,' she concluded lamely.

'I think I do know. I've looked at the matter from every point of view – and I've been driven to the conclusion that it is my duty to tell Leslie that I believe it is possible that Dick can be restored to himself; there my responsibility ends. It will be for her to decide what she will do.'

'I don't think you've any right to put such a responsibility on her. She has enough to bear. She is poor – how could she afford such an operation?'

'That is for her to decide,' persisted Gilbert stubbornly.

'You say you think that Dick can be cured. But are you *sure* of it?'

"Certainly not. Nobody could be sure of such a thing. There may have been lesions of the brain itself, the effect of which can never be removed. But if, as I believe, his loss of memory and other faculties is due merely to the pressure on the brain centres of certain depressed areas of bone, then he can be cured.'

'But it's only a possibility!' insisted Anne. 'Now, suppose you tell Leslie and she decides to have the operation. It will cost a great deal. She will have to borrow the money, or sell her little property. And suppose the operation is a failure and Dick remains the same. How will she be able to pay back the money she borrows or make a living for herself and that big helpless creature if she sells the farm?'

'Oh, I know – I know. But it is my duty to tell her. I can't get away from that conviction.'

'Oh, I know the Blythe stubbornness,' groaned Anne. 'But don't do this solely on your own responsibility. Consult Doctor Dave.'

'I *have* done so,' said Gilbert reluctantly.

'And what did he say?'

'In brief – as you say – leave well enough alone. Apart from his prejudice against new-fangled surgery, I'm afraid he looks at the case from your point of view – don't do it, for Leslie's sake.'

'There now,' cried Anne triumphantly. 'I do think, Gilbert, that you ought to abide by the judgement of a man nearly eighty, who has seen a great deal and saved scores of lives himself – surely his opinion ought to weigh more than a mere boy's.'

'Thank you.'

'Don't laugh. It's too serious.'

'That's just my point. It *is* serious. Here is a man who is a helpless burden. He may be restored to reason and usefulness –'

'He was so very useful before,' interjected Anne witheringly.

'He may be given a chance to make good and redeem the past. His wife doesn't know this. I do. It is therefore my duty to tell her that there is such a possibility. That, boiled down, is my decision.'

'Don't say "decision" yet, Gilbert. Consult somebody else. Ask Captain Jim what he thinks about it.'

'Very well. But I'll not promise to abide by his opinion, Anne. This is something a man must decide for himself. My conscience would never be easy if I kept silent on the subject.'

'Oh, your conscience!' moaned Anne. 'I suppose that Uncle Dave has a conscience too, hasn't he?'

'Yes. But I am not the keeper of his conscience. Come, Anne, if this affair did not concern Leslie – if it were a purely abstract case, you would agree with me – you know you would.'

'I wouldn't,' vowed Anne, trying to believe it herself. 'Oh, you can argue all night, Gilbert, but you won't convince me. Just you ask Miss Cornelia what she thinks of it.'

'You're driven to the last ditch, Anne, when you bring up Miss Cornelia as a reinforcement. She will say, "Just like a man", and rage furiously. No matter. This is no affair for Miss Cornelia to settle. Leslie alone must decide it.'

'You know very well how she will decide it,' said Anne, almost in tears. 'She has ideals of duty, too. I don't see how you can take such a responsibility on your shoulders. *I* couldn't.'

> 'Because right is right, to follow right
> Were wisdom in the scorn of consequence.'

quoted Gilbert.

'Oh, you think a couplet of poetry a convincing argument!' scoffed Anne. 'That is so like a man.'

And then she laughed in spite of herself. It sounded so like an echo of Miss Cornelia.

'Well, if you won't accept Tennyson as an authority, perhaps you will believe the words of a Greater than he,' said Gilbert seriously. ' "Ye shall know the truth and the truth shall make you free." I believe that, Anne, with all my heart. It's the greatest and grandest verse in the Bible – or in any literature – and the *truest*, if there are comparative degrees of trueness. And it's the first duty of a man to tell the truth, as he sees it and believes it.'

'In this case the truth won't make poor Leslie free,' sighed Anne. 'It will probably end in still more bitter bondage for her. Oh, Gilbert, I *can't* think you are right.'

CHAPTER 30

Leslie Decides

A SUDDEN OUTBREAK of a violent type of influenza at the Glen and down at the fishing village kept Gilbert so busy for the next fortnight that he had no time to pay the promised visit to Captain Jim. Anne hoped against hope that he had abandoned the idea about Dick Moore, and, resolving to let sleeping dogs lie, she said no more about the subject. But she thought of it incessantly.

'I wonder if it would be right for me to tell him that Leslie cares for Owen,' she thought. 'He would never let her suspect that he knew, so her pride would not suffer, and it *might* convince him that he should let Dick Moore alone. Shall I – shall I? No, after all, I cannot. A promise is sacred, and I've no right to betray Leslie's secret. But oh, I never felt so worried over anything in my life as I do over this. It's spoiling the spring – it's spoiling everything.'

One evening Gilbert abruptly proposed that they go down and see Captain Jim. With a sinking heart Anne agreed, and they set forth. Two weeks of kind sunshine had wrought a miracle in the bleak landscape over which Gilbert's crow had flown. The hills and fields were dry and brown and warm, ready to break into bud and blossom; the harbour was laughter-shaken again; the long harbour road was like a gleaming red ribbon; down on the dunes a crowd of boys, who were out smelt-fishing, were burning the thick, dry sand-hill grass of the preceding summer. The flames swept over the dunes rosily, flinging their cardinal banners against the dark gulf beyond, and illuminating the channel and the fishing village. It was a picturesque scene which would at other times have delighted Anne's eyes; but she was not enjoying this walk. Neither was Gilbert. Their usual good-comradeship and Josephian community of taste and viewpoint were sadly lacking. Anne's disapproval of the whole project showed itself in the haughty uplift of her head and the studied politeness of her remarks. Gilbert's mouth was set in all the Blythe obstinacy, but his eyes were troubled. He meant to do what he believed to be his duty; but to be at outs with Anne was a high price to pay. Altogether, both were glad when they reached the light – and remorseful that they should be glad.

Captain Jim put away the fishing net upon which he was working, and welcomed them joyfully. In the searching light of the spring evening he looked older than Anne had ever seen him. His hair had grown much greyer, and the strong old hand shook a little. But his blue eyes were clear and steady, and the staunch soul looked out through them gallant and unafraid.

Captain Jim listened in amazed silence while Gilbert said what he had come to say. Anne, who knew how the old man worshipped Leslie, felt quite sure that he would side with her, although she had not much hope that this would influence Gilbert. She was therefore surprised beyond measure when Captain Jim, slowly and sorrowfully, but unhesitatingly, gave it as his opinion that Leslie should be told.

'Oh, Captain Jim, I didn't think you'd say that,' she

exclaimed reproachfully. 'I thought you wouldn't want to make more trouble for her.'

Captain Jim shook his head.

'I don't want to. I know how you feel about it, Mistress Blythe – just as I feel meself. But it ain't our feelings we have to steer by through life – no, no, we'd make shipwreck mighty often if we did that. There's only the one safe compass and we've got to set our course by that – what it's right to do. I agree with the doctor. If there's a chance for Dick, Leslie should be told of it. There's no two sides to that, in my opinion.'

'Well,' said Anne, giving up in despair, 'wait until Miss Cornelia gets after you two men.'

'Cornelia'll rake us fore and aft, no doubt,' assented Captain Jim. 'You women are lovely critters, Mistress Blythe, but you're just a mite illogical. You're a highly eddicated lady and Cornelia isn't, but you're like as two peas when it comes to that. I dunno's you're any the worse for it. Logic is a sort of hard, merciless thing, I reckon. Now, I'll brew a cup of tea and we'll drink it and talk of pleasant things, jest to calm our minds a bit.'

At least, Captain Jim's tea and conversation calmed Anne's mind to such an extent that she did not make Gilbert suffer so acutely on the way home as she had deliberately intended to do. She did not refer to the burning question at all, but she chatted amiably of other matters, and Gilbert understood that he was forgiven under protest.

'Captain Jim seems very frail and bent this spring. The winter has aged him,' said Anne sadly. 'I am afraid that he will soon be going to seek lost Margaret. I can't bear to think of it.'

230

'Four Winds won't be the same place when Captain Jim "sets out to sea",' agreed Gilbert.

The following evening he went to the house up the brook. Anne wandered dismally around until his return.

'Well, what did Leslie say?' she demanded when he came in.

'Very little. I think she felt rather dazed.'

'And is she going to have the operation?'

'She is going to think it over and decide very soon.'

Gilbert flung himself wearily into the easy chair before the fire. He looked tired. It had not been an easy thing for him to tell Leslie. And the terror that had sprung into her eyes when the meaning of what he told her came home to her was not a pleasant thing to remember. Now, when the die was cast, he was beset with doubts of his own wisdom.

Anne looked at him remorsefully; then she slipped down on the rug beside him and laid her glossy red head on his arm.

'Gilbert, I've been rather hateful over this. I won't be any more. Please just call me red-headed and forgive me.'

By which Gilbert understood that, no matter what came of it, there would be no I-told-you-so's. But he was not wholly comforted. Duty in the abstract is one thing; duty in the concrete is quite another, especially when the doer is confronted by a woman's stricken eyes.

Some instinct made Anne keep away from Leslie for the next three days. On the third evening Leslie came down to the little house and told Gilbert that she had made up her mind; she would take Dick to Montreal and have the operation.

She was very pale and seemed to have wrapped herself in

her old mantle of aloofness. But her eyes had lost the look which had haunted Gilbert; they were cold and bright; and she proceeded to discuss details with him in a crisp, business-like way. There were plans to be made and many things to be thought over. When Leslie had got the information she wanted she went home. Anne wanted to walk part of the way with her.

'Better not,' said Leslie curtly. 'Today's rain has made the ground damp. Good night.'

'Have I lost my friend?' said Anne, with a sigh. 'If the operation is successful and Dick Moore finds himself again Leslie will retreat into some remote fastness of her soul where none of us can ever find her.'

'Perhaps she will leave him,' said Gilbert.

'Leslie would never do that, Gilbert. Her sense of duty is very strong. She told me once that her Grandmother West always impressed upon her the fact that when she assumed any responsibility she must never shirk it, no matter what the consequences might be. That is one of her cardinal rules. I suppose it's very old-fashioned.'

'Don't be bitter, Anne-girl. You know you don't think it old-fashioned — you know you have the very same idea of the sacredness of assumed responsibilities yourself. And you are right. Shirking responsibilities is the curse of our modern life — the secret of all the unrest and discontent that is seething in the world.'

'Thus saith the preacher,' mocked Anne. But under the mockery she felt that he was right; and she was very sick at heart for Leslie.

A week later Miss Cornelia descended like an avalanche upon the little house. Gilbert was away and Anne was compelled to bear the shock of the impact alone.

Miss Cornelia hardly waited to get her hat off before she began.

'Anne, do you mean to tell me it's true what I've heard — that Dr Blythe has told Leslie Dick can be cured, and that she is going to take him to Montreal to have him operated on?'

'Yes, it is quite true, Miss Cornelia,' said Anne bravely.

'Well, it's inhuman cruelty, that's what it is,' said Miss Cornelia, violently agitated. 'I did think Dr Blythe was a decent man. I didn't think he could have been guilty of this.'

'Dr Blythe thought it was his duty to tell Leslie that there was a chance for Dick,' said Anne with spirit, 'and,' she added, loyalty to Gilbert getting the better of her, 'I agree with him.'

'Oh, no, you don't, dearie,' said Miss Cornelia. 'No person with any bowels of compassion could.'

'Captain Jim does.'

'Don't quote that old ninny to me,' cried Miss Cornelia. 'And I don't care who agrees with him. Think — *think* what it means to that poor, hunted, harried girl.'

'We *do* think of it. But Gilbert believes that a doctor should put the welfare of a patient's mind and body before all other considerations.'

'That's just like a man. But I expected better things of you, Anne,' said Miss Cornelia, more in sorrow than in wrath; then she proceeded to bombard Anne with precisely the same arguments with which the latter had attacked Gilbert; and Anne valiantly defended her husband with the weapons he had used for his own protection. Long was the fray, but Miss Cornelia made an end at last.

'It's an iniquitous shame,' she declared, almost in tears. 'That's just what it is – an iniquitous shame. Poor, poor Leslie!'

'Don't you think Dick should be considered a little, too?' pleaded Anne.

'Dick! Dick Moore! *He's* happy enough. He's a better-behaved and more reputable member of society now than he ever was before. Why, he was a drunkard and perhaps worse. Are you going to set him loose again to roar and to devour?'

'He may reform,' said poor Anne, beset by foe without and traitor within.

'Reform your grandmother!' retorted Miss Cornelia. 'Dick Moore got the injuries that left him as he is in a drunken brawl. He *deserves* his fate. It was sent on him for a punishment. I don't believe the doctor has any business to tamper with the visitations of God.'

'Nobody knows how Dick was hurt, Miss Cornelia. It may not have been in a drunken brawl at all. He may have been waylaid and robbed.'

'Pigs *may* whistle, but they've poor mouths for it,' said Miss Cornelia. 'Well, the gist of what you tell me is that the thing is settled and there's no use in talking. If that's so I'll hold my tongue. I don't propose to wear *my* teeth out gnawing files. When a thing has to be I give in to it. But I like to make mighty sure first that it *has* to be. Now, I'll devote *my* energies to comforting and sustaining Leslie. And after all,' added Miss Cornelia, brightening up hopefully, 'perhaps nothing can be done for Dick.'

CHAPTER 31

The Truth Makes Free

LESLIE, having once made up her mind what to do, proceeded to do it with characteristic resolution and speed. House-cleaning must be finished with first, whatever issues of life and death might await beyond. The grey house up the brook was put into flawless order and cleanliness, with Miss Cornelia's ready assistance. Miss Cornelia, having said her say to Anne, and later on to Gilbert and Captain Jim — sparing neither of them, let it be assured — never spoke of the matter to Leslie. She accepted the fact of Dick's operation, referred to it when necessary in a business-like way, and ignored it when it was not. Leslie never attempted to discuss it. She was very cold and quiet during these beautiful spring days. She seldom visited Anne, and though she was invariably courteous and friendly, that very courtesy was an icy barrier between her and the people of the little house. The old jokes and laughter and chumminess of common things could not reach her over it. Anne refused to feel hurt. She knew that Leslie was in the grip of a hideous dread — a dread that wrapped her away from all little glimpses of happiness and hours of pleasure. When one great passion seizes possession of the soul all other feelings are crowded aside. Never in all her life had Leslie Moore shuddered away from the future with more intolerable terror. But she went forward as unswervingly in the path she had elected as the martyrs of old walked their chosen way, knowing the end of it to be the fiery agony of the stake.

The financial question was settled with greater ease than Anne had feared. Leslie borrowed the necessary money from Captain Jim, and, at her insistence, he took a mortgage on the little farm.

'So that is one thing off the poor girl's mind,' Miss Cornelia told Anne, 'and off mine too. Now, if Dick gets well enough to work again he'll be able to earn enough to pay the interest on it; and if he doesn't I know Captain Jim'll manage some way that Leslie won't have to. He said as much to me. "I'm getting old, Cornelia," he said, "and I've no chick or child of my own. Leslie won't take a gift from a living man, but mebbe she will from a dead one." So it will be all right as far as *that* goes. I wish everything else might be settled as satisfactorily. As for that wretch of a Dick, he's been awful these last few days. The devil was in him, believe *me*! Leslie and I couldn't get on with our work for the tricks he'd play. He chased all her ducks one day around the yard till most of them died. And not one thing would he do for us. Sometimes, you know, he'll make himself quite handy, bringing in pails of water and wood. But this week if we sent him to the well he'd try to climb down into it. I thought once, "If you'd only shoot down there head-first everything would be nicely settled."'

'Oh, Miss Cornelia!'

'Now, you needn't Miss Cornelia me, Anne, dearie. *Anybody* would have thought the same. If the Montreal doctors can make a rational creature out of Dick Moore they're wonders.'

Leslie took Dick to Montreal early in May. Gilbert went

with her, to help her and make the necessary arrangements for her. He came home with the report that the Montreal surgeon whom they had consulted agreed with him that there was a good chance of Dick's restoration.

'Very comforting,' was Miss Cornelia's sarcastic comment.

Anne only sighed. Leslie had been very distant at their parting. But she had promised to write. Ten days after Gilbert's return the letter came. Leslie wrote that the operation had been successfully performed and that Dick was making a good recovery.

'What does she mean by "successfully?" ' asked Anne. 'Does she mean that Dick's memory is really restored?'

'Not likely – since she says nothing of it,' said Gilbert. 'She uses the word "successfully" from the surgeon's point of view. The operation has been performed and followed by normal results. But it is too soon to know whether Dick's faculties will be eventually restored, wholly or in part. His memory would not be likely to return to him all at once. The process will be gradual, if it occurs at all. Is that all she says?'

'Yes – there's her letter. It's very short. Poor girl, she must be under a terrible strain. Gilbert Blythe, there are heaps of things I long to say to you, only it would be mean.'

'Miss Cornelia says them for you,' said Gilbert with a rueful smile. 'She combs me down every time I encounter her. She makes it plain to me that she regards me as little better than a murderer, and that she thinks it a great pity that Dr Dave ever let me step into his shoes. She even told me that the Methodist doctor over the harbour was to be preferred before me. With Miss Cornelia the force of condemnation can no farther go.'

'If Cornelia Bryant was sick it would not be Doctor Dave or the Methodist doctor she would send for,' sniffed Susan. 'She would have you out of your hard-earned bed in the middle of the night, doctor, dear, if she took a spell of misery, that she would. And then she would likely say your bill was past all reason. But do not mind her, doctor, dear. It takes all kinds of people to make a world.'

No further word came from Leslie for some time. The May days crept away in a sweet succession and the shores of Four Winds Harbour greened and bloomed and purpled. One day in late May, Gilbert came home to be met by Susan in the stable-yard.

'I am afraid something has upset Mrs Doctor, doctor, dear,' she said mysteriously. 'She got a letter this afternoon and since then she has just been walking round the garden and talking to herself. You know it is not good for her to be on her feet so much, doctor, dear. She did not see fit to tell me what her news was, and I am no pry, doctor, dear, and never was, but it is plain something has upset her. And it is not good for her to be upset.'

Gilbert hurried rather anxiously to the garden. Had anything happened at Green Gables? But Anne, sitting on the rustic seat by the brook, did not look troubled, though she was certainly much excited. Her eyes were their greyest, and scarlet spots burned on her cheeks.

'What has happened, Anne?'

Anne gave a queer little laugh.

'I think you'll hardly believe it when I tell you, Gilbert. *I* can't believe it yet. As Susan said the other day, "I feel like a fly coming to life in the sun — dazed-like." It's all so incredible. I've read the letter a score of times and every time it's just the same – I can't believe my own eyes. Oh, Gilbert, you were right – so right. I can see that clearly enough now – and I'm so ashamed of myself – and will you ever really forgive me?'

'Anne, I'll shake you if you don't grow coherent. Redmond would be ashamed of you. *What* has happened?'

'You won't believe it – you won't believe it –'

'I'm going in to phone for Uncle Dave,' said Gilbert pretending to start for the house.

'Sit down, Gilbert. I'll try to tell you. I've had a letter, and oh, Gilbert, it's all so amazing – so incredibly amazing – we never thought – not one of us ever dreamed –'

'I suppose,' said Gilbert, sitting down with a resigned air, 'the only thing to do in a case of this kind is to have patience and go at the matter categorically. Whom is your letter from?'

'Leslie – and oh, Gilbert –'

'Leslie! Whew! What has she to say? What's the news about Dick?'

Anne lifted the letter and held it out, calmly dramatic in a moment.

'There is *no* Dick! The man we have thought Dick Moore – whom everybody in Four Winds has believed for twelve years to be Dick Moore – is his cousin, George Moore, of Nova Scotia, who, it seems, always resembled him very strikingly. Dick Moore died of yellow fever thirteen years ago in Cuba.'

CHAPTER 32

Miss Cornelia Discusses the Affair

'AND DO YOU MEAN to tell me, Anne, dearie, that Dick Moore has turned out not to be Dick Moore at all but somebody else? Is *that* what you phoned up to me today?'

'Yes, Miss Cornelia. It is very amazing, isn't it?'

'It's — it's — just like a man,' said Miss Cornelia helplessly. She took off her hat with trembling fingers. For once in her life Miss Cornelia was undeniably staggered.

'I can't seem to sense it, Anne,' she said. 'I've heard you say it — and I believe you — but I can't take it in. Dick Moore is dead — has been dead all these years — and Leslie is free?'

'Yes. The truth has made her free. Gilbert was right when he said that verse was the grandest in the Bible.'

'Tell me everything, Anne, dearie. Since I got your phone I've been in a regular muddle, believe *me*. Cornelia Bryant was never so kerflummuxed before.'

'There isn't a very great deal to tell. Leslie's letter was short. She didn't go into particulars. This man — George Moore — has recovered his memory and knows who he is. He says Dick took yellow fever in Cuba, and the *Four Sisters* had to sail without him. George stayed behind to nurse him. But he died very shortly afterwards. George did not write Leslie because he intended to come right home and tell her himself.'

'And why didn't he?'

'I suppose his accident must have intervened. Gilbert says it is quite likely that George Moore remembers nothing of his accident, or what led to it, and may never remember it. It probably happened very soon after Dick's death. We may find out more particulars when Leslie writes again.'

'Does she say what she is going to do? When is she coming home?'

'She says she will stay with George Moore until he can leave the hospital. She has written to his people in Nova Scotia. It seems that George's only near relative is a married sister much older than himself. She was living when George sailed on the *Four Sisters*, but of course we do not know what may have happened since. Did you ever see George Moore, Miss Cornelia?'

'I did. It is all coming back to me. He was here visiting his Uncle Abner eighteen years ago, when he and Dick would be about seventeen. They were double cousins, you see. Their fathers were brothers and their mothers were twin sisters, and they did look a terrible lot alike. Of course,' added Miss Cornelia scornfully, 'it wasn't one of those freak resemblances you read of in novels where two people are so much alike that they can fill each other's places and their nearest and dearest can't tell between them. In those days you could tell easy enough which was George and which was Dick, if you saw them together and near at hand. Apart, or some distance away, it wasn't so easy. They played lots of tricks on people and thought it great fun, the two scamps. George Moore was a little taller and a good deal fatter than Dick – though neither of them was what you would call fat – they were both of the lean kind. Dick had higher colour than George, and his hair was a shade lighter. But their features were just alike, and they both had that queer freak of eyes – one blue and one hazel. They weren't much alike in any other way, though. George was a real nice fellow, though he was a scallawag for mischief, and some said he had a liking for a glass even then. But everybody liked him better than Dick. He spent about a month here. Leslie never saw him; she was only about eight or nine then and I remember now that she spent that whole winter over harbour with her Grandmother West. Captain Jim was away, too – that was the winter he was wrecked on the Magdalens. I don't suppose either he or Leslie had ever heard about the Nova Scotia cousin looking so much like Dick. Nobody ever thought of him when Captain Jim brought Dick – George, I should say – home. Of course, we all thought Dick had changed considerable – he'd got so lumpish and fat. But we put that down to what had happened to him, and no doubt that was the reason, for, as I've said, George wasn't fat to begin with either. And there was no other way we could have guessed, for the man's senses were clean gone. I can't see that it is any wonder we were all deceived. But it's a staggering thing. And Leslie has sacrificed the best years of her life to nursing a man who hadn't any claim on her! Oh, drat the men! No matter what they do, it's the wrong thing. And no matter who they are, it's somebody they shouldn't be. They do exasperate me.'

'Gilbert and Captain Jim are men, and it is through them that the truth has been discovered at last,' said Anne.

'Well, I admit that,' conceded Miss Cornelia reluctantly. 'I'm sorry I raked the doctor off so. It's the first time in my life I've ever felt ashamed of anything I said to a man. I don't know as I shall tell him so, though. He'll just have to take it for granted. Well, Anne, dearie, it's a mercy the Lord doesn't answer all our prayers. I've been praying hard right along that the operation wouldn't cure Dick. Of course, I didn't put it just quite so plain. But that was what was in the back of my mind, and I have no doubt the Lord knew it.'

'Well, He has answered the spirit of your prayer. You really wished that things shouldn't be made any harder for Leslie. I'm afraid that in my secret heart I've been hoping the operation wouldn't succeed, and I am wholesomely ashamed of it.'

'How does Leslie seem to take it?'

'She writes like one dazed. I think that, like ourselves, she hardly realizes it yet. She says, "It all seems like a strange dream to me, Anne." That is the only reference she makes to herself.'

'Poor child! I suppose when the chains are struck off a prisoner he'd feel queer and lost without them for a while. Anne, dearie, there's a thought keeps coming into my mind. What about Owen Ford? We both know Leslie was fond of him. Did it ever occur to you that he was fond of her?'

'It – did – once,' admitted Anne, feeling that she might say so much.

'Well, I hadn't any reason to think he was, but it just appeared to me he *must* be. Now, Anne, dearie, the Lord knows I'm not a matchmaker, and I scorn all such things. But if I were you and writing to that Ford man I'd just mention, casual-like, what has happened. That is what *I'd* do.'

'Of course I will mention it when I write him,' said Anne, a trifle distantly. Somehow, this was a thing she could not discuss with Miss Cornelia. And yet, she had to admit that the same thought had been lurking in her mind ever since she had heard of Leslie's freedom. But she would not desecrate it by free speech.

'Of course there is no great rush, dearie. But Dick Moore's been dead for thirteen years and Leslie has wasted enough of her life for him. We'll just see what comes of it. As for this George Moore, who's gone and come back to life when everyone thought he was dead and done for, just like a man, I'm real sorry for him. He won't seem to fit in anywhere.'

'He is still a young man, and if he recovers completely, as seems likely, he will be able to make a place for himself again. It must be very strange for him, poor fellow. I suppose all these years since his accident will not exist for him.'

CHAPTER 33

Leslie Returns Home

A FORTNIGHT LATER Leslie Moore came home alone to the old house where she had spent so many bitter years. In the June twilight she went over the fields to Anne's, and appeared with ghost-like suddenness in the scented garden.

'Leslie!' cried Anne in amazement. 'Where have you sprung from? We never knew you were coming. Why didn't you write? We would have met you.'

'I couldn't write, somehow, Anne. It seemed so futile to try to say anything with pen and ink. And I wanted to get back quietly and unobserved.'

Anne put her arms about Leslie and kissed her. Leslie returned the kiss warmly. She looked pale and tired, and she gave a little sigh as she dropped down on the grasses beside a great bed of daffodils that were gleaming through the pale, silvery twilight like golden stars.

'And you have come home alone, Leslie?'

'Yes. George Moore's sister came to Montreal and took him home with her. Poor fellow, he was sorry to part with me – though I was a stranger to him when his memory first came back. He clung to me in those first hard days when he was trying to realize that Dick's death was not the thing of yesterday that it seemed to him. It was all very hard for him. I helped him all I could. When his sister came it was easier for him, because it seemed to him only the other day that he had seen her last. Fortunately she had not changed much, and that helped him too.'

'It is all so strange and wonderful, Leslie. I think we none of us realize it yet.'

'I cannot. When I went into the house over there an hour ago I felt that it *must* be a dream – that Dick must be there, with his childish smile, as he had been for so long. Anne, I seem stunned yet. I'm not glad or sorry – or *anything*. I feel as if something had been torn suddenly out of my life and left a terrible hole. I feel as if I couldn't be *I* – as if I must have changed into somebody else and couldn't get used to it. It gives me a horrible lonely, dazed, helpless feeling. It's good to see you again – it seems as if you were a sort of anchor for my drifting soul. Oh, Anne, I dread it all – the gossip and wonderment and questioning. When I think of that I wish that I need not have come home at all. Dr Dave was at the station when I came off the train – he brought me home. Poor old man, he feels very badly because he told me years ago that nothing could be done for Dick. "I honestly thought so, Leslie," he said to me today. "But I should have told you not to depend on my opinion – I should have told you to go to a specialist. If I had you would have been saved many bitter years, and poor George Moore many wasted ones. I blame myself very much, Leslie." I told him not to do that – he had done what he thought right. He has always been so kind to me – I couldn't bear to see him worrying over it.'

'And Dick – George, I mean? Is his memory fully restored?'

'Practically. Of course, there are a great many details he can't recall yet – but he remembers more and more every day. He went out for a walk on the evening after Dick was buried. He had Dick's money and watch on him; he meant to bring them home to me, along with my letter. He admits he went to a place where the sailors resorted – and he remembers drinking – and nothing else. Anne, I shall never forget the moment he remembered his own name. I saw him looking at me with an intelligent but puzzled expression. I said, "Do you know me, Dick?" He answered, "I never saw you before. Who are you? And my name is not Dick. I am George Moore, and Dick died of yellow fever yesterday! Where am I? What has happened to me?" I – I fainted, Anne. And ever since I have felt as if I were in a dream.'

'You will soon adjust yourself to this new state of things, Leslie. And you are young – life is before you – you will have many beautiful years yet.'

'Perhaps I shall be able to look at it in that way after a while, Anne. Just now I feel too tired and indifferent to think about the future. I'm – I'm – Anne, I'm lonely. I miss Dick. Isn't it all very strange? Do you know, I was really fond of poor Dick – George, I suppose I should say – just as I would have been fond of a helpless child who depended on me for everything. I would never have admitted it – I was really ashamed of it – because, you see, I had hated and despised Dick so much before he went away. When I heard that Captain Jim was bringing him home I expected I would just feel the same to him. But I never did – although I continued to loathe him as I remembered him before. From the time he came home I felt only pity – a pity that hurt and wrung me. I supposed then that it was just because his accident had made him so helpless and changed. But now I believe it was because there was really a different personality there. Carlo

247

knew it, Anne – I know now that Carlo knew it. I always thought it strange that Carlo shouldn't have known Dick. Dogs are usually so faithful. But *he* knew it was not his master who had come back, although none of the rest of us did. I had never seen George Moore, you know. I remember now that Dick once mentioned casually that he had a cousin in Nova Scotia who looked as much like him as a twin; but the thing had gone out of my memory, and in any case I would never have thought it of any importance. You see, it never occurred to me to question Dick's identity. Any change in him seemed to me just the result of the accident.

'Oh, Anne, that night in April when Gilbert told me he thought Dick might be cured! I can never forget it. It seemed to me that I had once been a prisoner in a hideous cage of torture, and then the door had been opened and I could get out. I was still chained to the cage, but I was not in it. And that night I felt that a merciless hand was drawing me back into the cage – back to a torture even more terrible than it had once been. I didn't blame Gilbert. I felt he was right. And he had been very good – he said that if, in view of the expense and uncertainty of the operation, I should decide not to risk it, he would not blame me in the least. But I knew how I ought to decide – and I couldn't face it. All night I walked the floor like a mad woman, trying to compel myself to face it. I couldn't, Anne – I thought I couldn't – and when morning broke I set my teeth and resolved that I *wouldn't*. I would let things remain as they were. It was very wicked, I know. It would have been a just punishment for such wickedness if I had just been left to abide by that decision. I kept to it all day. That afternoon I had to go up to the Glen to do some shopping. It was one of Dick's quiet, drowsy days, so I left him alone. I was gone a little longer than I had expected, and he missed me. He felt lonely. And when I got home he ran to meet me just like a child, with such a pleased smile on his face. Somehow, Anne, I just gave way then. That smile on his poor vacant face was more than I could endure. I felt as if I were denying a child the chance to grow and develop. I knew that I must give him his chance, no matter what the consequences might be. So I came over and told Gilbert. Oh, Anne, you must have thought me hateful in those weeks before I went away. I didn't mean to be – but I couldn't think of anything except what I had to do, and everything and everybody about me were like shadows.'

'I know – I understood, Leslie. And now it is all over – your chain is broken – there is no cage.'

'There is no cage,' repeated Leslie absently, plucking at the fringing grasses with her slender brown hands. 'But – it doesn't seem as if there were anything else, Anne. You – you remember what I told you of my folly that night on the sand-bar? I find one doesn't get over being a fool very quickly. Sometimes I think there are people who are fools for ever. And to be a fool – of that kind – is almost as bad as being a – a dog on a chain.'

'You will feel very differently after you get over being tired and bewildered,' said Anne, who, knowing a certain thing that Leslie did not know, did not feel herself called upon to waste overmuch sympathy.

Leslie laid her splendid golden head against Anne's knee.

'Anyhow, I have *you*,' she said. 'Life can't be altogether empty with such a friend. Anne, pat my head – just as if I were a little girl – *mother* me a bit – and let me tell you while my stubborn tongue is loosed a little just what you and your comradeship have meant to me since that night I met you on the rock shore.'

CHAPTER 34

The Ship o' Dreams Comes to Harbour

ONE MORNING, when a windy golden sunrise was billowing over the gulf in waves of light, a certain weary stork flew over the bar of Four Winds Harbour on his way from the Land of Evening Stars. Under his wing was tucked a sleepy, starry-eyed little creature. The stork was tired, and he looked wistfully about him. He knew he was somewhere near his destination, but he could not yet see it. The big white lighthouse on the red sandstone cliff had its good points; but no stork possessed of any gumption would leave a new, velvet baby there. An old grey house, surrounded by willows, in a blossomy brook valley, looked more promising, but did not seem quite the thing either. The staring green abode farther on was manifestly out of the question. Then the stork brightened up. He had caught sight of the very place – a little white house nestled against a big, whispering fir-wood, with a spiral of blue smoke winding up from its kitchen chimney – a house which just looked as if it were meant for babies. The stork gave a sigh of satisfaction, and softly alighted on the ridge-pole.

Half an hour later Gilbert ran down the hall and tapped on the spare-room door. A drowsy voice answered him and in a moment Marilla's pale scared face peeped out from behind the door.

'Marilla, Anne has sent me to tell you that a certain young

gentleman has arrived here. He hasn't brought much luggage with him, but he evidently means to stay.'

'For pity's sake!' said Marilla blankly. 'You don't mean to tell me, Gilbert, that it's all over. Why wasn't I called?'

'Anne wouldn't let us disturb you when there was no need. Nobody was called until about two hours ago. There was no "passage perilous" this time.'

'And – and – Gilbert – will this baby live?'

'He certainly will. He weighs ten pounds and – why, listen to him. Nothing wrong with his lungs, is there? The nurse says his hair will be red. Anne is furious with her, and I'm tickled to death.'

That was a wonderful day in the little house of dreams.

'The best dream of all has come true,' said Anne, pale and rapturous. 'Oh, Marilla, I hardly dare believe it, after that horrible day last summer. I have had a heartache ever since then – but it is gone now.'

'This baby will take Joy's place,' said Marilla.

'Oh, no, no, *no*, Marilla. He can't – nothing can ever do that. He has his own place, my dear, wee man-child. But little Joy has hers, and always will have it. If she had lived she would have been over a year old. She would have been toddling around on her tiny feet and lisping a few words. I can see her so plainly, Marilla. Oh, I know now that Captain Jim was right when he said God would manage better than that my baby would seem a stranger to me when I found her Beyond. I've learned *that* this past year. I've followed her development day by day and week by week – I always shall. I shall know just how she grows from year to year – and when I meet her again I'll know her – she won't be a stranger. Oh,

Marilla, *look* at his dear, darling toes! Isn't it strange they should be so perfect?'

'It would be stranger if they weren't,' said Marilla crisply. Now that all was safely over Marilla was herself again.

'Oh, I know – but it seems as if they couldn't be quite *finished*, you know – and they are, even to the tiny nails. And his hands – *just* look at his hands, Marilla.'

'They appear to be a good deal like hands,' Marilla conceded.

'See how he clings to my finger. I'm sure he knows me already. He cries when the nurse takes him away. Oh, Marilla, do you think – you don't think, do you – that his hair is going to be red?'

'I don't see much hair of any colour,' said Marilla. 'I wouldn't worry about it, if I were you, until it becomes visible.'

'Marilla, he *has* hair – look at that fine little down all over his head. Anyway, nurse says his eyes will be hazel and his forehead is exactly like Gilbert's.'

'And he has the nicest little ears, Mrs Doctor, dear,' said Susan. 'The first thing I did was to look at his ears. Hair is deceitful and noses and eyes change, and you cannot tell what is going to come of them, but ears is ears from start to finish, and you always know where you are with them. Just look at their shape – and they are set right back against his precious head. You will never need to be ashamed of his ears, Mrs Doctor, dear.'

Anne's convalescence was rapid and happy. Folks came and worshipped the baby, as people have bowed before the kingship of the new-born since long before the Wise Men of the East knelt in homage to the Royal Babe of the Bethlehem manger. Leslie, slowly finding herself amid the new conditions of her life, hovered over it, like a beautiful, golden-crowned Madonna. Miss Cornelia nursed it as knackily as could any mother in Israel. Captain Jim held the small creature in his big brown hands and gazed tenderly at it, with eyes that saw the children who had never been born to him.

'What are you going to call him?' asked Miss Cornelia.

'Anne has settled his name,' answered Gilbert.

'James Matthew — after the two finest gentlemen I've ever known — not even saving your presence,' said Anne with a saucy glance at Gilbert.

Gilbert smiled.

'I never knew Matthew very well; he was so shy we boys couldn't get acquainted with him — but I quite agree with you that Captain Jim is one of the rarest and finest souls God ever clothed in clay. He is so delighted over the fact that we have given his name to our small lad. It seems he has no other namesake.'

'Well, James Matthew is a name that will wear well and not fade in the washing,' said Miss Cornelia. 'I'm glad you didn't load him down with some high-falutin, romantic name that he'd be ashamed of when he gets to be a grandfather. Mrs William Drew at the Glen has called her baby Bertie Shakespeare. Quite a combination, isn't it? And I'm glad you haven't had much trouble picking on a name. Some folks have an awful time. When the Stanley Flaggs' first boy was born there was so much rivalry as to who the child should be named for, that the poor little soul had to go for two years without a name. Then a brother came along and there it was — "Big Baby" and "Little Baby". Finally they called Big Baby Peter and Little Baby Isaac, after the two grandfathers, and had them both christened together. And each tried to see if it couldn't howl the other down. You know that Highland Scotch family of MacNabs back of the Glen? They've got twelve boys and the oldest and the youngest are both called Neil – Big Neil and Little Neil in the same family. Well, I s'pose they ran out of names.'

'I have read somewhere,' laughed Anne, 'that the first child is a poem but the tenth is very prosy prose. Perhaps Mrs MacNab thought that the twelfth was merely an old tale re-told.'

'Well, there's something to be said for large families,' said Miss Cornelia, with a sigh. 'I was an only child for eight years and I did long for a brother and sister. Mother told me to pray for one – and pray I did, believe *me*. Well, one day Aunt Nellie came to me and said, "Cornelia, there is a little brother for you upstairs in your ma's room. You can go up and see him." I was so excited and delighted I just flew upstairs. And old Mrs Flagg lifted up the baby for me to see. Lord, Anne, dearie, I never was so disappointed in my life. You see, I'd been praying for *a brother two years older than myself*.'

'How long did it take you to get over your disappointment?' asked Anne, amid her laughter.

'Well, I had a spite at Providence for a good spell, and for weeks I wouldn't even look at the baby. Nobody knew why, for I never told. Then he began to get real cute, and held out his wee hands to me, and I began to get fond of him. But I didn't get really reconciled to him until one day a school chum came to see him and said she thought he was awful small for his age. I just got boiling mad, and I sailed right

255

into her, and told her she didn't know a nice baby when she saw one, and ours was the nicest baby in the world. And after that I just worshipped him. Mother died before he was three years old and I was sister and mother to him both. Poor little lad, he was never strong, and he died when he wasn't much over twenty. Seems to me I'd have given anything on earth, Anne, dearie, if he'd only lived.'

Miss Cornelia sighed. Gilbert had gone down and Leslie, who had been crooning over the small James Matthew in the dormer window, laid him asleep in his basket and went her way. As soon as she was safely out of earshot Miss Cornelia bent forward and said in a conspirator's whisper:

'Anne, dearie, I'd a letter from Owen Ford yesterday. He's in Vancouver just now, but he wants to know if I can board him for a month later on. *You* know what that means. Well, I hope we're doing right.'

'We've nothing to do with it – we couldn't prevent him from coming to Four Winds if he wanted to,' said Anne quickly. She did not like the feeling of matchmaking Miss Cornelia's whispers gave her; and then she weakly succumbed herself.

'Don't let Leslie know he is coming until he is here,' she said. 'If she found out I feel sure she would go away at once. She intends to go in the fall anyhow – she told me so the other day. She is going to Montreal to take up nursing and make what she can of her life.'

'Oh, well, Anne, dearie,' said Miss Cornelia, nodding sagely, 'that is all as it may be. You and I have done our part and we must leave the rest to Higher Hands.'

CHAPTER 35

Politics at Four Winds

WHEN ANNE came downstairs again the Island, as well as all Canada, was in the throes of a campaign preceding a general election. Gilbert, who was an ardent Conservative, found himself caught in the vortex, being much in demand for speech-making at the various county rallies. Miss Cornelia did not approve of his mixing up in politics and told Anne so.

'Dr Dave never did it. Dr Blythe will find he is making a mistake, believe *me*. Politics is something no decent man should meddle with.'

'Is the government of the country to be left solely to the rogues then?' asked Anne.

'Yes – so long as it's Conservative rogues,' said Miss Cornelia, marching off with the honours of war. 'Men and politicians are all tarred with the same brush. The Grits have it laid on thicker than the Conservatives, that's all – *considerably* thicker. But Grit or Tory, my advice to Dr Blythe is to steer clear of politics. First thing you know, he'll be running an election himself, and going off to Ottawa for half the year and leaving his practice to go to the dogs.'

'Ah, well, let's not borrow trouble,' said Anne. 'The rate of interest is too high. Instead, let's look at Little Jem. It should be spelled with a G. Isn't he perfectly beautiful? Just see the dimples in his elbows. We'll bring him up to be a good Conservative, you and I, Miss Cornelia.'

'Bring him up to be a good man,' said Miss Cornelia. 'They're scarce and valuable; though, mind you, I wouldn't like to see him a Grit. As for the election, you and I may be thankful we don't live over harbour. The air there is blue these days. Every Elliott and Crawford and MacAllister is on the war-path, loaded for bear. This side is peaceful and calm, seeing there's so few men. Captain Jim's a Grit, but it's my opinion he's ashamed of it, for he never talks politics. There isn't any earthly doubt that the Conservatives will be returned with a big majority again.'

Miss Cornelia was mistaken. On the morning after the election Captain Jim dropped in at the little house to tell the news. So virulent is the microbe of party politics, even in a peaceable old man, that Captain Jim's cheeks were flushed and his eyes were flashing with all his old-time fire.

'Mistress Blythe, the Liberals are in with a sweeping majority. After eighteen years of Tory mismanagement this down-trodden country is going to have a chance at last.'

'I never heard you make such a bitter partisan speech before, Captain Jim. I didn't think you had so much political venom in you,' laughed Anne, who was not much excited over the tidings. Little Jem had said 'Wow-ga' that morning. What were principalities and powers, the rise and fall of dynasties, the overthrow of Grit or Tory, compared with that miraculous occurrence?

'It's been accumulating for a long while,' said Captain Jim, with a deprecating smile. 'I thought I was only a moderate Grit, but when the news came that we were in I found out how Gritty I really was.'

'You know the doctor and I are Conservatives.'

'Ah, well, it's the only bad thing I know of either of you, Mistress Blythe. Cornelia is a Tory, too. I called in on my way from the Glen to tell her the news.'

'Didn't you know you took your life in your hands?'

'Yes, but I couldn't resist the temptation.'

'How did she take it?'

'Comparatively calm, Mistress Blythe, comparatively calm. She says, says she, "Well, Providence sends seasons of humiliation to a country, same as to individuals. You Grits have been cold and hungry for many a year. Make haste to get warmed and fed, for you won't be in long." "Well, now, Cornelia," I says, "mebbe Providence thinks Canada needs a real long spell of humiliation." Ah, Susan, have *you* heard the news? The Liberals are in.'

Susan had just come in from the kitchen, attended by the odour of delectable dishes which always seemed to hover around her.

'Now, are they?' she said, with beautiful unconcern. 'Well, I never could see but that my bread rose just as light when Grits were in as when they were not. And if any party, Mrs Doctor, dear, will make it rain before the week is out, and save our kitchen garden from entire ruination, that is the party Susan will vote for. In the meantime, will you just step out and give me your opinion on the meat for dinner? I am fearing that it is very tough, and I think that we had better change our butcher as well as our Government.'

One evening, a week later, Anne walked down to the Point, to see if she could get some fresh fish from Captain Jim, leaving Little Jem for the first time. It was quite a tragedy. Suppose he cried? Suppose Susan did not know just

259

exactly what to do for him? Susan was calm and serene.

'I have had as much experience with him as you, Mrs Doctor, dear, have I not?'

'Yes, with him – but not with other babies. Why, I looked after three pairs of twins when I was a child, Susan. When they cried I gave them peppermint or castor oil quite coolly. It's quite curious now to recall how lightly I took all those babies and their woes.'

'Oh, well, if Little Jem cries, I will just clap a hot-water bag on his little stomach,' said Susan.

'Not too hot, you know,' said Anne anxiously. Oh, was it really wise to go?

'Do not you fret, Mrs Doctor, dear. Susan is not the woman to burn a wee man. Bless him, he has no notion of crying.'

Anne tore herself away finally and enjoyed her walk to the Point after all, through the long shadows of the sun-setting. Captain Jim was not in the living-room of the lighthouse, but another man was – a handsome, middle-aged man, with a strong, clean-shaven chin, who was unknown to Anne. Nevertheless, when she sat down he began to talk to her with all the assurance of an old acquaintance. There was nothing amiss in what he said or the way he said it, but Anne rather resented such a cool taking-for-granted in a complete stranger. Her replies were frosty, and as few as decency required. Nothing daunted, her companion talked on for several minutes, then excused himself and went away. Anne could have sworn there was a twinkle in his eye, and it annoyed her. Who was the creature? There was something vaguely familiar about him, but she was certain she had never seen him before.

'Captain Jim, who was that who just went out?' she asked, as Captain Jim came in.

'Marshall Elliott,' answered the captain.

'Marshall Elliott!' cried Anne. 'Oh, Captain Jim – it wasn't – yes, it *was* his voice – oh, Captain Jim, I didn't know him – and I was quite insulting to him! *Why* didn't he tell me? He must have seen I didn't know him.'

'He wouldn't say a word about it – he'd just enjoy the joke. Don't worry over snubbing him – he'll think it fun. Yes, Marshall's shaved off his beard at last and cut his hair. His party is in, you know. I didn't know him myself first time I saw him. He was up in Carter Flagg's store at the Glen the night after election day, along with a crowd of others, waiting for the news. About twelve the phone came through – the Liberals were in. Marshall just got up and walked out – he didn't cheer or shout – he left the others to do that, and they nearly lifted the roof off Carter's store, I reckon. Of course, all the Tories were over in Raymond Russell's store. Not much cheering *there*. Marshall went straight down the street to the side door of Augustus Palmer's barber shop. Augustus was in bed asleep, but Marshall hammered on the door until he got up and come down, wanting to know what all the racket was about.

' "Come into your shop and do the best job you ever did in your life, Gus," said Marshall. "The Liberals are in and you're going to barber a good Grit before the sun rises."

'Gus was mad as hops – partly because he'd been dragged out of bed, but more because he's a Tory. He vowed he wouldn't shave any man after twelve at night.

'"You'll do what I want you to do, sonny," said

261

Marshall, "or I'll jest turn you over my knee and give you one of those spankings your mother forgot."

'He'd have done it, too, and Gus knew it, for Marshall is as strong as an ox and Gus is only a midget of a man. So he gave in and towed Marshall into the shop and went to work. "Now," says he, "I'll barber you up, but if you say one word to me about the Grits getting in while I'm doing it, I'll cut your throat with this razor," says he. You wouldn't have thought mild Gus could be so bloodthirsty, would you? Shows what party politics will do for a man. Marshall kept quiet and got his hair and beard disposed of and went home. When his old housekeeper heard him come upstairs she peeked out of her bedroom door to see whether 'twas him or the hired boy. And when she saw a strange man striding down the hall with a candle in his hand she screamed blue murder and fainted dead away. They had to send for the doctor before they could bring her to, and it was several days before she could look at Marshall without shaking all over.'

Captain Jim had no fish. He seldom went out in his boat that summer, and his long tramping expeditions were over. He spent a great deal of his time sitting by his seaward window, looking out over the gulf, with his swiftly whitening head leaning on his hand. He sat there tonight for many silent minutes, keeping some tryst with the past which Anne would not disturb. Presently he pointed to the iris of the West:

'That's beautiful, isn't it, Mistress Blythe? But I wish you could have seen the sunrise this morning. It was a wonderful thing – wonderful. I've seen all kinds of sunrises come over that gulf. I've been all over the world, Mistress Blythe, and take it all in all, I've never seen a finer sight than a summer sunrise over the gulf. A man can't pick his time for dying, Mistress Blythe – jest got to go when the Great Captain gives His sailing orders. But if I could I'd go out when the morning comes across that water. I've watched it many a time and thought what a thing it would be to pass out through that great white glory to whatever was waiting beyant, on a sea that ain't mapped out on any airthly chart. I think, Mistress Blythe, that I'd find lost Margaret there.'

Captain Jim had often talked to Anne of lost Margaret since he had told her the old story. His love for her trembled in every tone – that love that had never grown faint or forgetful.

'Anyway, I hope when my time comes I'll go quick and easy. I don't think I'm a coward, Mistress Blythe – I've looked an ugly death in the face more than once without blenching. But the thought of a lingering death does give me a queer, sick feeling of horror.'

'Don't talk about leaving us, dear, *dear* Captain Jim,' pleaded Anne, in a choked voice, patting the old brown hand, once so strong, but now grown very feeble. 'What would we do without you?'

Captain Jim smiled beautifully.

'Oh, you'd get along nicely – nicely – but you wouldn't forget the old man altogether, Mistress Blythe – no, I don't think you'll ever quite forget him. The race of Joseph always remembers one another. But it'll be a memory that won't hurt – I like to think that my memory won't hurt my friends – it'll always be kind of pleasant to them, I hope and believe. It won't be very long now before lost Margaret calls me, for the last time. I'll be all ready to answer. I jest spoke of this because there's a little favour I want to ask you. Here's this poor old Matey of mine' – Captain Jim reached out a hand and poked the big, warm, velvety, golden ball on the sofa. The First Mate uncoiled himself like a spring with a nice, throaty, comfortable sound, half purr, half meow, stretched his paws in air, turned over and coiled himself up again. '*He*'ll miss me when I start on the Long V'yage. I can't bear to think of leaving the poor critter to starve, like he was left before. If anything happens to me will you give Matey a bite and a corner, Mistress Blythe?'

'Indeed I will.'

'Then that is all I had on my mind. Your little Jem is to have the few curious things I picked up – I've seen to that. And now I don't like to see tears in those pretty eyes, Mistress Blythe. I'll mebbe hang on for quite a spell yet. I heard you reading a piece of poetry one day last winter – one of Tennyson's pieces. I'd sorter like to hear it again, if you could recite it for me.'

Softly and clearly, while the sea-wind blew in on them, Anne repeated the beautiful lines of Tennyson's wonderful swan song – 'Crossing the Bar'. The old captain kept time gently with his sinewy hand.

'Yes, yes, Mistress Blythe,' he said, when she had finished, 'that's it, that's it. He wasn't a sailor, you tell me – I dunno how he could have put an old sailor's feelings into words like that, if he wasn't one. He didn't want any "sadness o' farewells" and neither do I, Mistress Blythe – for all will be well with me and mine beyant the bar.'

CHAPTER 36

Beauty for Ashes

'ANY NEWS from Green Gables, Anne?'

'Nothing very especial,' replied Anne, folding up Marilla's letter. 'Jake Donnell has been there shingling the roof. He is a full-fledged carpenter now, so it seems he has had his own way in regard to the choice of a life-work. You remember his mother wanted him to be a college professor. I shall never forget the day she came to the school and rated me for failing to call him St Clair.'

'Does anyone ever call him that now?'

'Evidently not. It seems that he has completely lived it down. Even his mother has succumbed. I always thought that a boy with Jake's chin and mouth would get his own way in the end. Diana writes me that Dora has a beau. Just think of it – that child!'

'Dora is seventeen,' said Gilbert. 'Charlie Sloane and I were both mad about you when you were seventeen, Anne.'

'Really, Gilbert, we must be getting on in years,' said Anne with a half-rueful smile, 'when children who were six when we thought ourselves grown up are old enough now to have beaux. Dora's is Ralph Andrews – Jane's brother. I remember him as a little, round, fat, white-headed fellow who was always at the foot of his class. But I understand he is quite a fine-looking young man now.'

'Dora will probably marry young. She's of the same type

as Charlotta the Fourth – she'll never miss her first chance for fear she might not get another.'

'Well, if she marries Ralph I hope he will be a little more up-and-coming than his brother Billy,' mused Anne.

'For instance,' said Gilbert, laughing, 'let us hope he will be able to propose on his own account. Anne, would you have married Billy if he had asked you himself, instead of getting Jane to do it for him?'

'I might have.' Anne went off into a shriek of laughter over the recollection of her first proposal. 'The shock of the whole thing might have hypnotized me into some such rash and foolish act. Let us be thankful he did it by proxy.'

'I had a letter from George Moore yesterday,' said Leslie, from the corner where she was reading.

'Oh, how is he?' asked Anne interestedly, yet with an unreal feeling that she was inquiring about someone whom she did not know.

'He is well, but he finds it very hard to adapt himself to all the changes in his old home and friends. He is going to sea again in the spring. It's in his blood, he says, and he longs for it. But he told me something that made me glad for him, poor fellow. Before he sailed on the *Four Sisters* he was engaged to a girl at home. He did not tell me anything about her in Montreal, because he said he supposed she would have forgotten him and married someone else long ago, and with him, you see, his engagement and love was still a thing of the present. It was pretty hard on him, but when he got home he found she had never married and still cared for him. They are to be married this fall. I'm going to ask him to bring her over here for a little trip; he says he wants to come and see the place where he lived so many years without knowing it.'

'What a nice little romance,' said Anne, whose love for the romantic was immortal. 'And to think,' she added with a sigh of self-reproach, 'that if I had had my way George Moore would never have come up from the grave in which his identity was buried. How I did fight against Gilbert's suggestion! Well, I am punished: I shall never be able to have a different opinion from Gilbert's again! If I try to have he will squelch me by casting George Moore's case up to me!'

'As if even that would squelch a woman!' mocked Gilbert. 'At least do not become my echo, Anne. A little opposition gives spice to life. I do not want a wife like John MacAllister's over the harbour. No matter what he says, she at once remarks in that drab, lifeless little voice of hers, "That is very true, John, dear me!" '

Anne and Leslie laughed. Anne's laughter was silver and Leslie's golden, and the combination of the two was as satisfactory as a perfect chord in music.

Susan, coming in on the heels of the laughter, echoed it with a resounding sigh.

'Why, Susan, what is the matter?' asked Gilbert.

'There's nothing wrong with Little Jem, is there, Susan?' cried Anne, starting up in alarm.

'No, no, calm yourself, Mrs Doctor, dear. Something has happened, though. Dear me, everything has gone catawampus with me this week. I spoiled the bread, as you know too well – and I scorched the doctor's best shirt bosom – and I broke your big platter. And now, on the top of all this, comes word that my sister Matilda has broken her leg and wants me to go and stay with her for a spell.'

267

'Oh, I'm very sorry – sorry that your sister has met with such an accident, I mean,' exclaimed Anne.

'Ah, well, man was made to mourn, Mrs Doctor, dear. That sounds as if it ought to be in the Bible, but they tell me a person named Burns wrote it. And there is no doubt that we are born to trouble as the sparks fly upward. As for Matilda, I do not know what to think of her. None of our family ever broke their legs before. But whatever she has done she is still my sister, and I feel that it is my duty to go and wait on her if you can spare me for a few weeks, Mrs Doctor, dear.'

'Of course, Susan, of course. I can get some one to help me while you are gone.'

'If you cannot I will not go, Mrs Doctor, dear, Matilda's leg to the contrary notwithstanding. I will not have you worried, and that blessed child upset in consequence, for any number of legs.'

'Oh, you must go to your sister at once, Susan. I can get a girl from the cove, who will do for a time.'

'Anne, will you let me come and stay with you while Susan is away?' exclaimed Leslie. 'Do! I'd love to – and it would be an act of charity on your part. I'm so horribly lonely over there in that big barn of a house. There's so little to do – and at night I'm worse than lonely – I'm frightened and nervous in spite of locked doors. There was a tramp around two days ago.'

Anne joyfully agreed, and next day Leslie was installed as an inmate of the little house of dreams. Miss Cornelia warmly approved of the arrangement.

'It seems providential,' she told Anne in confidence. 'I'm sorry for Matilda Clow, but since she had to break her leg it couldn't have happened at a better time. Leslie will be here while Owen Ford is in Four Winds, and those old cats up at the Glen won't get the chance to meow, as they would if she was living over there alone and Owen going to see her. They are doing enough of it as it is, because she doesn't put on mourning. I said to one of them, "If you mean she should put on mourning for George Moore, it seems to me more like his resurrection than his funeral; and if it's Dick you mean, I confess *I* can't see the propriety of going into weeds for a man who died thirteen years ago and good riddance then!" And when old Louisa Baldwin remarked to me that she thought it very strange that Leslie should never have suspected it wasn't her own husband *I* said, "*You* never suspected it wasn't Dick Moore, and you were next-door neighbour to him all his life, and by nature you're ten times as suspicious as Leslie." But you can't stop some people's tongues, Anne, dearie, and I'm real thankful Leslie will be under your roof while Owen is courting her.'

Owen Ford came to the little house one August evening when Leslie and Anne were absorbed in worshipping the baby. He paused at the open door of the living-room, unseen by the two within, gazing with greedy eyes at the beautiful picture. Leslie sat on the floor with the baby in her lap, making ecstatic dabs at his fat little hands as he fluttered them in the air.

'Oh, you dear, beautiful, beloved baby,' she mumbled, catching one wee hand and covering it with kisses.

'Isn't him ze darlingest itty sing,' crooned Anne, hanging over the arm of her chair adoringly. 'Dem itty wee pads are ze very tweetest handies in ze whole big world, isn't dey, you darling itty man.'

Anne, in the months before Little Jem's coming, had pored diligently over several wise volumes, and pinned her faith to one in especial, *Sir Oracle on the Care and Training of Children*. Sir Oracle implored parents by all they held sacred never to talk 'baby talk' to their children. Infants should invariably be addressed in classical language from the moment of their birth. So should they learn to speak English undefiled from their earliest utterance. 'How,' demanded Sir Oracle, 'can a mother reasonably expect her child to learn correct speech, when she continually accustoms its impressionable grey matter to such absurd expressions and distortions of our noble tongue as thoughtless mothers inflict every day on the helpless creatures committed to their care? Can a child who is constantly called "tweet itty wee singie" ever attain to any proper conception of his own being and possibilities and destiny?'

Anne was vastly impressed with this, and informed Gilbert that she meant to make it an inflexible rule never, under any circumstances, to talk 'baby talk' to her children. Gilbert agreed with her, and they made a solemn compact on the subject – a compact which Anne shamelessly violated the very first moment Little Jem was laid in her arms. 'Oh, the darling itty wee sing!' she had exclaimed. And she had continued to violate it ever since. When Gilbert teased her she laughed Sir Oracle to scorn.

'He never had any children of his own, Gilbert – I am positive he hadn't or he would never have written such rubbish. You just can't help talking baby talk to a baby. It comes natural – and it's *right*. It would be inhuman to talk to those tiny, soft, velvety little creatures as we do to great big boys and girls. Babies want love and cuddling and all the sweet baby talk they can get, and Little Jem is going to have it, bess his dear itty heartums.'

'But you're the worst I ever heard, Anne,' protested Gilbert, who, not being a mother but only a father, was not wholly convinced yet that Sir Oracle was wrong. 'I never heard anything like the way you talk to that child.'

'Very likely you never did. Go away — go away. Didn't I bring up three pairs of Hammond twins before I was eleven? You and Sir Oracle are nothing but cold-blooded theorists. Gilbert, *just* look at him! He's smiling at me — he knows what we're talking about. And oo dest agwees wif evy word muzzer says, don't oo, angel-lover?'

Gilbert put his arm about them. 'Oh, you mothers!' he said. 'You mothers! God knew what He was about when He made you.'

So Little Jem was talked to and loved and cuddled: and he throve as became a child of the house of dreams. Leslie was quite as foolish over him as Anne was. When their work was done and Gilbert was out of the way they gave themselves over to shameless orgies of love-making and ecstasies of adoration, such as that in which Owen Ford had surprised them.

Leslie was the first to become aware of him. Even in the twilight Anne could see the sudden whiteness that swept over her beautiful face, blotting out the crimson of lip and cheeks.

Owen came forward, eagerly, blind for a moment to Anne.

'Leslie!' he said, holding out his hand. It was the first time he had ever called her by her name; but the hand Leslie gave him was cold; and she was very quiet all the evening, while

271

Anne and Gilbert and Owen laughed and talked together. Before his call ended she excused herself and went upstairs. Owen's gay spirits flagged and he went away soon after with a downcast air.

Gilbert looked at Anne.

'Anne, what are you up to? There's something going on that I don't understand. The whole air here tonight has been charged with electricity. Leslie sits like the muse of tragedy; Owen Ford jokes and laughs on the surface, and watches Leslie with the eyes of his soul. You seem all the time to be bursting with some suppressed excitement. Own up. What secret have you been keeping from your deceived husband?'

'Don't be a goose, Gilbert,' was Anne's conjugal reply. 'As for Leslie, she is absurd and I'm going up to tell her so.'

Anne found Leslie at the dormer window of her room. The little place was filled with the rhythmic thunder of the sea. Leslie sat with locked hands in the misty moonshine – a beautiful, accusing presence.

'Anne,' she said in a low, reproachful voice, 'did you know Owen Ford was coming to Four Winds?'

'I did,' said Anne brazenly.

'Oh, you should have told me, Anne,' Leslie cried passionately. 'If I had known I would have gone away – I wouldn't have stayed to meet him. You should have told me. It wasn't fair of you, Anne – oh, it wasn't fair!'

Leslie's lips were trembling and her whole form was tense with emotion. But Anne laughed heartlessly. She bent over and kissed Leslie's upturned, reproachful face.

'Leslie, you are an adorable goose. Owen Ford didn't rush from the Pacific to the Atlantic from a burning desire to see *me*. Neither do I believe that he was inspired by any wild and frenzied passion for Miss Cornelia. Take off your tragic airs, my dear friend, and fold them up and put them away in lavender. You'll never need them again. There are some people who can see through a grindstone when there is a hole in it, even if you cannot. I am not a prophetess, but I shall venture on a prediction. The bitterness of life is over for you. After this you are going to have the joys and hopes — and I dare say the sorrows, too — of a happy woman. The omen of the shadow of Venus did come true for you, Leslie. The year in which you saw it brought your life's best gift for you — your love for Owen Ford. Now, go right to bed and have a good sleep.'

Leslie obeyed orders in so far that she went to bed: but it may be questioned if she slept much. I do not think she dared to dream wakingly; life had been so hard for this poor Leslie, the path on which she had had to walk had been so straight, that she could not whisper to her own heart the hopes that might wait on the future. But she watched the great revolving light bestarring the short hours of the summer night, and her eyes grew soft and bright and young once more. Nor, when Owen Ford came next day, to ask her to go with him to the shore, did she say him nay.

CHAPTER 37

Miss Cornelia Makes a Startling Announcement

MISS CORNELIA sailed down to the little house one drowsy afternoon, when the gulf was the faint, bleached blue of hot August seas, and the orange lilies at the gate of Anne's garden held up their imperial cups to be filled with the molten gold of August sunshine. Not that Miss Cornelia concerned herself with painted oceans or sun-thirsty lilies. She sat in her favourite rocker in unusual idleness. She sewed not, neither did she spin. Nor did she say a single derogatory word concerning any portion of mankind. In short, Miss Cornelia's conversation was singularly devoid of spice that day, and Gilbert, who had stayed home to listen to her, instead of going a-fishing, as he had intended, felt himself aggrieved. What had come over Miss Cornelia? She did not look cast down or worried. On the contrary, there was a certain air of nervous exultation about her.

'Where is Leslie?' she asked — not as if it mattered much either.

'Owen and she went raspberrying in the woods back of her farm,' answered Anne. 'They won't be back before supper-time — if then.'

'They don't seem to have any idea that there is such a thing as a clock,' said Gilbert. 'I can't get to the bottom of that affair. I'm certain you women pulled strings. But Anne, undutiful wife, won't tell me. Will you, Miss Cornelia?'

'No, I shall not. But,' said Miss Cornelia, with the air of one determined to take the plunge and have it over, 'I will tell you something else. I came today on purpose to tell it. I am going to be married.'

Anne and Gilbert were silent. If Miss Cornelia had announced her intention of going out to the channel and drowning herself the thing might have been believable. This was not. So they waited. Of course Miss Cornelia had made a mistake.

'Well, you both look sort of kerflummuxed,' said Miss Cornelia, with a twinkle in her eyes. Now that the awkward moment of revelation was over Miss Cornelia was her own woman again. 'Do you think I'm too young and inexperienced for matrimony?'

'You know – it *is* rather staggering,' said Gilbert, trying to gather his wits together. 'I've heard you say a score of times that you wouldn't marry the best man in the world.'

'I'm not going to marry the best man in the world,' retorted Miss Cornelia. 'Marshall Elliott is a long way from being the best.'

'Are you going to marry Marshall Elliott?' exclaimed Anne, recovering her power of speech under this second shock.

'Yes. I could have had him any time these twenty years if I'd lifted my finger. But do you suppose I was going to walk into church beside a perambulating haystack like that?'

'I am sure we are very glad – and we wish you all possible happiness,' said Anne, very flatly and inadequately, as she felt. She was not prepared for such an occasion. She had never imagined herself offering betrothal felicitations to Miss Cornelia.

275

'Thanks, I knew you would,' said Miss Cornelia. 'You are the first of my friends to know it.'

'We shall be so sorry to lose you, though, dear Miss Cornelia,' said Anne, beginning to be a little sad and sentimental.

'Oh, you won't lose me,' said Miss Cornelia unsentimentally. 'You don't suppose I would live over harbour with all those MacAllisters and Elliotts and Crawfords, do you? "From the conceit of the Elliotts, the pride of the MacAllisters and the vain-glory of the Crawfords, good Lord deliver us." Marshall is coming to live at my place. I'm sick and tired of hired men. That Jim Hastings I've got this summer is positively the worst of the species. He would drive anyone to getting married. What do you think? He upset the churn yesterday and spilled a big churning of cream over the yard. And not one whit concerned about it was he! Just gave a foolish laugh and said cream was good for the land. Wasn't that like a man? I told him I wasn't in the habit of fertilizing my back yard with cream.'

'Well, I wish you all manner of happiness too, Miss Cornelia,' said Gilbert, solemnly; 'but,' he added, unable to resist the temptation to tease Miss Cornelia, despite Anne's imploring eyes, 'I fear your day of independence is done. As you know, Marshall Elliott is a very determined man.'

'I like a man who can stick to a thing,' retorted Miss Cornelia. 'Amos Grant, who used to be after me long ago, couldn't. You never saw such a weather-vane. He jumped into the pond to drown himself once and then changed his mind and swum out again. Wasn't that like a man? Marshall would have stuck to it and drowned.'

'And he has a bit of a temper, they tell me,' persisted Gilbert.

'He wouldn't be an Elliott if he hadn't. I'm thankful he has. It will be real fun to make him mad. And you can generally do something with a tempery man when it comes to repenting time. But you can't do anything with a man who just keeps placid and aggravating.'

'You know he's a Grit, Miss Cornelia.'

'Yes, he *is*,' admitted Miss Cornelia rather sadly. 'And of course there is no hope of making a Conservative of him. But at least he is a Presbyterian. So I suppose I shall have to be satisfied with that.'

'Would you marry him if he were a Methodist, Miss Cornelia?'

'No, I would not. Politics is for this world, but religion is for both.'

'And you may be a "relict" after all, Miss Cornelia.'

'Not I. Marshall will live me out. The Elliotts are long-lived, and the Bryants are not.'

'When are you to be married?' asked Anne.

'In about a month's time. My wedding dress is to be navy blue silk. And I want to ask you, Anne, dearie, if you think it would be all right to wear a veil with a navy blue dress. I've always thought I'd like to wear a veil if I ever got married. Marshall says to have it if I want to. Isn't that like a man?'

'Why shouldn't you wear it if you want to?' asked Anne.

'Well, one doesn't want to be different from other people,' said Miss Cornelia, who was not noticeably like anyone else on the face of the earth. 'As I say, I do fancy a veil. But maybe it shouldn't be worn with any dress but a white one. Please tell me, Anne, dearie, what you really think. I'll go by your advice.'

'I don't think veils are usually worn with any but white dresses,' admitted Anne, 'but that is merely a convention, and I am like Mr Elliott, Miss Cornelia. I don't see any good reason why you shouldn't have a veil if you want one.'

But Miss Cornelia, who made her calls in calico wrappers, shook her head.

'If it isn't the proper thing I won't wear it,' she said, with a sigh of regret for a lost dream.

'Since you are determined to be married, Miss Cornelia,' said Gilbert solemnly, 'I shall give you the excellent rules for the management of a husband which my grandmother gave my mother when she married my father.'

'Well, I reckon I can manage Marshall Elliott,' said Miss Cornelia placidly. 'But let us hear your rules.'

'The first one is, catch him.'

'He's caught. Go on.'

'The second one is, feed him well.'

'With enough pie. What next?'

'The third and fourth are – keep your eye on him.'

'I believe you,' said Miss Cornelia emphatically.

CHAPTER 38

Red Roses

THE GARDEN of the little house was a haunt beloved of bees and reddened by late roses that August. The little house folk lived much in it, and were given to taking picnic suppers in the grassy corner beyond the brook and sitting about in it through the twilights when great night moths sailed athwart the velvet gloom. One evening Owen Ford found Leslie alone in it. Anne and Gilbert were away, and Susan, who was expected back that night, had not yet returned.

The northern sky was amber and pale green over the fir tops. The air was cool, for August was nearing September, and Leslie wore a crimson scarf over her white dress. Together they wandered through the little, friendly, flower-crowded paths in silence. Owen must go soon. His holiday was nearly over. Leslie found her heart beating wildly. She knew that this beloved garden was to be the scene of the binding words that must seal their as yet unworded understanding.

'Some evenings a strange odour blows down the air of this garden, like a phantom perfume,' said Owen. 'I have never been able to discover from just what flower it comes. It is elusive and haunting and wonderfully sweet. I like to fancy it is the soul of Grandmother Selwyn passing on a little visit to the old spot she loved so well. There should be a lot of friendly ghosts about this little old house.'

'I have lived under its roof only a month,' said Leslie, 'bu
I love it as I never loved the house over there where I hav
lived all my life.'

'This house was builded and consecrated by love,' sai
Owen. 'Such houses *must* exert an influence over those wh
live in them. And this garden – it is over sixty years old an
the history of a thousand hopes and joys is written in it
blossoms. Some of those flowers were actually set out by th
schoolmaster's bride, and she has been dead for thirty years
Yet they bloom on every summer. Look at those red roses
Leslie – how they queen it over everything else!'

'I love the red roses,' said Leslie. 'Anne likes the pink one
best, and Gilbert likes the white. But I want the crimson
ones. They satisfy some craving in me as no other flowe
does.'

'These roses are very late – they bloom after all the other
have gone – and they hold all the warmth and soul of th
summer come to fruition,' said Owen, plucking some of th
glowing, half-opened buds. 'The rose is the flower of love –
the world has acclaimed it so for centuries. The pink rose
are love hopeful and expectant – the white roses are lov
dead or forsaken – but the red roses – ah, Leslie, what are th
red roses?'

'Love triumphant,' said Leslie in a low voice.

'Yes – love triumphant and perfect. Leslie, you know –
you understand. I have loved you from the first. And I *know*
you love me – I don't need to ask you. But I want to hear you
say it – my darling – my darling!'

Leslie said something in a very low and tremulous voice
Their hands and lips met; it was life's supreme moment fo
them, and as they stood there in the old garden, with its

many years of love and delight and sorrow and glory, he crowned her shining hair with the red, red rose of a love triumphant.

Anne and Gilbert returned presently, accompanied by Captain Jim. Anne lighted a few sticks of driftwood in the fireplace, for love of the pixy flames, and they sat around it for an hour of good fellowship.

'When I sit looking at a driftwood fire it's easy to believe I'm young again,' said Captain Jim.

'Can you read futures in the fire, Captain Jim?' asked Owen.

Captain Jim looked at them all affectionately, and then back again at Leslie's vivid face and glowing eyes.

'I don't need the fire to read your future,' he said. 'I see happiness for all of you – all of you – for Leslie and Mr Ford – and the Doctor here and Mistress Blythe – and Little Jem – and children that ain't born yet but will be. Happiness for you all – though, mind you, I reckon you'll have your troubles and worries and sorrows, too. They're bound to come – and no house, whether it's a palace or a little house of dreams, can bar 'em out. But they won't get the better of you if you face 'em *together* with love and trust. You can weather any storm with them two for compass and pilot.'

The old man rose suddenly and placed one hand on Leslie's head and one on Anne's.

'Two good, sweet women,' he said. 'True and faithful and to be depended on. Your husbands will have honour in the gates because of you – your children will rise up and call you blessed in the years to come.'

There was a strange solemnity about the little scene. Anne and Leslie bowed as those receiving a benediction. Gilbert suddenly brushed his hand over his eyes; Owen Ford was rapt as one who can see visions. All were silent for a space. The little house of dreams added another poignant and unforgettable moment to its store of memories.

'I must be going now,' said Captain Jim slowly at last. He took up his hat and looked lingeringly about the room.

'Good night, all of you,' he said, as he went out.

Anne, pierced by the unusual wistfulness of his farewell, ran to the door after him.

'Come back soon, Captain Jim,' she called, as he passed through the little gate hung between the firs.

'Ay, ay,' he called cheerily back to her. But Captain Jim had sat by the old fireside of the house of dreams for the last time.

Anne went slowly back to the others.

'It's so – so pitiful to think of him going all alone down to that lonely Point,' she said. 'And there is no one to welcome him there.'

'Captain Jim is such good company for others that one can't imagine him being anything but good company for himself,' said Owen. 'But he must often be lonely. There was a touch of the seer about him tonight – he spoke as one to whom it had been given to speak. Well, I must be going, too.'

Anne and Gilbert discreetly melted away; but when Owen had gone Anne returned, to find Leslie standing by the hearth.

'Oh, Leslie – I know – and I'm so glad, dear,' she said, putting her arms about her.

'Anne, my happiness frightens me,' whispered Leslie. 'It seems too great to be real – I'm afraid to speak of it – to think of it. It seems to me that it must just be another dream of this

282

house of dreams and it will vanish when I leave here.'

'Well, you are not going to leave here – until Owen takes you. You are going to stay with me until that time comes. Do you think I'd let you go over to that lonely, sad place again?'

'Thank you, dear. I meant to ask you if I might stay with you. I didn't want to go back there – it would seem like going back into the chill and dreariness of the old life again. Anne, Anne, what a friend you've been to me – "a good, sweet woman – true and faithful and to be depended on" – Captain Jim summed you up.'

'He said "women", not "woman",' smiled Anne. 'Perhaps Captain Jim sees us both through the rose-coloured spectacles of his love for us. But we can try to live up to his belief in us, at least.'

'Do you remember, Anne,' said Leslie slowly, 'that I once said – that night we met on the shore – that I hated my good looks? I did – then. It always seemed to me that if I had been homely Dick would never have thought of me. I hated my beauty because it had attracted him, but now – oh, I'm glad that I have it. It's all I have to offer Owen – his artist soul delights in it. I feel as if I do not come to him quite empty-handed.'

'Owen loves your beauty, Leslie. Who would not? But it's foolish of you to say or think that that is all you bring him. *He* will tell you that – I needn't. And now I must lock up. I expected Susan back tonight, but she has not come.'

'Oh, yes, here I am, Mrs Doctor, dear,' said Susan entering unexpectedly from the kitchen, 'and puffing like a hen drawing rails at that! It's quite a walk from the Glen down here.'

'I'm glad to see you back, Susan. How is your sister?'

'She is able to sit up, but of course she cannot walk yet. However, she is very well able to get on without me now, for her daughter has come home for her vacation. And I am thankful to be back, Mrs Doctor, dear. Matilda's leg was broken and no mistake, but her tongue was not. She would talk the legs off an iron pot, that she would, Mrs Doctor, dear, though I grieve to say it of my own sister. She was always a great talker and yet she was the first of our family to get married. She really did not care much about marrying James Clow, but she could not bear to disoblige him. Not but what James is a good man – the only fault I have to find with him is that he always starts to say grace with such an unearthly groan, Mrs Doctor, dear. It always frightens my appetite clear away. And speaking of getting married, Mrs Doctor, dear, is it true Cornelia Bryant is going to be married to Marshall Elliott?'

'Yes, quite true, Susan.'

'Well, Mrs Doctor, dear, it does *not* seem to me fair. Here is me, who never said a word against the men, and I cannot get married nohow. And there is Cornelia Bryant, who is never done abusing them, and all she has to do is to reach out her hand and pick one up, as it were. It is a very strange world, Mrs Doctor, dear.'

'There's another world, you know, Susan.'

'Yes,' said Susan with a heavy sigh, 'but, Mrs Doctor dear, there is neither marrying nor giving in marriage there.'

CHAPTER 39

Captain Jim Crosses the Bar

ONE DAY in late September Owen Ford's book came at last. Captain Jim had gone faithfully to the Glen post-office every day for a month, expecting it. This day he had not gone, and Leslie brought his copy home with hers and Anne's.

'We'll take it down to him this evening,' said Anne, excited as a schoolgirl.

The walk to the Point on that clear, beguiling evening along the red harbour road was very pleasant. Then the sun dropped down behind the western hills into some valley that must have been full of lost sunsets, and at the same instant the big light flashed out on the white tower of the point.

'Captain Jim is never late by the fraction of a second,' said Leslie.

Neither Anne nor Leslie ever forgot Captain Jim's face when they gave him the book – *his* book, transfigured and glorified. The cheeks that had been blanched of late suddenly flamed with the colour of boyhood; his eyes glowed with all the fire of youth; but his hands trembled as he opened it.

It was called simply *The Life-book of Captain Jim*, and on the title-page the names of Owen Ford and James Boyd were printed as collaborators. The frontispiece was a photograph of Captain Jim himself, standing at the door of the lighthouse, looking across the gulf. Owen Ford had 'snapped' him one day while the book was being written. Captain Jim had known this, but he had not known that the picture was to be in the book.

'Just think of it,' he said, 'the old sailor right there in a real printed book. This is the proudest day of my life. I'm like to bust, girls. There'll be no sleep for me tonight. I'll read my book clean through before sun-up.'

'We'll go right away and leave you free to begin it,' said Anne.

Captain Jim had been handling the book in a kind of reverent rapture. Now he decidedly closed it and laid it aside.

'No, no, you're not going away before you take a cup of tea with the old man,' he protested. 'I couldn't hear to that — could you, Matey? The life-book will keep, I reckon. I've waited for it this many a year. I can wait a little longer while I'm enjoying my friends.'

Captain Jim moved about getting his kettle on to boil, and setting out his bread and butter. Despite his excitements he did not move with his old briskness. His movements were slow and halting. But the girls did not offer to help him. They knew it would hurt his feelings.

'You just picked the right evening to visit me,' he said, producing a cake from his cupboard. 'Leetle Joe's mother sent me down a big basket full of cakes and pies today. A blessing on all good cooks, says I. Look at this purty cake, all frosting and nuts. 'Tain't often I can entertain in such style. Set in, girls, set in! We'll "tak a cup o' kindness yet for auld lang syne".'

The girls 'set in' right merrily. The tea was up to Captain Jim's best brewing. Little Joe's mother's cake was the last word in cakes; Captain Jim was the prince of gracious hosts, never even permitting his eyes to wander to the corner where the life-book lay, in all its bravery of green and gold. But when his door finally closed behind Anne and Leslie they knew that he went straight to it, and as they walked home they pictured the delight of the old man poring over the printed pages wherein his own life was portrayed with all the charm and colour of reality itself.

'I wonder how he will like the ending – the ending I suggested,' said Leslie.

She was never to know. Early the next morning Anne awakened to find Gilbert bending over her, fully dressed, and with an expression of anxiety on his face.

'Are you called out?' she asked drowsily.

'No. Anne, I'm afraid there's something wrong at the Point. It's an hour after sunrise now, and the light is still burning. You know it has always been a matter of pride with Captain Jim to start the light the moment the sun sets, and put it out the moment it rises.'

Anne sat up in dismay. Through her window she saw the light blinking palely against the blue skies of dawn.

'Perhaps he has fallen asleep over his life-book,' she said anxiously, 'or become so absorbed in it that he has forgotten the light.'

Gilbert shook his head.

'That wouldn't be like Captain Jim. Anyway, I'm going down to see.'

'Wait a minute and I'll go with you,' exclaimed Anne. 'Oh, yes, I must – Little Jem will sleep for an hour yet, and I'll call Susan. You may need a woman's help if Captain Jim is ill.'

It was an exquisite morning, full of tints and sounds at

once ripe and delicate. The harbour was sparkling and dimpling like a girl; white gulls were soaring over the dunes; beyond the bar was a shining, wonderful sea. The long fields by the shore were dewy and fresh in that first fine, purely tinted light. The wind came dancing and whistling up the channel to replace the beautiful silence with a music more beautiful still. Had it not been for the baleful star on the white tower that early walk would have been a delight to Anne and Gilbert. But they went softly with fear.

Their knock was not responded to. Gilbert opened the door and they went in.

The old room was very quiet. On the table were the remnants of the little evening feast. The lamp still burned on the corner stand. The First Mate was asleep in a square of sunshine by the sofa.

Captain Jim lay on the sofa, with his hands clasped over the life-book, open at the last page, lying on his breast. His eyes were closed and on his face was a look of the most perfect peace and happiness – the look of one who has long sought and found at last.

'He is asleep?' whispered Anne tremulously.

Gilbert went to the sofa and bent over him for a few moments. Then he straightened up.

'Yes, he sleeps – well,' he said quietly. 'Anne, Captain Jim has crossed the bar.'

They could not know precisely at what hour he had died, but Anne always believed that he had had his wish and went out when the morning came across the gulf. Out on that shining tide his spirit drifted, over the sunrise sea of pearl and silver, to the haven where lost Margaret waited, beyond the storms and calms.

CHAPTER 40

Farewell to the House of Dreams

CAPTAIN JIM was buried in the little over-harbour graveyard, very near to the spot where the wee white lady slept. His relatives put up a very expensive, very ugly 'monument' – a monument at which he would have poked sly fun had he seen it in life. But his real monument was in the hearts of those who knew him, and in the book that was to live for generations.

Leslie mourned that Captain Jim had not lived to see the amazing success of it.

'How he would have delighted in the reviews – they are almost all so kindly. And to have seen his life-book heading the lists of the best-sellers – oh, if he could just have lived to see it, Anne!'

But Anne, despite her grief, was wiser.

'It was the book itself he cared for, Leslie – not what might be said of it – and he had it. He had read it all through. That last night must have been one of the greatest happiness for him – with the quick, painless ending he had hoped for in the morning. I am glad for Owen's sake and yours that the book is such a success – but Captain Jim was satisfied – I *know*.'

The lighthouse star still kept its nightly vigil; a substitute keeper had been sent to the Point, until such time as an all-wise Government could decide which of many applicants was best fitted for the place – or had the strongest pull. The

First Mate was at home in the little house, beloved by Anne and Gilbert and Leslie, and tolerated by a Susan who had small liking for cats.

'I can put up with him for the sake of Captain Jim, Mrs Doctor, dear, for I liked the old man. And I will see that he gets bite and sup, and every mouse the traps account for. But do not ask me to do more than that, Mrs Doctor, dear. Cats is cats, and take my word for it, they will never be anything else. And at least, Mrs Doctor, dear, do keep him away from the blessed wee man. Picture to yourself how awful it would be if he was to suck the darling's breath.'

'That might be fitly called a *cat*-astrophe,' said Gilbert.

'Oh, you may laugh, doctor, dear, but it would be no laughing matter.'

'Cats never suck babies' breaths,' said Gilbert. 'That is only an old superstition, Susan.'

'Oh, well, it may be a superstition or it may not, doctor, dear. All that I know is, it has happened. My sister's husband's nephew's wife's cat sucked their baby's breath, and the poor innocent was all but gone when they found it. And superstition or not, if I find that yellow beast lurking near our baby I will whack him with the poker, Mrs Doctor, dear.'

Mr and Mrs Marshall Elliott were living comfortably and harmoniously in the green house. Leslie was busy with sewing, for she and Owen were to be married at Christmas. Anne wondered what she would do when Leslie was gone.

'Changes come all the time. Just as soon as things get really nice they change,' she said with a sigh.

'The old Morgan place up at the Glen is for sale,' said Gilbert, apropos of nothing in especial.

'Is it?' asked Anne indifferently.

'Yes. Now that Mr Morgan has gone, Mrs Morgan wants to go to live with her children in Vancouver. She will sell cheaply, for a big place like that in a small village like the Glen will not be very easy to dispose of.'

'Well, it's certainly a beautiful place, so it is likely she will find a purchaser,' said Anne, absently, wondering whether she should hemstitch or feather-stitch Little Jem's 'short' dresses. He was to be shortened the next week, and Anne felt ready to cry at the thought of it.

'Suppose we buy it, Anne?' remarked Gilbert quietly.

Anne dropped her sewing and stared at him.

'You're not in earnest, Gilbert?'

'Indeed I am, dear.'

'And leave this darling spot – our house of dreams?' said Anne incredulously. 'Oh, Gilbert, it's – it's unthinkable!'

'Listen patiently to me, dear. I know just how you feel about it. I feel the same. But we've always known we would have to move some day.'

'Oh, but not so soon, Gilbert – not just yet.'

'We may never get such a chance again. If we don't buy the Morgan place someone else will – and there is no other house in the Glen we would care to have, and no other really good site on which to build. This little house is – well, it is and has been what no other house can ever be to us, I admit, but you know it is out-of-the-way down here for a doctor. We have felt the inconvenience, though we've made the best of it. And it's a tight fit for us now. Perhaps, in a few years, when Jem wants a room of his own, it will be entirely too small.'

'Oh, I know – I know,' said Anne, tears filling her eyes. 'I know all that can be said against it, but I love it so – and it's so beautiful here.'

'You would find it very lonely here after Leslie goes – and Captain Jim has gone too. The Morgan place is beautiful, and in time we would love it. You know you have always admired it, Anne.'

'Oh, yes, but – but – this has all seemed to come up so suddenly, Gilbert. I'm dizzy. Ten minutes ago I had no thought of leaving this dear spot. I was planning what I meant to do for it in the spring – what I meant to do in the garden. And if we leave this place who will get it? It *is* out-of-the-way, so it's likely some poor, shiftless, wandering family will rent it – and overrun it – and oh, that would be desecration. It would hurt me horribly.'

'I know. But we cannot sacrifice our own interests to such considerations, Anne-girl. The Morgan place will suit us in every essential particular – we really can't afford to miss such a chance. Think of that big lawn with those magnificent old trees; and of that splendid hardwood grove behind it – twelve acres of it. What a play place for our children! There's a fine orchard, too, and you've always admired that high brick wall around the garden with the door in it – you've thought it was so like a story-book garden. And there is almost as fine a view of the harbour and the dunes from the Morgan place as from here.'

'You can't see the lighthouse star from it.'

'Yes. You can see it from the attic window. *There's* another advantage, Anne-girl – you love big garrets.'

'There's no brook in the garden.'

'Well, no, but there is one running through the maple grove into the Glen pond. And the pond itself isn't far away.

You'll be able to fancy you have your own Lake of Shining Waters again.'

'Well, don't say anything more about it just now, Gilbert. Give me time to think – to get used to the idea.'

'All right. There is no great hurry, of course. Only – if we decide to buy, it would be well to be moved in and settled before winter.'

Gilbert went out, and Anne put away Little Jem's short dresses with trembling hands. She could not sew any more that day. With tear-wet eyes she wandered over the little domain where she had reigned so happy a queen. The Morgan place was all that Gilbert claimed. The grounds were beautiful, the house old enough to have dignity and repose and traditions, and new enough to be comfortable and up-to-date. Anne had always admired it; but admiring is not loving; and she loved this little house of dreams so much. She loved *everything* about it – the garden she had tended, and which so many women had tended before her – the gleam and sparkle of the little brook that crept so roguishly across the corner – the gate between the creaking fir-trees – the old red sandstone step – the stately Lombardies – the two tiny quaint glass cupboards over the chimney-piece in the living-room – the crooked pantry door in the kitchen – the two funny dormer windows upstairs – the little jog in the staircase – why, these things were a part of her! How could she leave them?

And how this little house, consecrated aforetime by love and joy, had been re-consecrated for her by her happiness and sorrow! Here she had spent her bridal moon; here wee Joyce had lived her one brief day; here the sweetness of motherhood had come again with Little Jem; here she had heard the exquisite music of her baby's cooing laughter; here beloved friends had sat by her fireside. Joy and grief, birth and death, had made sacred for ever this little house of dreams.

And now she must leave it. She knew that, even while she had contended against the idea to Gilbert. The little house was outgrown. Gilbert's interests made the change necessary; his work, successful though it had been, was hampered by his location. Anne realized that the end of their life in this dear place drew nigh, and that she must face the fact bravely. But how her heart ached!

'It will just be like tearing something out of my life,' she sobbed. 'And oh, if I could hope that some nice folk would come here in our place – or even that it would be left vacant. That itself would be better than having it overrun with some horde who know nothing of the geography of dreamland, and nothing of the history that has given this house its soul and its identity. And if such a tribe come here the place will go to rack and ruin in no time – an old place goes down so quickly if it is not carefully attended to. They'll tear up my garden – and let the Lombardies get ragged – and the paling will come to look like a mouth with half the teeth missing – and the roof will leak – and the plaster fall – and they'll stuff pillows and rags in broken window panes – and everything will be out-at-elbows.'

Anne's imagination pictured forth so vividly the coming degeneration of her dear little house that it hurt her as severely as if it had already been an accomplished fact. She sat down on the stairs and had a long, bitter cry. Susan found her there and inquired with much concern what the trouble was.

'You have not quarrelled with the doctor, have you now, Mrs Doctor, dear? But if you have, do not worry. It is a thing quite likely to happen with married couples, I am told, although I have had no experience that way myself. He will be sorry, and you can soon make it up.'

'No, no, Susan, we haven't quarrelled. It's only – Gilbert is going to buy the Morgan place, and we'll have to go and live at the Glen. And it will break my heart.'

Susan did not enter into Anne's feelings at all. She was, indeed, quite rejoiced over the prospect of living at the Glen. Her one grievance against her place in the little house was its lonesome location.

'Why, Mrs Doctor, dear, it will be splendid. The Morgan house is such a fine, big one.'

'I hate big houses,' sobbed Anne.

'Oh, well, you will not hate them by the time you have half a dozen children,' remarked Susan calmly. 'And this house is too small already for us. We have no spare room, since Mrs Moore is here, and that pantry is the most aggravating place I ever tried to work in. There is a corner every way you turn. Besides, it is out-of-the-world down here. There is really nothing at all but scenery.'

'Out of your world perhaps, Susan – but not out of mine,' said Anne with a faint smile.

'I do not quite understand you, Mrs Doctor, dear, but of course I am not well educated. But if Dr Blythe buys the Morgan place he will make no mistake, and that you may tie to. They have water in it, and the pantries and closets are beautiful, and there is not another such cellar in P.E. Island, so I have been told. Why, the cellar here, Mrs Doctor, dear, has been a heart-break to me, as well you know.'

'Oh, go away, Susan, go away,' said Anne forlornly. 'Cellars and pantries and closets don't make a *home*. Why don't you weep with those who weep?'

'Well, I never was much hand for weeping, Mrs Doctor, dear. I would rather fall to and cheer people up than weep with them. Now, do not you cry and spoil your pretty eyes. This house is very well and has served your turn, but it is high time you had a better.'

Susan's point of view seemed to be that of most people. Leslie was the only one who sympathized understandingly with Anne. She had a good cry, too, when she heard the news. Then they both dried their tears and went to work at the preparations for moving.

'Since we must go let us go as soon as we can and have it over,' said poor Anne with bitter resignation.

'You know you will like that lovely old place at the Glen after you have lived in it long enough to have dear memories woven about it,' said Leslie. 'Friends will come there, as they have come here – happiness will glorify it for you. Now, it's just a house to you – but the years will make it a home.'

Anne and Leslie had another cry the next week when they shortened Little Jem. Anne felt the tragedy of it until evening when in his long nightie she found her own dear baby again.

'But it will be rompers next – and then trousers – and in no time he will be grown-up,' she sighed.

'Well, you would not want him to stay a baby always, Mrs Doctor, dear, would you?' said Susan. 'Bless his innocent heart, he looks too sweet for anything in his little short dresses, with his dear feet sticking out. And think of the save in the ironing, Mrs Doctor, dear.'

'Anne, I have just had a letter from Owen,' said Leslie,

entering with a bright face. 'And, oh! I have such good news. He writes me that he is going to buy this place from the church trustees and keep it to spend our summer vacations in. Anne, are you not glad?'

'Oh, Leslie, "glad" isn't the word for it! It seems almost too good to be true. I shan't feel half so badly now that I know this dear spot will never be desecrated by a vandal tribe, or left to tumble down in decay. Why, it's lovely! It's lovely!'

One October morning Anne wakened to the realization that she had slept for the last time under the roof of her little house. The day was too busy to indulge regret and when evening came the house was stripped and bare. Anne and Gilbert were alone in it to say farewell. Leslie and Susan and Little Jem had gone to the Glen with the last load of furniture. The sunset light streamed in through the curtainless windows.

'It has all such a heart-broken, reproachful look, hasn't it?' said Anne. 'Oh, I shall be so homesick at the Glen tonight!'

'We have been very happy here, haven't we, Anne-girl?' said Gilbert, his voice full of feeling.

Anne choked, unable to answer. Gilbert waited for her at the fir-tree gate, while she went over the house and said farewell to every room. She was going away; but the old house would still be there, looking seaward through its quaint windows. The autumn winds would blow around it mournfully, and the grey rain would beat upon it and the white mists would come in from the sea to enfold it; and the moonlight would fall over it and light up the old paths where the schoolmaster and his bride had walked. There on that

297

old harbour shore the charm of story would linger; the wind would still whistle alluringly over the silver sand-dunes; the waves would still call from the red rock-coves.

'But we will be gone,' said Anne through her tears.

She went out, closing and locking the door behind her. Gilbert was waiting for her with a smile. The lighthouse star was gleaming northward. The little garden, where only marigolds still bloomed, was already hooding itself in shadows.

Anne knelt down and kissed the worn old step which she had crossed as a bride.

'Good-bye, dear little house of dreams,' she said.